# THE EYE
## of the
# NAVIGATOR

## A LEILANI KEALOHA HAWAIIAN THRILLER

Book 2 of the Leilani Kealoha Trilogy

BY

# CHUCK MORGAN

# DEDICATION

To the truth-seekers who refuse to be silenced —
May your courage echo louder than corruption.

And your love for family burns brighter than betrayal.

This story is for the ones who stand firm

Even when paradise turns its back.

# Chapter One

## Paradise Disrupted

Detective Leilani Kealoha preferred the hour before dawn. Most people saw it as the tail end of the night, a time for ghosts and regrets, but she found it perfect for picking apart crime scenes. Less noise, less traffic and thanks to the warm trade winds drifting across the island, less of the sticky-sweet tang of human sweat that always bloomed once the sun fully woke.

She rolled up to the Aloha Shores Resort with her window down and her radio turned off. The patrol units had been dispatched at 4:10 a.m.. When Leilani reached the sprawling drive, lights were strobing against the resort's low-slung portico, painting blue stripes across the columns and sending restless shadows running for cover. The usual suspects, bored valets, security staff with arms crossed over uniforms, a couple of guests in robes and sandals, clustered in knots behind yellow tape. One uniform, a sergeant she recognized from last year's Christmas party, was busily shepherding them to the side entrance.

Leilani parked in the valet slot and ignored the boy who tried to wave her elsewhere. She grabbed her battered messenger bag from the passenger seat, squinted up at the lightening sky, and ducked under the crime tape. Her boots made flat echoes on the white marble, still glossy from last night's waxing.

Inside, the lobby had been transformed. Usually a temple to understated luxury, now an anthill of activity. Technicians with cameras were kneeling on the rug, shooting from weird angles. A forensic cart in the corner spilled out latex gloves and evidence bags like a cornucopia of bureaucratic dread. The concierges, stripped of their polite force fields, clustered behind the desk, faces drawn and bloodless.

"Detective Kealoha," said a voice to her right. She turned to see Officer Lum, out of his rookie phase, not yet sure how to fill out his own uniform.

"Morning, Lum," Leilani said, checking her watch, although she already knew the time. "Which way to the fireworks?"

He led her down a hallway lined with potted palms, talking as they walked. "Victim is the hotel itself," Lum said. "Safe room in the admin suite, ground floor. Nobody was hurt, at least not physically. The night manager found the breach at four oh-three, after getting a silent alarm from central."

"And the manager?" Leilani asked.

"In his office, with a trauma blanket and three cups of coffee. Wants to sue the company that sold her the safe." Lum managed a weak grin. "You want to talk to her first?"

"Not yet," said Leilani. "I'll look at the scene first."

Lum nodded, standing back as she approached the safe room entrance. More tape, but this time a strip of plastic stretched across the door at knee level. She stepped over it, ducked through, and exhaled a short, surprised breath.

It was a mess, but not the kind she was used to. No

violence, but the violence of efficiency.

The safe room was more of a closet, albeit one lined with reinforced steel panels and a CCTV camera staring glassily from the corner. A bank of safety deposit drawers, all numbered, filled the far wall. One of them, number 21, the lucky blackjack, had been levered open with surgical precision, its lock left dangling like the molted carapace of some unfortunate beetle.

Below the drawers, a standalone safe sat squat and indignant. The electronic keypad punched out, and a panel on the side peeled away to expose its digital heart. Scattered on the floor were velvet-lined cases, empty now, but still imprinted with the forms of high-carat stones. Among them, a handful of latex glove tips snipped off and discarded, and a tight, gray coil of fiberoptic cable.

Leilani let out a low whistle. "Somebody brought their A-game," she muttered.

A hotel security guard, mid-forties, trim but losing the battle with his belt, sleeves rolled up past the elbows, was waiting in the corner, nervously clutching a clipboard.

"Detective," he said, with the automatic deference of someone who'd seen a lot of uniforms. "I'm James Stovall. Director of security." He offered his hand, remembered the gloves, and withdrew it. "I've worked at this resort for fifteen years. Never seen anything like this."

"That makes two of us, James." Leilani crouched by the open safe, keeping her movements slow and deliberate. "Walk me through the system."

James set the clipboard on the nearest table and pulled up a chair. "That safe is a Yamasaki T-2000. It's top of the line, installed last November. It's got three layers — biometric, PIN code, plus a timed access that can't be bypassed without management override." He shot a glance at the exposed side panel, and at Leilani, as if afraid she'd blame him personally for the breach.

She traced a finger along the keypad's ragged edge. "You said there's a time lock?"

"Yes, ma'am. With the correct thumbprint and PIN, you can't open it until the window hits. The window's random, set by our back-end system, synced to Tokyo time. Two people have override codes, the GM and myself."

"Either of you lose a badge recently?"

"No, ma'am. And the biometric? It's supposed to be idiot-proof." James looked at the safe as if it had betrayed him.

Leilani nodded, standing to scan the room with fresh eyes. "What's missing?"

James cleared his throat. "The hotel keeps guests' jewelry in short-term custody while they use the spa or beach. Mostly for VIPs, high rollers. Last night we had three watches, some custom rings and a jadeite necklace from the casino owner's wife."

"And?"

"And all gone except the necklace. They left that one in the case."

Leilani blinked. "Any reason?"

He hesitated. "It's cursed. Or so the staff likes to say."

"Our thief has a sense of humor." She smiled, not that it reached her eyes. "Or they know something we don't."

She circled the crime scene, glancing up at the CCTV. The lens was still red, but a strip of black electrical tape had been pasted over it with surgical neatness. A move so basic and effective it made her want to applaud.

"Who else had access to this room last night?" she asked.

"The desk manager and I, and the night janitor, but he's only here for thirty minutes after closing." James produced a log from his clipboard. "Badge in and out, every door trip logged."

Leilani thumbed through the paper. "How about off the books? Any maintenance work, vendor deliveries?"

James frowned. "No, but..." He reached into a pocket and produced a sealed plastic bag. Inside was a chunk of matte black plastic, snapped off at the corner and wired with micro-filaments. "I found this wedged under the cabinet."

She took the bag, turning it over in her hand. "Looks like part of an RFID spoofer. Or maybe a signal jammer."

James nodded, glum. "That's what I thought. So much for idiot-proof."

Leilani tucked the bag into her own evidence pouch. "You did good, James. This wasn't an inside job, at least not by you."

He smiled, thin and haunted.

Leilani drifted toward the windows, letting the day's first light spill across the tile. She scanned the floor, her breath hitching as she saw the shape.

On the white marble floor, drawn in a fat line of turquoise chalk, was a Hawaiian petroglyph, two concentric spirals, arms radiating out like the sun, or the eye of a hurricane. The line work was unsteady but confident, as if the artist had copied from memory rather than a design.

She kneeled beside it, careful not to smudge. "You see this, James?"

He shuffled over, peering down. "Kids vandalize the pool sometimes, but nobody gets into the admin suites."

Leilani snapped a photo, zoomed in for a detail shot. She sensed the low, hard thump of her heart, not fear, but anticipation. This wasn't only a break-in. There was something else going on.

She straightened, dusting her hands on her jeans. "I'll need your camera logs, James. Every second from midnight to now."

"Yes, ma'am."

"And a list of everyone who's checked out over the last twelve hours. Staff, too."

He scribbled notes, eager for the task.

Leilani glanced back at the petroglyph, the spirals catching the sunlight and sending a brief, spectral glint up the wall. Whoever did this wanted attention, and she was more than happy to give it.

"Thank you, James," she said, her voice calm as ever.

She made her way out, stepping past the chalk spiral and into the fresh wash of morning.

The manager's office was a glass jewel box perched above the palms and infinity pool, high enough for a sightline over the sand and out to where the Pacific bled into the horizon. Leilani stood in the doorway, taking in the details. A mid-century desk, two club chairs in cream leather, and a Japanese sand garden raked to precise angles on a credenza by the window. She clocked a faint trace of scotch in the air, layered under the sharper top note of disinfectant.

The manager, Henry Matsu, according to his doorplate, rose from his desk as she entered. He was in his early fifties, with a tan this side of orange and a hairline that clung to the last defense line above his ears. His smile was a horizontal crack in a face otherwise fixed in panic.

"Detective Kealoha," he said, extending his hand. He kept it out a second too long before withdrawing it and fussed with his tie instead. "Would you care for some coffee? I brewed it myself."

She declined with a shake of her head. "Thank you, but I'm good. Mind if I record our conversation?"

"Please do," he said, nodding so hard his glasses

threatened to leap off his nose. He gestured to the chairs, and they both sat, Leilani balancing her tablet on one knee.

"Before we start, let me say, I'm deeply embarrassed this happened here. At my property. I pride myself on discretion and safety. This…" He faltered, glancing out the window at the perfect morning. "It's a violation."

"There were other victims," Leilani said, keeping her voice flat. "We'll keep it quiet as long as we can, but once insurance gets involved, the story usually finds its way out. It's best to get in front of it."

He looked like he might vomit. "How bad is it?"

Leilani tapped her stylus on the tablet, running through her notes. "You lost three guest deposits and a hotel jewelry collection. We're working on the list of items, but our initial estimate is." She waited for his reaction.

He winced. "North of two million. The sapphire watch alone was worth half a million. Christ."

"Would you mind walking me through last night's events?"

Matsu splayed his hands on the desk as if preparing for a séance. "I left the property at ten, after the Friday luau. Our guests were the usual crowd: couples, families, a handful of business types. Security rotation is by the book, with two roving guards inside and another on the beach side. After hours, everything is locked down except the casino and pool bar, both with their own cameras and security."

He pointed at the monitor on his desk, where a digital schematic of the hotel glowed faintly. "My head of security, James, runs a tight ship. All badge ins and outs are logged, as you'll see. The room is accessed by management and security."

"And no one else has the override code?"

His mouth twisted. "Officially, yes. In practice, there's an emergency kit in my office safe containing a physical key and an encrypted thumb drive, but it's in a tamper-proof bag. Still sealed when I checked this morning."

Leilani nodded, scrolling down. "Do you have any enemies, Mr. Matsu? Business rivals? Disgruntled ex-employees?"

He laughed, short and raw. "I run a five-star hotel on Oahu. Every week is a new grudge. But corporate usually handles that. My job is to keep the guests happy and the money coming in."

"Any recent staff turnover?"

He chewed his lip. "One bellhop was fired last month for drugs. Two servers quit abruptly, but they moved to the Four Seasons. No drama, better pay."

Leilani jotted it down. More for show than need. "Last night, was anyone acting off? Any service calls to the admin wing?"

"No, but there was a room change at 1:22 a.m. A guest in the penthouse suite moved down to a lower floor. Complained about a leaking AC vent." He spread his hands again, helpless. "I'm happy to pull up the logs for you."

"Please do. And the security footage, too. Midnight to four a.m."

Matsu swiveled his chair, hands trembling as he typed on the keyboard. His desktop was a shrine to efficiency. No photos of kids or pets. Some golden-hued business cards and a coaster with the resort logo. He clicked through a series of folders, found the right feed, and projected it onto the wall monitor.

They watched in silence. At 2:37 a.m., a figure in a maintenance jumpsuit crossed the lobby, pushing a utility cart. The uniform matched the house style, but the face was lost in shadow. The person kept their head down, moved with the brisk certainty of someone who belonged.

"That's not one of ours," Matsu said. "Maintenance clocks out at midnight."

"Did you recognize the badge?" she asked.

He paused the video, zooming in. "It's too blurry. But we use color-coded lanyards. See." He tapped the screen. "Red is housekeeping. Maintenance is blue. That's green. Green is for outside contractors, like HVAC or pest control."

"And you had no contractors scheduled last night?"

He hesitated, reviewing his calendar. "No, but we do quarterly bug checks. Next one's not until June." He looked up, worried. "I can pull the vendor list for you."

Leilani was about to respond when the footage flickered. The timestamp jumped forward ninety seconds, skipping from 2:38:14 to 2:39:45. When it resumed, the lobby was empty, and the utility cart was gone.

She rewound it, letting it play again, slower. "Who edits your security footage?" she asked.

"Nobody," Matsu said, a cold sweat forming on his forehead. "It's all cloud-based. Triple redundancy. You think someone hacked it?"

"I think someone planned this carefully," said Leilani, not looking away from the screen. "Is it possible for someone to access the system remotely?"

He nodded, paling. "Technically yes. But they'd need credentials."

She made another note. "Anyone new on your IT team? Consultants, recent hires?"

"No, but our lead admin's been out sick for two weeks. IT's being handled by a temp from corporate."

Leilani wrote it down. "Name and contact?"

He searched his files, reading from the screen: "Rafiq Nawaz, out of L.A."

"Good," she said. "Anything else unusual during the last seventy-two hours?"

He considered. "I got a call from a blocked number at 3:11 a.m. I didn't recognize the voice. A man, or a woman trying to sound like a man? They said. You're not safe, Henry. Not yet. The caller disconnected."

"Did you report it?"

"I." He stopped, looking down. "I was going to. It didn't seem real until I found the safe this morning."

Leilani closed her tablet and stood. "Thank you, Mr. Matsu. I'll need a copy of your call log and a list of your high-value guests for the past month."

He nodded, defeat settling in his bones. "Anything you need, Detective."

Leilani crossed to the window. Down by the pool, a flock of early risers practiced yoga on the dew-slick grass. She inhaled deeply, willing her brain to see connections. Her eyes caught on a cluster of framed photographs on the far wall. Matsu, arm-in-arm with a rotating cast of city officials, local developers and resort board members. In one, he stood at the ribbon-cutting ceremony for the new spa wing, beaming with the same forced pride she'd seen moments ago.

She made a mental note of the faces, their order, the subtle signals of alliance and hierarchy.

"Anything else?" he asked, already wilting behind his desk.

"Just this," Leilani said. "You're sure your own people are clean?"

He bristled, a flare of pride through the nerves. "My people are like family, Detective. We take care of our own."

She smiled, polite and unreadable. "That's what I'm counting on."

She thanked Matsu stood and walked out of the office. Out in the corridor, she thumbed a message to her tech unit. I need a full background on the temp IT hire, and a dump of all phone traffic to Matsu's number after midnight.

The first hint of adrenaline sizzled in her chest. She'd seen professional work before. Whoever pulled this off was local enough to draw the petroglyph, smart enough to hack the cloud, and brazen enough to toy with their mark. She doubted it was just about money.

Her stomach growled, a physical reminder she hadn't eaten since dinner. She made her way down to the resort café, and as she waited for her coffee, watched the guests trickle in. Every face is a new potential mask, every gesture a possible lie.

Leilani couldn't help but grin. For once, the morning looked like it might be interesting.

When she doubled back, the lobby had emptied. The sun had finally cleared the horizon, turning the hotel's east wall into a sheet of gold. Outside, the birds were having a party in the palms. Inside, the noise came from the soft slap of her own footsteps and the distant whir of a floor buffer.

She let herself in, letting the door fall closed behind her. The room smelled faintly of latex and bleach, like a dentist's office crossed with a server farm. She walked straight to the spiral on the marble, her spiral now, and crouched to eye level, getting as close as she dared.

The lines looked hand-drawn, but not in the way of a bored kid doodling on his math worksheet. Whoever drew it cared about form, or at least wanted to look like they did. The curves were steady; the turns exact. Leilani pulled out her phone and took a series of close-ups. First the entire spiral, afterward the place where the lines doubled back on themselves, and lastly the end point, where the chalk had crumbled under sudden pressure.

She sat back on her haunches and thumbed the photos into her tablet's search function. The database had been stitched together by a university team, a wild mix of Polynesian glyphs, logograms and ancient stone carvings. She keyed in concentric spirals, cross-referenced with Hawaii and Oahu. In less than a minute, she had a match. The Papahānaumokuākea petroglyph, better known as "the eye of the navigator." Old as the islands themselves, it was supposed to guide travelers or warn off outsiders.

Leilani stared at the screen, then at the chalk. "You're not a warning," she murmured. "You're a signature."

A throat cleared behind her. She looked up to see one forensic tech, a woman with close-cropped hair and an evidence satchel slung over one shoulder, hovering in the doorway.

"Detective?" the tech said. "You wanted preliminary?"

Leilani stood, dusting her hands on her jeans. "Hit me."

The tech opened her satchel and produced two clear bags. In one was the RFID spoofer James had found. In the other, two diamond-tipped drill bits. "No prints, obviously. These are commercial, off-the-shelf but pricey. Whoever did this, they did their homework. Bypass was clean, no alarms triggered until the safe was already open."

"And the chalk?"

She shrugged. "Kids' art supplies, nothing special. But they wore gloves, didn't smudge any fingerprints on the marble or the door."

Leilani nodded, already feeling the shape of the case in her bones. "Security system, could it be hacked externally?"

The tech grinned, a little admiring. "Could? Sure. But the patch level on this hotel's system is two revisions behind. The exploit's been floating around since last year. An amateur could have brute-forced it with time and a laptop."

Leilani experienced a pulse of irritation. "Anything else?"

"The cart used by the perp matches the ones in housekeeping," the tech said. "But that one's missing. The housekeeping boss says it vanished last night and showed up this morning in a dumpster behind the ABC Store. No hair, no fibers, nothing. Probably wiped down."

"Thanks." Leilani checked the door. "Get me a full list of employees and contractors who logged badge activity last night and ping the casino for guest comps or unusual charges after midnight."

The tech nodded, already texting.

Alone again, Leilani kneeled one last time by the spiral, letting her mind drift. Most thieves wanted to erase themselves from a crime scene. This one left a calling card. Why? To taunt? To lay claim? Or to deliver a message?

She snapped a last shot of the glyph, after which she stood and swept the room with one last look. A tightness in her chest told her she'd been here before. It was at that moment that a puzzle snapped into focus, and she realized the answers were going to hurt.

She walked out, already dialing her mother, her best source for the stories no database would touch. As the line rang, Leilani glanced once more at the chalk spiral, and wondered what kind of navigator would leave such an unmistakable mark.

She was about to find out.

# Chapter Two

## Symbols and Suspicions

The conference room at HPD headquarters had been upgraded with a new projector, though it still stank of burned coffee and nervous sweat. Leilani stood at the podium, a manila folder fat with photos and printouts balanced on her palm, and watched the slow-motion turf war unfold across the table.

To her left, the Chief of Detectives occupied the chair like it was an enemy fortress, one elbow anchored, the other hand drumming an unending Morse code onto the laminated surface. His eyes fixed on the phone sitting in front of him. On his right, the department's PR chief sat with arms folded, all business casual and barely concealed contempt for the detective's idea of fashion. At the far end, two city attorneys passed a legal pad back and forth, conferring in whispers, one eye always on the clock. The person who looked halfway interested was the new Assistant Chief, a short, square woman in a crisply pressed uniform who regarded Leilani with a mix of curiosity and predation.

"Whenever you're ready, Detective Kealoha," said the Chief of Ds, not looking up from his phone.

Leilani keyed the first slide, a montage of three different resort lobbies—one on the windward coast, one in Waikiki proper, and the third on the North Shore. In each, police tape lacerated the entrance, and in each, a small circle of forensic techs squatted over something out of frame.

"Three high-value property crimes in under two weeks," Leilani began. "No witnesses, no usable prints, no forced entry. Each location had state-of-the-art security, yet the suspect was in and out in under twelve minutes, according to time stamps."

The Chief slid his gaze up, thumb hovering over the mute button. "We've heard this part already."

"I know," said Leilani, modulating her voice with deliberate patience. She advanced the slide. Now the photo zoomed in on the first crime scene, a safe room door with a small, turquoise chalk spiral marked dead center. "What's new is this. At each site, the perpetrator left a signature. It's a petroglyph, locally known as the eye of the navigator."

The city attorneys peered at the screen, unimpressed.

Leilani pressed on. "The symbol predates Western contact by centuries, but it's not something you'd see on tourist T-shirts. Our working theory is the thief is kamaʻāina or has access to someone with specialized knowledge."

The PR chief snorted. "A homegrown cat burglar. That's what we're going with?"

Leilani fixed him with a stare. "It's better than blaming it on outside agitators just because it fits a headline."

Assistant Chief Mori cut in, her voice flat as poured concrete. "Detective, the Board of Tourism is blowing up my inbox. They want someone in handcuffs by the end of the week. Are you close?"

"I've got a person of interest," said Leilani, "But nothing we can take to a judge. The suspect wore gloves, avoided cameras, and spoofed the RFID system at all three resorts. Each time, they left behind part of a jammer device and used a different method to defeat the safe."

"So not a single amateur," the Chief of Ds said. He leaned forward, finally pocketing his phone. "That's the part that worries me."

Leilani's jaw tightened. "They're good. But they're also sending a message, Chief. These marks," she gestured at the petroglyph. "They're not signatures. They're taunts."

"And you're sure it's not a prank?" asked one attorney, who hadn't bothered to introduce himself. "Some kid with a TikTok channel?"

"If it is, he's the next Houdini," Leilani said, unable to keep the irritation from her voice. "We've matched fiberoptic fragments from each scene, and all point to custom builds. This guy is an engineer moonlighting as a thief, or vice versa."

The Chief resumed drumming, the tempo up a notch. "So, what do you need?"

"I need a couple more bodies to canvass resort staff and run background on current employees, especially recent hires and maintenance contractors. I also want to bring in a cultural consultant. The glyph is accurate, but the style is off. I think we're dealing with someone who's learned enough to fake being authentic."

The PR chief objected, but the Chief shot him a look that shut him up. "Fine. You can have two from Vice and a language expert from the University pool, but keep it off overtime. The last thing I need is a cost overrun for a glorified art project."

"Understood, Chief."

The city attorneys scribbled a note and said. "Have you notified the FBI?"

"They're looped in," said Leilani. "So far, nothing crosses state lines. We can handle it."

"Can we?" said the Chief of Ds. He pushed back his chair, the wheels squealing in protest. "These resorts pump millions into our economy every month, Detective. If the tourism board thinks HPD can't protect their assets, I'll be taking phone calls from the Governor, and the mayor. I need this wrapped up yesterday."

Leilani nodded once. She kept her posture squared, refusing to let her frustration show. "Okay, I'll get you a suspect by Friday."

"Good." The Chief of Ds stood. "Dismissed."

The attorneys and the PR chief made a beeline for the door. Mori lingered, hands behind her back.

"You've got instincts, Kealoha," Mori said, low enough so she could hear. "Don't let the old guard wear them out of you."

Leilani let the compliment hang, wary it might be bait. "Thanks, ma'am."

"Anything you don't want in the official record?"

asked Mori, eyes sharp.

Leilani thought about the chalk, the feeling that the marks were less about pride and more about misdirection. She shook her head. "Not yet. I'll let you know."

Mori smiled a sliver's worth and followed the others.

The conference room was cold and empty, stripped of all its institutional menace now that the show was over. Leilani packed her files back into the folder and took a long breath through her nose, trying to calm the fluttering in her chest. She'd fought for years to earn these moments of autonomy, coming to realize the leash was longer, but no less tight.

On the way out, she paused at the window, looking down at the city below. Morning traffic crawled along Beretania, punctuated by blue rental mopeds and the stray skateboarder weaving through. The sunlight struck the ocean in the far distance, turning it into a slick, dazzling sheet. It almost made you forget the predators that swam beneath.

Leilani pressed her forehead to the glass, willing the weight on her shoulders to ease. It didn't. Not even a little.

Leilani drove east along King Street until the buildings shrank and the trees grew fat with rain. Her mother's house, pale blue with a rusting tin roof and ginger plants crowding the porch, always looked like it was about to be reclaimed by the jungle. The driveway was choked with weeds. The mailbox was a coconut, carved with the family name in block letters:

KEALOHA.

She knocked once, twice, and stepped in, knowing the door would be unlocked and her mother somewhere within earshot.

"Kitchen," called a voice from the back.

Leilani navigated the narrow hall, blinking at the clutter, wooden masks, baskets, a parade of framed hula portraits, all Naalei's students, going back decades. The kitchen was its own world, a fog of ginger and brewing oolong, sunlight dappling the counter through battered louver windows. Her mother stood at the stove, stirring a chipped pot, her back as straight as a flagpole and her hair bundled in a fist of gray.

"Didn't think you'd come so soon," said Naalei, without turning.

"You called me," Leilani said, setting the folder of photos on the table.

"I called you last week," said her mother, pulling down a tin of honey from the cupboard. "Today, you come because you need something."

Leilani grinned, conceding the point. "I always need something."

She grabbed a seat, letting her shoulder slump. Naalei's house did that. It peeled off her cop armor and left the girl underneath, all hunger, and opinions. The table was set for two, as if her mother had been expecting her at this very moment, which, of course she had.

Naalei ladled tea into two mugs, one branded with

the Kamehameha School logo, the other a souvenir from a Vegas buffet. She slid the Vegas cup to Leilani, wiped her hands on the hem of her dress and sat across from her.

"Let me see."

Leilani spread the photos, the spiral glyph front and center. She slid a magnified shot across the wood grain.

Naalei held the photo close, narrowing her eyes until the lines blurred. "I know this one. It's the eye of the navigator. They say it guides the lost, warns the greedy."

"Or taunts the stubborn," Leilani said, sipping her tea.

Her mother didn't smile, but her eyes crinkled. "It's old, but this," she tapped the photo, "is new. Whoever did this has seen the real thing, but their hands are too clean. It's copied, not lived."

"I thought you might say that," said Leilani.

She leaned back, arms folded. "In the stories, the eye belongs to the trickster. Maui, or sometimes the mo'o, lizard spirits, who steal things to hide them again."

"Sounds about right," Leilani muttered.

Naalei studied her daughter over the rim of her mug. "They left it on purpose."

Leilani nodded. "Three times. Three different resorts, all in the same two weeks."

"It's not for you. It's for someone watching."

Leilani's mouth twitched. "Who?"

But Naalei had moved on, shuffling to the pantry. She emerged with a small dish, poured salt and a splash of rum, and set it next to the photo.

Leilani groaned. "Ma, not the rituals."

Her mother ignored her, dusting the rim of the dish with a pinch of turmeric and saying a quiet chant under her breath. When she finished, she placed both hands on the table, palms flat.

"Traditions matter," Naalei said. "But they are not toys. This thief uses your ancestors' marks like a mask at Halloween. Don't give them power they don't deserve."

Leilani poked at the dish. "You think it's a smokescreen?"

"I think it's a costume," said Naalei. "And not a very good one. But a bad actor can stir up trouble if the audience is foolish."

Leilani watched her mother's face for a long moment. "You ever see anything like this before?"

"In the old days, yes. It was always about land, or family honor. Sometimes both. But this? It smells of money."

Leilani thought about the Chief of Ds, the resorts, the urgent phone calls and the threat to the local economy. "Yeah," she said. "It smells like money to me, too."

Her mother took her hand, surprising her. The grip was warm and dry and impossibly strong.

"You will catch them," said Naalei, as if reciting a prophecy. "Don't chase shadows. Chase the person behind them."

Leilani let the words settle. Outside, a couple of mynah birds bickered in the breadfruit tree. Inside, her mother poured more tea. She rummaged in the fridge for papaya halves dusted with lime and chili salt.

As they ate, Leilani filled her mother in on the other details: the safe room, the missing jewelry, the tampered cameras. Her mother listened, saying little. Shaking her head at the right moments and asked for more details at the end.

"So," said Naalei. "Who do you trust to help you?"

Leilani answered without thinking. "Nobody yet. Possibly the new assistant chief. But the rest, they want an answer that fits in a press release."

Her mother raised a papaya slice. "Trust yourself. Your father always said you were the stubbornest of all his children. Prove him right."

Leilani laughed, and the tension in her shoulders vanished. She finished her tea, wiped her mouth, and gathered up the photos. "I'll be back when I have more."

"Bring your son next time," Naalei said, already loading dishes into the sink. "He needs to learn who he is."

"I'll try," said Leilani, and meant it.

She kissed her mother on the forehead, gathered her evidence, and stepped back into the humid green world. The driveway still overflowed with weeds. The coconut mailbox was still listing, but as she walked by, she noticed the fresh flowers tucked into the top.

She smiled. No matter how hard she tried to outrun her legacy, it always waited at home.

She slipped into her city issued Explorer and pulled onto the road, her mind already churning through new angles, but her body relaxed in a way she hadn't in weeks.

When she reached into her pocket, she found a small version of the spiral, carved on a stone. She laughed, wondering when her mother had placed it there.

Pickup time at Kahala Elementary was organized chaos. Soccer balls arced across the blacktop, teachers herded loose children like wrangling cats, and the curbside buzzed with parents double-parked and calling names out of car windows. Leilani sipped an iced coffee she didn't remember buying, squinting at the swarm until she spotted Kai, last out the door, shirt untucked, hair already coming loose from his morning bun.

He jogged with the loping enthusiasm of someone who trusted the ground to rise and meet him. His backpack, patched with Star Wars and Dwayne "The Rock" Johnson, bounced like a buoy in a hurricane. He scanned the sidewalk, saw her, and launched into a sprint.

"Mom!" he hollered, skidding to a stop so close he fogged the passenger window.

She popped the lock. "Hey, Detective Kai."

He slid in, dropping his bag on the floorboards with a heavy thunk. He wore his case face, eyebrows furrowed, lips pursed as he unzipped the front pocket and produced a spiral notebook.

"You didn't answer your phone," he said, flipping to a dog-eared page. "There was an incident."

She put the car in gear, easing into the queue of departing parents. "What kind of incident?"

"Suspicious disappearance. Mr. Chang's lunch box went missing during recess. No one saw anything. He says it was a bento with those little octopus hot dogs, and he's super bummed."

She nodded, feigning gravity. "An inside job."

"That's what I said." He glanced at his notebook, where he'd diagrammed the playground in painstaking detail. "I already questioned Aiden and Jasmine, but they had alibis. I think it was probably Chloe, because she had mustard stains on her hands."

Leilani grinned. "But you don't have hard evidence."

"Not yet." Kai's face clouded. "But I will."

She reached over, ruffled his hair, and watched the worry fade from his eyes. He leaned into the contact.

"Did you catch any bad guys today?" he asked, notebook poised for notes.

"Not yet," she said. "But I'm getting close. The thief left a clue. A drawing."

His eyes lit up. "Like a riddle?"

She nodded. "Kind of. A spiral. It's an old symbol; could be a warning or possibly a trick."

Kai mulled this over, doodling a spiral in the margin. "Did you dust for fingerprints?"

"We tried," said Leilani, "but they wore gloves."

He looked deeply disappointed. "That's not fair."

"Criminals rarely play fair, Kai."

He absorbed this with a long, solemn nod, before changing tactics. "Can I see your badge?"

She glanced around, checked her mirrors, and pulled it from her belt. She held it up, glinting in the late sun. Kai studied it with reverence, before he set about examining the micro-etchings on the edges.

"Do all detectives have the same badge?"

"Mostly," she said. "But each has a number. Mine is 1068."

"Is that your secret code?"

"In a way," said Leilani. "If you memorize the numbers, you'll always know who you can trust."

He liked this logic and jotted something in his book. They rode in companionable silence, the air heavy with the scent of miso soup from Kai's thermos and the faint, lingering ginger from her mother's kitchen.

At the next stoplight, Kai piped up. "How do you know when someone's lying?"

She considered the question. "Most liars look away. The best ones look you right in the eye, but they can't keep the details straight."

Kai mulled it over. "So you ask a lot of questions?"

"All the time," she said. "Sometimes it's not the answer that gives it away, but how fast they want to move on."

Kai leaned his forehead against the glass, watching a father struggle with an armful of soccer gear and a screaming toddler. "You think I'd be a good detective?"

"You're already better than most of the guys at my station," said Leilani, deadpan. "But don't tell them I said that."

He laughed, leaned back and closed his eyes. "I'm going to solve the lunchbox case before Monday."

"I know you will."

At the next light, Kai's hand found hers, a quick squeeze before he let go and rummaged in his bag for homework. She felt the pressure in her chest, different from the weight at work, more like a small warm stone. It surprised her every time.

"Mom?" he said, halfway to sleep. "If you catch your thief, can I help interrogate them?"

She smiled, turning onto their street. "You can watch. But you have to promise not to correct my technique."

He gave a sleepy laugh, then drifted off, head lolling with each bump in the road.

As Leilani pulled into the driveway, she let the day's tensions flatten out. Her phone buzzed with a message from her tech unit, more lab results, probably nothing new, but for once, she let it wait.

She turned off the Explorer, letting the quiet settle.

For the first time in days, she wasn't alone.

# Chapter Three

## Federal Interference

The Makai Grand Hotel took luxury to cartoonish extremes, from the gilded portico that arched like a cathedral to the valet team in matching lavender shirts, each ready to bow like a samurai at the drop of a parking stub. Leilani pulled into the loading zone, her battered Explorer setting off car alarms as it slotted between two electric blue Teslas. The doorman opened her door before she could kick it. He stood back, eyes professionally blank but tracking the dust on her boots.

She left the engine running and strode straight into the lobby. The AC hit like a slap, blasting her in the face with scented air, plumeria, ocean, something chemical lurking under the surface. A waterfall tumbled down three stories of polished basalt. Koi, the size of subway sandwiches, paddled in a pond circled by nervous tech execs and tanned influencers pretending to ignore the swirl of uniformed officers blocking the main hallway.

This was the big leagues. Which meant, she should have guessed, feds.

Her stomach tightened as she clocked the tall silhouette in the center of the scene. The man wore a crisp, dove-gray suit, his tie the same blue as the police helicopter. He moved with a velocity that said I've never missed a flight in my life, all direct lines and precise, economical steps. HPD's finest orbited him like moons around an exoplanet.

She drifted up behind the closest patrol, who tried and failed to mask a grimace of recognition. "Detective Kealoha," the cop said, handing her a sanitized evidence bag with a practiced flick. "They told me to send you to the scene lead."

She arched an eyebrow. "You mean the guy with the federal hair?"

He bit the inside of his cheek and nodded. "He's already gone over everything twice."

"Figures," she said, already moving.

She took a moment to case the perimeter. The lobby floor was cordoned off with velvet rope and a single narrow strip of crime scene tape. She noticed the forensic team in the back, their movement crisp, efficient, but subdued. There was a whiff of nervousness in the air, a sense of big brother watching. The hotel staff, usually world champions of calm, stood rigid and wide-eyed behind the front desk.

The safe room, she'd been told, was on the second floor, admin wing, halfway between the spa and the executive conference suite. The elevator had its own concierge, who checked her badge, offered a pressed handkerchief in case she was too warm, and pointed her to the right corridor. Leilani took the stairs, unwilling to let her brain cool down.

At the end of the marble hall, two HPD officers stood guard over a glass door etched with a stylized wave. Through the panel she could see him, Special Agent Isaac Torres, already mid-conversation with a woman in a Chanel skirt suit. He was tall and sharp-angled, every detail down to his shoes purebred and spit-polished.

He turned as she entered, and for a heartbeat, his face registered surprise, and defaulted to charming neutrality. He extended a hand.

"Detective Kealoha," he said.

"Special Agent Torres." She shook his hand. "Didn't expect to see you here."

"I was in the neighborhood and thought I'd check up on my favorite HPD detective."

Leilani laughed. "Sure you were. No, really. What's going on?" she asked.

The hotel manager hovered by the doorway, clutching a tablet and radiating stress. She kept glancing from Torres to Leilani, as if waiting for one to devour the other.

Torres gestured at the carnage in the safe room, and afterward at the woman in the Chanel suit, who was making a rapid tally of empty velvet boxes and silk bags with a sort of surgical detachment.

"Detective," Torres said. "The Bureau has reason to believe this isn't a standalone."

She looked past him into the room. It was less of a safe and more of a bank vault, floor-to-ceiling stainless, digital control panel, palm scanner, and a backup generator on a shelf. The contents, or what was left, were scattered in concentric rings like someone had detonated a jewelry grenade. It was, in its own way, beautiful.

"So, you read my case notes?" Leilani said, giving

him a sideways glance.

Torres took the bait, but his smile didn't waver. "We were hoping you'd brief us in person. And maybe explain this."

He held up his phone, showing a picture of the spiral drawn on the marble floor. She stared at his phone. The image was different, and her throat caught.

She couldn't help it; her face tightened. The mark was bigger than before, and this time the lines doubled back, as if the artist had changed their mind mid-stroke. At the center, a tiny dot circled in red pen. Forensics had already gone to town.

"Did the Chief of Ds call you in?" she asked. "Or did your people want a vacation on the government dime?"

Torres put up both palms. "Not my call, Detective. But the Bureau's white-collar unit is interested because of certain, let's say, financial irregularities. Two guests at the hotel are under observation for international wire fraud. Both had assets in this safe room."

"Lucky for them, the thief got here first," Leilani said.

"Or unlucky," Torres replied. "We think it may be a message."

She stepped into the room, careful not to touch anything. The usual trace of latex was overpowered by the sweet scent of mango disinfectant. She scanned the surfaces, her eyes moving faster than her feet. Every drawer was open, every cubby rifled, but there was no sign of forced entry, and the electronic lock blinked a friendly green.

She crouched, letting her gaze drift to the edges. The pattern on the marble was too clean, too practiced, as if someone had rehearsed it in advance. She took out her phone and snapped a series of high-res shots.

Torres stood behind her, not looming, but always in her periphery. "You have a theory?"

"Too early," she said. "But this is different from the others. Cleaner. More time spent on the mark. And." She trailed off, fished a latex glove from her pocket, and ran a finger along the outer spiral. There, tucked in the crook of the symbol, a tiny nick in the marble. Not deep, but intentional.

She pointed. "Our guy's escalating. Or getting more confident."

Torres followed her finger, then pulled out a pad and made a note. "Appreciate the eye, Detective."

She rose, stripped off the glove. "Who's in charge of the evidence chain?"

Torres ticked his pen towards the Chanel suit, who turned at once and introduced herself as the Bureau's local forensic lead. They did the usual dance, names, business cards, who had what authority and when. Leilani recognized a stone wall when she saw one. She made a circuit through the room with the forensic lead, pointing out items she wanted collected and catalogued. She turned, but didn't see Isaac anywhere.

She stepped back out into the hall. Alone, she let her composure crack enough to mutter a curse. She'd worked too hard on this case to have it lifted by mainland suits with a taste for TV drama.

Still, a part of her, the competitive part, relished the pressure. If the thief was trying to show off, so could she.

Down in the lobby, the doorman greeted her with a folded note, the paper smooth and heavy as a wedding invitation.

FROM THE DESK OF SPECIAL AGENT ISAAC TORRES, FBI. MEET ME BY THE KOI POND.

She folded it, slipped it in her pocket, and made her way through the knot of tourists and business travelers. Torres was already waiting, his jacket off, sleeves rolled, looking as comfortable as a man could look in a garden full of garish statuary and plastic flamingos.

"Leilani," he said, not smiling. "Walk with me."

She shrugged, then paced him around the pond, counting three turns before he spoke again.

"I get the sense you don't want us here." She hadn't wanted him on her last case either. A double murder involving crooked politicians, corrupt developers, and a master criminal known as Mastermind. They had worked well together and their friendship had grown as well, but she didn't like the feds swooping in on her cases.

She didn't answer.

He tried again. "I'm not here to step on toes. But this is bigger than you think. The two guests I mentioned. We've been tracking them for eighteen months. If someone is targeting them, it's no coincidence."

"Possibly," Leilani said. "Or someone's cashing in on the tourist circuit."

He paused at a bench, turned to face her full-on. "I'd like us to work together, like last time, but without the getting shot part." Leilani laughed, and her hand moved instinctively to her shoulder while he touched a still sensitive spot on his chest. "You know this case better than anyone. I know the players on the financial side."

"Fine," she said, after a moment. "But I don't do paperwork, and I don't wait for permission."

He grinned. "Good. Glad to see nothing's changed."

They sat, and she smiled at him. "How are you healing?"

He smiled. "It only hurts when I laugh or move. You?"

She touched her upper arm again. "Still gets tight once in a while, but not bad."

They watched the koi surface, hungry for food or gossip. The tension broke. Her phone buzzed. A text from forensics.

*SAFE ROOM PRINTS CLEAN, DNA HIT IS FEMALE, BELONGS TO HOTEL MAID. NOTHING ELSE.*

She looked at Torres. "Our thief wears gloves, avoids cameras, and leaves a calling card."

He nodded. "The spiral. A message?"

Leilani gazed at the water, at her own reflection warped by ripples. She was good at puzzles, better than most. But this one seemed different. Not like the other three thefts.

She stood up, dusted her hands on her jeans. "We're going to need more coffee."

Torres laughed. "Now you sound like a fed, but not that crap at your headquarters."

Torres headed inside the lobby while she walked over to the outside coffee bar and ordered two large coffees.

The hotel was on full alert now, security buzzing, managers whispering in corners. As she stepped through the lobby, Leilani spotted Torres exchanging numbers with the chief of security. She hated to admit it, but the man worked fast.

Outside, the sun had burned off the last of the morning haze. The sky was bluer than the lights on the patrol cars, and the palms stood dead still, as if holding their breath for what would happen next. She walked up and handed him a coffee cup. He nodded and took a sip.

"Exactly the way I like it," he said with a smile.

Leilani pulled out her phone and stared at the picture of the spiral. The thief had left her a message, all right. Now, she had to figure out if it was meant for her, or for the man who'd walked into her case and refused to leave.

Either way, she was ready to find the answer.

The Makai Grand's "executive suite" conference room was a study in contradictions. On one side, an acre of glass, with the Pacific framed in such electric blue it looked computer-generated. On the other, a twelve-foot slab of koa wood polished to an aggressive sheen, ringed with ergonomic chairs that cost more than Leilani's car. The room hummed with recycled air and nervous energy.

Isaac Torres had already commandeered the head of the table, a line of Bureau-branded notepads arrayed before him like chess pieces. He was rolling the cap of his Montblanc between two fingers, eyes on his phone but clearly listening to everything. Leilani took a seat off-center, close enough to catch the sunrise, but far enough to avoid being caught in his tactical stare.

The hotel manager arrived first, trailing a scent of aftershave and misery. His nameplate read KOJI TANIMURA, but the badge on his lapel said I'M HERE TO HELP. He carried a folder so thick it threatened to explode.

"Thank you both for coming," Tanimura began, voice sanded down to the grit beneath. "We're still doing inventory, but." He broke off as Isaac raised a hand.

"We'll get to the list in a second," said Isaac. "For now, let's focus on access. How many employees have physical access to the safe room?"

"Four," Tanimura answered instantly. "Myself, Marcus Kwan, our head of security, and two assistant managers. But we also have rotating maintenance and IT personnel for scheduled checks."

"And guests?"

"None. Zero. The guests with property in the safe

room are VIPs, and their assets are inventoried by management."

"Was anyone acting unusual in the days leading up to the incident?"

Tanimura hesitated. "A couple of high-profile guests checked out early. Russian, both. But that's not unusual during summit season."

Isaac nodded, making a note. "Do you keep logs of all badge entries and exits?"

"Digitally, yes. I've printed them out." Tanimura slid the folder forward, hands trembling slightly. "But, um, there's a ninety-second gap at 2:19 this morning. The system shows no activity, but the safe was breached in that window."

Leilani reached for the list, flipping pages with a light touch. "Does the gap coincide with a power failure or a maintenance event?"

He shook his head. "No. Power was steady. No blips, no alarms."

Torres looked up from his notes, fixing Tanimura with a stare that could freeze boiling water. "Any recent staff terminations? Threats? Suspensions?"

"We had one security staffer resign last week," Tanimura said. "But he left amicably. Moved to the mainland for family."

"Who was on duty last night?"

Tanimura checked a note. "Marcus was on security duty, plus a floater from Allied Security, but the latter does hourly walk-bys."

Leilani jotted the name, then added, "Can we get security footage from all entrances for the last forty-eight hours?"

Tanimura nodded, but his voice stuttered. "Yes, but I reviewed it already. There's nothing. Whoever did this, they never showed up on camera."

Isaac drummed his pen. "We need a list of everyone with admin access to the digital system."

Tanimura's composure crumbled a little more. "Of course."

Leilani watched his face, cataloguing every twitch. He wasn't lying, but he was frightened of more than the police.

The manager left them with the binder. The minute the door closed, Torres muttered, "He's hiding something."

Leilani blinked. "You read it too?"

He smirked. "That's what we're paid to do."

Next in was Marcus Kwan, the hotel security chief. He came in with a stiff military posture, wearing the resort's navy suit jacket like a flak vest. His forehead glistened, and his hands couldn't settle, first at his cuffs, smoothing the file, and clasping each other so tight the knuckles turned white.

Torres asked the first question, his tone pure Bureau. "Mr. Kwan, please confirm for the record your role here at Makai Grand."

Kwan cleared his throat. "Director of Security. Seven years. I manage all physical and digital assets, and supervise a team."

Torres cut him off. "We'll need your entire team's home addresses and prior employment history. Also, has anyone on staff reported threats, bribes, or attempts to compromise them over the last six months?"

"Absolutely not," Kwan said, voice a hair too loud.

Leilani leaned in, hands folded, eyes softening as if they were in a neighbor's kitchen. "Marcus, I'm guessing you're ex-military?"

He glanced at her, wary. "Yes. Navy."

She smiled. "You know what it's like to follow the chain of command. But if someone higher up told you to look the other way for an hour, how would you handle it?"

Kwan shifted in his seat, throat working. "I wouldn't."

"You're sure?"

He stared at his hands. "Yes, Detective."

Torres made a show of writing that down. "Let's move to the digital records. Who maintains your server?"

Kwan blinked, relief flooding his face at the safe topic. "Our IT firm, Pacific Byte. But I have override access. So do Mr. Tanimura and one hotel board member. Everyone else needs two-factor authentication."

"Was there a remote login last night?"

Kwan opened his own folder, hands finally steady.

"No evidence of one. But there was a two-minute lag at 2:18 AM, which lines up with the badge reader gap."

Leilani locked on. "Who's the board member with access?"

"Evan Shigeta," Kwan said. "He hasn't visited the property in a month, but he could technically log in from anywhere."

Isaac's pen froze. "And his relationship to the Makai Grand?"

Kwan hesitated. "He's the owner's son-in-law."

Leilani caught the tremor in his voice, filed it away. "You know him well?"

Kwan nodded, eyes darting toward the door. "We served together."

"What branch?" Torres asked.

"Submarines. Pearl Harbor," Kwan said, not meeting their eyes.

Leilani softened her tone further. "You seem tense, Marcus. Are you worried about repercussions?"

He shook his head, a drop of sweat tracing down his temple. "No, ma'am. I'm embarrassed this happened on my watch."

She gave him a look that said, You're not alone. "What can you tell us about the mark left on the marble?"

Kwan straightened, grateful for a technical question. "It's like Polynesian navigational glyphs. I've seen them in museums, sometimes at heiau sites.

But this one, the triple spiral, it's rare."

"Have you seen it before on the property?" Isaac asked.

"Never," said Kwan

Torres turned to Leilani. "Anything else?"

She let the silence build a moment, then asked, "Marcus, did you know the security camera in the safe room was partially covered with tape last night?"

He blinked, confusion flickering. "That's not possible. I inspected it at ten p.m. It was clean."

"And at two a.m.?"

He hesitated. "I… wasn't in the area."

Leilani cocked her head. "Your logs say you made a round at 1:55."

He looked down. "I may have misremembered."

"People do," she said, not letting up. "But you're detail oriented. Which makes me think you noticed something strange and didn't want to put it in writing."

Kwan's face paled. "I didn't want to jump to conclusions."

"What conclusions?" Isaac asked, tone suddenly sharper.

Kwan finally looked up, eyes hollow. "There was a guest wandering near the admin hall, around one. I asked her to return to her suite, and she did, but she seemed… lost. I thought she was drunk."

"Which guest?" Isaac asked.

Kwan swallowed. "Her name's on the register. I'll get it for you."

Leilani nodded, standing up. "Thank you, Marcus."

As he left, Torres let out a low whistle. "That was impressive."

She shrugged. "Old-school island hospitality. If you act like you're family, people forget you're a cop."

He grinned. "You got more out of him in ten minutes than I would in an hour."

"But he's still holding back," she said. "He knows more than he's telling."

Torres's smile vanished. "Could be. Or might fear losing his job."

Leilani gathered her notes. "We should run the guest registry, see if there's a pattern. And I want a look at Kwan's service record."

Torres picked up his notepad. "I'll have Quantico check for international links on the owner's son-in-law."

She glanced at the window, at the horizon so bright it made her eyes water. "It's never the obvious one."

Torres followed her gaze. "You mean the suspect, or the method?"

She shrugged. "Both."

Downstairs, the lobby had thinned, the parade of guests reduced to a trickle of retirees and honeymooners. In the corner, Tanimura stood alone, hands wringing each other like wet towels.

"He's hiding something," Leilani murmured.

Torres didn't look convinced. "I want to see proof. Not hunches."

Leilani didn't argue. She watched the tide, waiting for the next wave.

The sky over the Makai Grand had shifted from blue to the color of a bruised plum, storm clouds massing on the horizon. It had been a long day of interviews with nothing to show for it. Leilani watched the approaching storm. If she had been superstitious, scratch that, if she'd been any less stubborn, she might have taken the sky's warning to heart. But she'd been a cop too long to believe in weather as an omen. If anything, she liked a little turbulence.

She and Torres ducked back through the admin hall, now abandoned except for a cleaner swabbing up footprints with clinical indifference. The hotel's spa music still leaked from overhead, mocking their sense of urgency with a rain stick and ukulele.

They reached the safe room. This time, the forensic team had finished, so the two of them had the place to themselves.

Torres scanned the door; his profile set to doubtful but game. "I don't get it," he said. "The lock is untouched. The wiring's clean. Whoever got in here had the code or knew how to sidestep it. The alarm didn't make a blip."

Leilani kneeled on the floor, her palm bracing against the cool marble. The spiral mark was still fresh, this time rendered in dark, matte streaks, charcoal, not chalk. Up close, she saw the black flecks on the surrounding tile, and a faint dusting on the corner of the nearest cabinet.

She took out her phone, set it to macro, and started snapping. "We're dealing with someone who doesn't want to take things," she murmured. "They want to leave a fingerprint. But not a real one."

Torres folded his arms. "The mark's for show. It's a way to feed your ego when you're bored with taking money."

"Or it's a warning," Leilani said. "You saw the old stories. Some petroglyphs are guides. Some are threats."

He leaned in, lowering his voice. "I think you're seeing ghosts, Leilani. But if it gets us closer, I'll play along."

She studied the symbol again, eyes narrowed. At the outer edge, three tiny cross-marks radiated out from the main line, almost like notches on a tally stick. She checked her notes from the other sites. Three spirals at the first three scenes. All very similar. Now four, but this one was different. The thief was counting. Or keeping score.

She angled her phone for a better shot, but the lens glared. Torres, unasked, produced a penlight from his jacket and aimed it from the side, casting shadows that made the tiny cross-marks pop.

"Nice," she said. "You always carry a flashlight?"

"My dad was a homicide cop in Miami. Habit."

She filed it away. Perhaps he wasn't all Bureau.

Torres paced the vault, pausing at the backup generator. "You know what bugs me? Nobody else noticed the signature. Not the owner's son-in-law, the submarine guy."

She straightened, pocketing her phone. "Because he was never meant to be. The marks are for people like us. Investigators."

He chewed on that. "So, what's the message?"

"That the thief is smarter than us," she said, deadpan.

He grinned, grudging respect in his eyes. "Not hard. The Bureau's batting zero on this one."

Leilani glanced at the security panel. "Has anyone checked the motion sensor logs?"

"First thing I did. No anomalies," he said.

She perused the keypad, thinking of Kwan's hands, the way he'd clutched them together, holding on like he might slip out of his own skin. The security chief was hiding something. She'd bet her badge.

"Let's go for a walk," she said.

They exited into the corridor. The storm had arrived; rain lashed the glass wall in smears, the ocean now a gray static. Most guests had retreated to their rooms, but a few diehards still lounged under the porte-cochère, drinks sweating in their fists.

She led Torres through the employee hall, bypassing the main elevator for the fire stairs. He followed without complaint. At the bottom, the garage was dim and nearly empty, with a few rental SUVs and an electric golf cart on a charger. The air was thick with wet concrete.

She spotted Marcus Kwan immediately. He was standing near a white van, back turned, hunched into a phone call. He jerked his head up at their approach, thumb stabbing at the End button.

"Afternoon, Marcus," Leilani called.

He tried to mask his alarm with a smile. "Detective. Agent."

Torres kept it cordial. "Burning the midnight oil?"

Kwan shrugged, glancing at the van. "Checking the perimeter before heading home. That's all."

Leilani closed the distance. "Rough day?"

Kwan let out a strained laugh. "You could say that."

She nodded at the phone in his hand. "Anything interesting?"

"It's my wife. She's worried. You know, after all this."

Torres looked at Leilani. "Would you mind if we spoke to her?"

Kwan blanched. "I…she's not well. She's in bed already."

Leilani softened her tone. "We're not here to make it worse, Marcus. But I have to ask, were you expecting a call tonight?"

His jaw clenched. "No. I mean, yes. To check in with my wife."

She stepped closer. "Who was on the phone, really?"

For a split second, Kwan looked like he might bolt. Instead he slumped. "An old friend. We were in the Navy together. He heard about the theft. He's worried I'll get scapegoated."

"Name?" asked Torres, notebook poised.

Kwan hesitated. "Evan Shigeta."

Leilani recorded it. The board member. The submariner. She thanked Kwan, who shuffled away with the air of a man already sinking.

When they reached the parking garage, Torres exhaled. "You were right. He's hiding something."

She flashed him a sideways glance. "I told you."

He raised a hand, conceding. "From now on, we share everything. No more solo runs."

She smiled, letting the victory hang in the wet air. "Deal."

They lingered a moment, the thunder outside a distant drumbeat. Torres offered her a stick of gum, which she declined, laughing at himself for the gesture.

He eyed her. "We should go see the owner's son-in-law tomorrow."

"We?" she said, teasing.

He shrugged. "You don't play well with others. I don't either. That's why we work so well together."

She considered this, then nodded. "Fine. But I'm driving."

He grinned. "Just keep it under Mach One."

She almost laughed.

They stood silently, watching the storm pummel the city. The thief was out there somewhere, plotting their next move, the spiral mark growing with each success.

But so were they.

And Leilani liked her odds.

# Chapter Four

## Underworld Whispers

Chinatown didn't know how to sleep. At two a.m., the streets radiated an energy somewhere between dying battery and short circuit. Above the noodle joints and tattoo parlors, neon signs pulsed in unreadable kanji. The air tasted of car exhaust and frying oil, underlined by a faint thread of clove cigarettes. The thing that was sharper than the alleyway shadows were the eyes that lurked within them.

Leilani moved through the blur like a tide pool predator, low and careful. She ducked past a knot of off-duty service workers and into the Blue Bamboo, a bar so dedicated to anonymity it advertised by the faint sound of slack-key guitar leaking through its door. Inside, the darkness was deliberate, a tactical decision by the management. No one wanted to see or be seen. The décor was a muddle of fake Polynesia and battered Formica, barely lit by fish tanks that hummed ominously. Most of the patrons hunched over their drinks, faces lit blue from beneath like in a horror movie.

She spotted her mark instantly. Keoki had the posture of a hunted animal, elbows up around his beer, head dipped as if he might drink by osmosis. His hair was salt and pepper now, slicked with product, and his aloha shirt looked like it had never been unwrinkled in its entire lifespan. He glanced up as she approached, and for a heartbeat, she observed the man he'd been before the years and the stress and the two stints inside.

She slid into the booth opposite him, making sure not to brush his glass. "You look worse every time I see you," she said, voice flat but not unkind.

Keoki laughed, a papery sound. "And you look more cop. That's a talent, Detective." His eyes skittered sideways, tracking the bartender, the guy on the end stool, back to her. "Is it safe to talk here?"

"About as safe as anywhere." She signaled the bartender for a coffee, leaned in, lowering her voice enough for the acoustics to erase it in the noise.

Keoki ran a finger around his glass. "It's hot tonight, yeah? Not the weather. Lotta movement, lotta rumors."

She waited. Informants were like vending machines with a broken coin slot. If you pushed too hard, they jammed.

He scanned the bar again, and shrugged. "I heard about your problem at the Makai Grand. My cousin works janitorial there, part time. Says the place is crawling with HPD and some haole feds."

"Maybe we're thirsty," Leilani said. "But you didn't call me out for spa gossip."

He grimaced. "Don't get cute. You want info, you pay for info. That was always the deal."

She produced a slip of paper from her inside pocket, a receipt for a traffic warrant fixed three weeks ago, and slid it across the table. He snatched it up, checked the signature, and pocketed it without a word.

Keoki glanced around. He leaned in. "There's a new player. Not kama'āina, not mainland either. This guy, he moves like he's got clearance everywhere. Never the same car, never the same look. People call him the Host."

She frowned. "That's not really a good villain name."

Keoki laughed again, but it was a nervous tic. "He's not a villain, not like you think. More like a coordinator. He brings in the jobs, lines up the muscle and the brains, then vanishes before it pops off."

Leilani sipped her coffee, black and bitter. "Did he ever show up in person?"

"I saw him once at the All-In Diner, two weeks ago. He was talking to some Russian girl. Out of place, but not out of his element, if you know what I mean. Like he'd already cased the place before he sat down."

"Describe him."

Keoki hesitated, then plucked a bar napkin and a stubby pen from the table's condiment bin. His hands shook as he wrote. "Couldn't get a read. Local maybe, but light-skinned. Short hair, face like a math teacher, but the eyes were dead. Real dead." He doodled something on the napkin, then started scribbling numbers, not looking up as he talked.

"Here's the thing," he said, scribbling faster, voice dropping almost to a whisper. "Everyone's scared of him, but not because he'll kill you. It's what comes after. You vanish, but your accounts, your condo, your kid's trust, everything keeps moving like you're still around. He's into digital, not blood."

She watched him finish, then slid the napkin over.

It was a scrawl of routing numbers, random letters, and question marks. She recognized two bank codes. Both belonged to offshore laundromats that served the resorts.

"Who's this belong to?" she asked.

Keoki wiped his palms on his shirt. "High roller. Used to launder for the Waikiki strip. Not a squealer, but he's missing. Nobody's talking."

"Do you trust your source?"

"More than I trust you." It didn't sound like a joke.

She palmed the napkin, folding it into her wallet. "What's the Host want?"

"Nobody knows. He's not after money. Not really. It's about control. The new rumor is he's building a portfolio of people, assets, secrets. Like he wants to own Honolulu, one bite at a time."

Leilani didn't like the sound of that. She didn't like a lot of things about this story, least of all the way Keoki's hands wouldn't quit shaking.

"You got more?" she asked.

"No way. You already owe me double for what I said. You don't get it, Detective. This guy doesn't have to threaten. He lets you know he's there. The next day, your kid's teacher calls from a new phone number. Your parole officer retires early. You go to lunch, and there's a seat waiting, but you never ordered."

Leilani considered. "You want protection?"

He flinched. "That's what I'm saying. There's no protection. If you dig, you're already buried."

She was about to press him, but Keoki's eyes caught on something behind her, and he froze. Not a hard freeze, but a fractional shift, a stiffness in the spine. She didn't turn. Instead, she used the reflection in the glass behind his head.

Someone had joined the bar, dark suit, hair clipped high and tight, eyes scanning, not drinking. He looked almost like a security detail, but the confidence said otherwise.

Keoki drained the rest of his beer, wiped his mouth, and stood. "We're done. You didn't hear any of this from me."

He slipped out so fast he left the receipt. Leilani gathered her things, but didn't rush. She paid for her coffee in cash and left the napkin tip folded in her palm.

On her way out, she glanced at the watcher. The man didn't acknowledge her. He watched the TV, a basketball game replaying in a loop. Still, she spotted the earpicce, the way his hand hovered near his hip.

The rain had started again, a thin drizzle that turned the neon to bleeding colors. She stepped into the wet, and the door closed behind her, the noise of the Blue Bamboo replaced by the electric hum of the city at night.

She knew the napkin in her pocket was more dangerous than a loaded gun. And that someone, somewhere, was already aware she had it.

She hurried back to her car, never once looking back.

The FBI's Honolulu field office wasn't built for beauty. The walls wore the same sickly taupe as every government building from Anchorage to Guam, and the décor was a plaque commemorating the agency's 50th year on the island. The bullpen after hours was silent as an empty church. The overheads buzzed with cheap fluorescence, but Torres worked by the blue-white glow of his monitor, the rest of the room in darkness except for the fire exit sign and the blinking charge light on his laptop.

He looked like hell. Shirt sleeves rolled, tie on the desk, jawline stippled with the shadow of a twelve-hour day. The desk was buried under two weeks' worth of printouts, flagged emails, and three separate case folders, each labeled with his unforgiving scrawl: MAKAI GRAND, PACIFIC HAVEN, ALOHA SHORES. A manila envelope full of flagged wire transfer sheets crowned the mess.

Torres had long ago learned that most crimes were interesting on paper. Most times, murder got boring if you sifted through enough spreadsheets. But tonight, the numbers were like clues instead of chores.

He squinted at his monitor, switching between a spreadsheet and the Bureau's secure database. Each cell was a bullet hole, bleeding into the next. The pattern wasn't obvious, but it was there. Days before every major heist, there was a ripple, a sudden, out-of-pattern wire transfer. Small at first, then massive, always routed through the same chain of shell companies in the Caymans, and always scrubbed clean by a pro.

Torres tapped his pencil against his lip, and pulled

up the spreadsheet's metadata. The shell companies, SINOCO, BLUE RAVEN, LAGOON HOLDINGS, all had different owners, but every single one was set up in the past year. The email on file was a rotating string of numbers and symbols. Disposable, like a burner phone for the digital age.

He scribbled notes on a yellow legal pad, underlining keywords three times before crossing them out. He liked the tactile feel of paper, even if the Bureau preferred everything logged and encrypted. On his notepad, he started a tree. Resort Names branching to dates, to the shadow companies, to the sums. Below, he wrote. What's the pattern? Who benefits?

He stopped and massaged his temples. He missed working cases that smelled of blood and gunpowder. Not this white-collar shell game. But he was good at recognizing patterns. In his first year at Quantico, he'd memorized the entire suspect taxonomy for a bet, to prove he could. Numbers didn't lie, but they could hide.

He pulled up the timestamp of the last wire transfer. Three a.m., exactly two days before the Makai Grand job. He cross-referenced the login used to initiate the transfer. It pinged from a Tor server, bounced twice through Russia, ending in Singapore.

He smiled. "Found you," he said to nobody.

He opened a new window and built a diagram, nodes, and arrows linking the dots. He color-coded the different jobs. Blue for the first hit, green for the second, red for Makai Grand. With every line, the thing grew more complicated, but the center held. Someone orchestrated all of it, moving funds in and out like a chess player flicking pawns from the board.

Torres paused and glanced at the wall clock. 2:17 AM. He wondered if Kealoha was awake, probably was. He considered calling her, but remembered the look in her eyes the last time he'd interrupted her at home. Not tonight. She'd still be smarter than him in the morning.

He checked his inbox, found two more internal memos from D.C., both urging patience and cross-checking and keeping local assets in the loop. He ignored both. He made a note on the legal pad. "Trust instincts. Move fast."

He flipped to a fresh page and listed every name that appeared more than once in the background checks. Three popped. Two low-level clerks, one maintenance guy, all with squeaky clean records. But the fourth name, Rafiq Nawaz, the IT contractor at Aloha Shores, came up on an FBI white-collar watch list for suspected money laundering in San Jose four years prior. Never charged, but on the radar.

He typed up a quick background check on Nawaz, sent it to the Bureau's cyber task force, then sat back and rolled his shoulders. The air conditioner kicked in, rattling the windowpanes. It smelled faintly of something like cinnamon.

He studied the printouts, the names, the flowchart and the map on the wall with pins stuck into it. Each job was so perfect it hurt. No forced entry, no alarms, and zero evidence. But the wires, those couldn't be erased. They had to be rerouted. And whoever was running the show was getting greedy, bolder with each hit.

He noted the last line on his pad. The handwriting had changed, as if he'd written it in a hurry. Mastermind?

He grinned despite himself. He'd seen the term in Leilani's police reports, always used with skepticism. But it fit. Someone was running these jobs like an algorithm. Not stealing, but investing in chaos. Testing for weaknesses. Torres sensed the heat in his veins, as was typical before a break.

He opened the Mastermind case file, scanned through the previous notes, and started a new page. Connection, all three resorts, all wire funds, all started from the same digital footprint. A link to Nawaz, IT.

He printed the page and added it to the file, the stack thicker now than the Bureau's quarterly budget request.

He sat, letting the quiet settle. He thumbed Leilani's number on his cell, hovering his finger over Send. She'd be pissed. He put the phone down.

Instead, he propped his feet on the desk, took a last look at the board, and watched the shape of the thing finally come into focus. They had a suspect. The rest was details.

As Leilani reached her street, the rain had slowed to a fine, floating drizzle, blurring the streetlights into soft halos. She killed the headlights and coasted the last few yards, instinctively checking the rearview before stepping out. The quiet in her bones was different from the one in the city. It was honest, earned, a fatigue that grounded her. She opened the door with the back door key, shouldering it gently so it wouldn't stick and wake her so.

She expected darkness, or at least the dull, forgiving blue of the kitchen nightlight. Instead, the living room was a strobe of LEDs and the glow of the old TV. She found Kai on the carpet, surrounded by open detective novels, a clutch of battered composition books, and a web of neon-colored yarn tacked to the foot of the couch. He'd stacked toy magnifying glasses on the coffee table and staged an entire cast of action figures in a ragged half-circle around a plush Pikachu. The suspect was bound with a twist tie.

He was so focused on his cross-examination, doing both the accused and the interrogator's voices, that he didn't see her at first. His brow furrowed in concentration as he asked, "Where were you on the night of the chili spill, Mr. Sparkle?" and in a falsetto, "I was in the laundry room, I swear!" The kid had good instincts, but no poker face. Every emotion was scrawled across his cheeks, and when he looked up, the joy at seeing her wiped the scene away.

"Mom!" He rocketed up, nearly tripping on the web of yarn, and ran to her at full speed. And paused, not sure if he should hug or give a cool detective nod. He decided on both, wrapping his arms around her waist and tilting his head up, wide-eyed.

"You're home early," he said, trying for casual but missing by a mile.

She dropped her bag by the umbrella stand,

suppressing a groan as her shoulders finally slumped. "It's after one," she said. "Detective hours don't count as early."

He grinned, gap-toothed. "I was on a big case. Didn't want to sleep until I cracked it."

She mussed his hair. "It looks like you broke more cases than you solved, Junior."

He grabbed her hand and towed her to the center of the living room, skidding on his socked feet. "Wait, wait, you have to see this. I've got clues!"

The crime board he'd built on the coffee table would have put some rookies to shame. There were scribbled timelines, cutouts from local newspapers, and a diagram mapping out potential escape routes from a stick-figure drawing of the Makai Grand. In the middle, a sticky note read, MOTIVE???

She sat cross-legged, trying not to collapse. "Walk me through your theory, Detective Kealoha."

He pointed teacher-like with a cheap plastic ruler. "Okay. So first, the thief is good, right? But that means they probably messed up once, somewhere. That's how it always goes in the books. So, I checked all the robberies from the last year and made a list of every single time something got stolen, like lunch money at school." He pointed at the notepad. "There's a pattern. Every time there's a big heist, there's a little one first. Like it's practice."

Leilani's smile saddened. "That's smart. Too smart."

He bounced on his toes. "Right? So, I figured, what

if you follow the little ones? You can catch the big one before it happens?" He paused, searching for validation.

She met his gaze and experienced pride. "You might have cracked it, Kai. Next time I hit a wall, I'll bring you in for a consult."

He beamed, glancing sideways, as if remembering he was supposed to be cool. "So, um… did you catch the guy yet?"

"Not yet," she whispered. "But we have a really good lead." She ruffled his hair again. "Now, your turn. Did you brush your teeth?"

He made a show of sniffing his own breath. "Like five times. Gums, too."

She couldn't help it; she laughed, loud enough that it might wake the neighbor's dog. She scooped him up and dropped him onto the couch, then started tidying the crime scene, stacking the books and gathering the scattered clues. He watched her, fiddling with the magnifier, silent for a rare second.

"Mom," he said finally. "Can I ask you a real detective question?"

She braced herself. "Go ahead."

"What do you do if you know something bad is coming, but you can't stop it? All you can do is slow it down."

She froze. For a heartbeat, she wondered if he'd picked up something from the news, or from her face, the way the job sometimes left marks you couldn't scrub off.

"You tell someone you trust," she said, voice gentle. "And you do your best, even if it's not perfect."

He nodded, rolling the answer around in his head. "But what if that person gets hurt?"

She kneeled beside him, putting a hand on his shoulder. "You stay with them. You help them heal."

He smiled, but it was a small, worried thing. "I think you're the best detective in the world, Mom."

She kissed the top of his head. "You're not a bad partner yourself."

She shooed him toward the hallway. "Bedtime. And no more crime scenes until daylight, got it?"

"Got it," he called, scampering off.

She tidied and sat on the couch, letting the silence soak in. On the coffee table, Kai's notebook sat open to a page with bold block letters. SUSPECTS, MOTIVE, ALIBI. It made her want to cry and laugh at the same time.

She locked up, double-checked the windows, then peeked in on him before heading to her own room. He was already under the covers, but the notepad was clutched tight to his chest.

She whispered, "Good night, Detective."

His eyes were already closed, but he mumbled, "G'night, Mom. Dream of clues."

She turned out the hall light and, allowed herself a smile. Tomorrow would be another hard day.

But for now, she'd let the world go quiet.

# Chapter Five

## A Deadly Turn

Leilani hated late night calls, but she hated being second on the scene more. The drive to Honu Bay Resort was thirty minutes of winding switchbacks, headlights carving tunnels through the darkness and rain smearing the world to a blur. When she finally crested the last rise, the resort loomed below, one sprawling pearl set in the black bowl of the bay. Ocean to the right, jungle to the left, and, for tonight at least, an armada of police strobes tattooing the entrance in a wash of blue and white.

She killed her flashing lights at the gate. The guard shack was deserted, with a single Styrofoam coffee cup still spinning in the puddle on the ledge. She rolled through the gravel crunching under her tires, and followed the driveway toward the main building. Palm trees bowed under the wind, their fronds lashed sideways as if they were ducking the sirens.

A row of patrol cars blocked the porte-cochère. Leilani parked wherever she fit, killed the engine, and let her eyes adjust. The air was thick with salt and humidity. Past the valets' podium, a smear of yellow tape fluttered between two posts.

As she stepped out, a uniformed patrol officer, barely old enough to shave, met her at the curb. His nametag read F. MORALES.

"Detective Kealoha," he said, nerves making the syllables trip over each other. "They're expecting you upstairs."

"Show me," she said.

They moved through the lobby, which looked more obscene at two in the morning, a million dollars of lighting empty, every mirror reflecting the chaos outside. At the elevator, Morales fumbled with his card and punched the button for the twelfth floor. The ride up was silent aside from the burble of the lobby fountain still filtering in from below.

At twelve, the doors slid open onto another wall of tape. A night manager stood there, hands wringing a hotel towel. He was early forties, the man who wore ties in self-defense, now sweating through his collar as if every stain was a new criminal offense.

"I'm… I'm supposed to walk you through," he said, then realized how dumb it sounded and tried to fix it with a watery smile. "They're all waiting."

"Lead the way," said Leilani, keeping her hands in her pockets.

Suite 1204 was at the end of the hall. The carpet, usually plush and beige, was now a crime scene, with boot prints in every direction, a drag mark that made her heart race despite herself. The manager stopped short of the open double doors, gesturing weakly.

"Take a seat," Leilani told him. "If you remember anything else, I'll find you."

He nodded and vanished.

Inside, the lights were all the way up. Crime techs in bunny suits circled the room, snapping photos, scribbling notes. One looked up, saw Leilani, and gave her a sharp chin-jut out of respect. In the center of the marble floor, a body sprawled flat, arms akimbo, one cheek mashed against the grout line as if in supplication.

She knew before she glimpsed the face. The way the legs bowed, the right boot scuffed raw, the bulk of the frame inside the rent-a-cop blazer. John Maka'ala. The security officer was ex-HPD, two years retired and working the graveyard shift at Honu Bay. He'd taught her how to clear a hallway her second week on the job. He'd sent her bad dad jokes every Christmas. He'd called her Lani, like nobody else on the force.

He'd also been shot twice in the chest, at point-blank range. Blood ran black in the harsh light, pooled under his torso, streaked out in shaky arterial arcs where he'd tried to crawl. His arms reached forward, hands empty. No weapon.

Leilani stood there, not breathing, for a five-count. She stepped over the evidence markers and kneeled by his head.

He was older, heavier, his hairline running for the exit, but the jaw was unmistakable. The mouth looked ready for a joke. She shut her eyes long enough for the sting to pass, then opened them again. Back to work.

His blazer was open, shirt dark and sodden. A lanyard still hung from his neck, the plastic sleeve bent but readable: JOHN MAKA'ALA, SECURITY OFFICER. Below it, a smaller badge, tarnished but intact. HPD, issued 2002.

"Who found him?" Leilani asked, her voice steady.

A tech across the room piped up. "Night cleaner. She was doing turndown. Says he always made his rounds right before two. She thought it was weird when he didn't show. Saw the door open, found him like this."

"Anybody else in the room?"

"Not when she got here. No sign of forced entry, no glass broken. The suites under a VIP comp."

Leilani's eyes moved across the suite. The living area was untouched. TV muted, the remote still balanced on the arm of the couch. The minibar stood open, with one bottle missing. The bedroom door was ajar, the bed pristine, but a suitcase flopped open on the luggage bench. Inside, clothes folded with military precision, then scattered as if someone had rooted through in a hurry.

The bathroom door gaped wide. Through it, she saw a second smear of blood leading to the toilet. She followed it, avoiding the mess, and saw where John had tried to brace himself on the porcelain tank before he fell. There on the far wall above the sink was the spiral.

The petroglyph, done with a thick, wobbling finger, was drawn from the dark arterial ooze leaking down John's wrist. It was perfect, concentric, intentional, unmistakable. This time, it wasn't chalk or charcoal or marker. This was done in his blood.

Leilani stared at it, all the heat rushing from her chest to her hands. She forgot about the cameras, the forensics, and the body on the floor. She could see the line, the intent behind it, and what it meant.

Not a message. A declaration.

She steadied herself against the vanity as gravity set in. She knew the Mastermind had killed, or ordered the killings of at least two people, Sonny Alana, and Mako Pahoa, so he wasn't afraid of violence, but this string of robberies didn't show the same proclivity, until now.

Someone came up behind her. She didn't turn. "Get the photo, then cover it."

"Yes, ma'am," the tech replied softly and fast.

She pivoted back into the suite. Morales was back in the doorway, the manager still beside him, wringing his towel.

"Who else was in the building?" Leilani asked.

The manager said, "We're at thirty percent occupied. Most of the wing is empty except for one honeymoon couple and a group of Japanese retirees."

"Did anyone hear anything? Gunshots, yelling?"

His face turned ghost white. "No. The walls here are two layers, soundproofed. And there was a storm, thunder all night."

She nodded, filed it away. "Get me a list of all guest keycards used in the last six hours, and anyone who left or entered through the staff doors."

He nodded, eager to be helpful.

Leilani turned back to Morales. "Keep the hallway locked down. Nobody leaves the floor until I say. Do we know who was staying in this room and where that person is right now?"

"No, Detective."

"Do you think you could go find out?" she asked.

Morales bolted for the door, leaving Leilani with her thoughts.

She walked to the window and parted the curtains. The resort's grounds glimmered, rain-slick and empty. Down below, another set of headlights crawled up the drive. Probably Torres. He was always late, but never missed a party.

Leilani glanced at John once more, afterward at the spiral on the wall. She remembered his voice, the way he'd called her "Lani-girl" when she was a rookie. How he'd said, "Never turn your back on the ugly; it always gets uglier."

She had no intention of turning away.

She rolled her neck, tucked her hair behind her ears, and stepped back into the chaos. The city was already waking, and so was the hunt.

The next hour was work, nothing but. Leilani wrapped herself in the rituals. Gloves, notebook, two cameras, one digital and one instant, because prints didn't crash. She circled the body, framing shots of the wound, the spatter, the way the shirt bunched up beneath the armpit. The entry wounds were clean, a double tap to the sternum. John had gone down fighting, judging by the crescent of blood under each fingernail.

The techs respected her orbit. They boxed evidence, bagged the shell casings, and ran black lights over the bathroom. On the marble, she found two .38 rounds, hollow point, with no marks except from the factory. She logged each one, then shifted to the bedroom, careful to photograph the mess exactly as she found it.

The suitcase had been searched, but with precision. The packing order was disrupted, but nothing was dumped out. She held her phone flashlight over the folds, searching for residue or prints. Nothing. Not even a stray hair. She didn't find any ID or anything personal.

In the closet, she found a portable gun safe, open; the interior wiped down. Left inside was a printed page torn from a PDF manual, directions on how to reset the combination. She smoothed it with her hand, careful not to smudge it, and read the steps. Basic, unremarkable, but it confirmed her suspicion. The killer came to take more than a life. She wondered why someone was traveling with a gun safe. That was unusual.

She moved to the wall safe near the minibar. This one was fancy, flush with the wood paneling, numeric keypad still glowing green. It wasn't locked. She thumbed the door, half-expecting a booby trap, but it swung free to reveal the bare shelf inside. Not even dust.

Leilani smiled. Whoever hit the room knew exactly what they wanted, and how to take it without tripping the alarms.

But the blood was messy. The bullet wounds, brutal, almost angry. It didn't add up. The Mastermind had always been careful, never leaving anything but a taunt. Why break the pattern now?

She turned towards the spiral on the bathroom wall. The symbol was already flaking; the edges drying into a black crust. Up close, she noted where the fingertip had pressed too hard and streaked the line. A moment of hesitation, or exhaustion. The spiral ended with a dot, the kind a child makes to finish a sentence. It looked back at her.

"This was personal," she said to nobody.

Behind her, the suite door clicked open. She didn't turn, but she noted a change in the air. The aftershave, the exacting tread, the way even a sigh sounded like it was weighing options.

Isaac Torres leaned in the doorway, his Bureau badge already out, eyes raking the room.

"Couldn't wait for me?" he said, voice pitched low.

Leilani took one last photo. She straightened. "You're late."

"I had to wait for my agent to land." He didn't elaborate. Instead, he walked the perimeter of the suite, hands clasped behind his back like a docent on a tour of the macabre. He paused at the body, the shell casings, and at the spiral.

He whistled softly. "Jesus. He upped his game."

She shrugged, more fatigue than bravado. "Or lost his cool."

Torres pulled out his phone and started scanning the space, mirroring her earlier movements. "Surveillance is wiped. Hard drives were pulled and replaced with blanks. Exactly like the Makai Grand job," he said.

She made a note. "Safe's empty, too. No prints, not even a fiber. Also found a portable gun safe. No gun."

He walked over to the safe. "We'll have our people on it by dawn. The prints might be under the overlay."

She allowed herself to smile a half-smile. "You always bring the optimism."

"It's our weapon against the smart ones."

He moved to the bathroom, gazed at the symbol, and then at the streak of blood trailing down the sink.

"Is that an HPD retirement badge on his lapel?" he asked.

"Yeah. John Maka'ala," she said flatly.

Torres' mouth made a shape like it might speak, but nothing came out.

"I worked with him," she said. "Before he took this gig. He was solid. He always volunteered for the graveyard shift."

"Was he in Iraq?" Torres asked.

"Twice," she replied. "Would have made captain if he'd played politics. Instead, he retired and took a rent-a-cop job for the health plan. Why?"

"He has the look of a soldier, clean shaven, hair high and tight. Doesn't seem like he would be an easy target."

"He wouldn't be," said Leilani. "He had a lot of street smarts."

They stood in silence, both watching the spiral dry.

"I can't believe this," Torres said.

Leilani let her hands fall to her sides, gloves sticky from the camera grip. "The Mastermind has killed before, but this isn't a message. It's a challenge."

He nodded. "You think he knew it was John?"

She thought about it. "If he's half as smart as I think, he knew exactly who'd be guarding this suite, what nights he worked, what time he made his rounds."

Torres ran a hand through his hair, then turned to face her. "This changes everything, you know."

"I do," she said. "But I don't know what his next move will be. After this kind of violence, I'd expect him to lie low for a while. Who knows?"

He considered it. "Agreed, but so far he hasn't done anything we expected."

She smiled. "Guess we'd better work fast."

He leaned against the doorframe, letting his eyes go out of focus, like he was replaying the scene in his head.

"You want a drink?" he asked, nodding at the minibar.

She raised an eyebrow. "Is that an FBI interrogation technique?"

"Call it trauma protocol."

She hesitated, then shrugged. "Sure."

He kneeled, dug around, and produced two miniature bottles, gin, and bourbon. He handed her the gin.

"I'll get you the bullet analysis and a list of any guests checked in with the same profile as our last two cases," he said, unsealing the bourbon with his thumb. "But I'm betting this guy used the tunnels again."

She popped the gin. "You ever going to tell me how you know about those?"

He stared, a little smile cutting through the gloom. "After we close the case."

They drank, not a toast but a shared surrender. The gin was cheap and burned all the way down.

Torres said, "You want the room for a few minutes?"

She shook her head. "Already said goodbye. Besides, I have to find the manager, get guest lists before everyone starts lawyering up."

He nodded, straightened, and stepped to the door. But he hesitated, hand on the frame.

"I'm sorry, Leilani."

The hours before sunrise blurred into a marathon of door-knocks and note-taking. Leilani and Torres started with the night staff, working down the list by shift start time, then by distance from the suite. Each interview peeled back another layer, though not always the one she wanted.

The turndown maid, an older woman with a church voice and the hands of a gardener, described finding John on the floor. She wept as she did it, shivering despite the robe the hotel had loaned her. Leilani walked her through the timeline.

"He always checked the corridor before I entered," the maid said. "Tonight, he didn't." She dabbed her eyes. "But I thought he was busy."

"No unusual sounds?" Leilani asked. "Arguments, shots?"

The woman shook her head. "No. Well, the TV from the next room. And the wind, always the wind."

Torres gave her tissues and said nothing. He had a rare gift for silence, knew when a word would help, and when it would fill the void.

Next was a kitchen runner, who was more annoyed than scared. "We're not supposed to use the guest elevator, but sometimes I do. With cops all over, I can't get anything to the suites on time. Sucks, man."

He was halfway out the door before Leilani flagged him. "Did you see the security officer tonight?"

The runner shrugged. "He's in the lobby, talking with the bell captain. Looked pissed off."

She noted that and moved on.

The front desk agent was a college student, sleep deprived and riding the thin edge of panic. He'd checked John in for his shift, confirmed that the dead man had signed the log at 12:04. After that, no record until the maid's frantic call at 2:17.

"Any visitors?" Leilani pressed.

The clerk paged through the system. "Not for that room. But we had a comped guest in 1208. Left at ten, like you said. But then." He hesitated, cheeks reddening. "This is off the record, right?"

"Of course," Torres said.

The clerk lowered his voice. "Sometimes guests trade rooms. Not officially. But the staff get tipped to look the other way. Happens more in the busy months."

"So, there could've been a different person in the suite originally?" Leilani asked.

He nodded, eager to be helpful. "It's possible."

"Who was registered in 1204?" she asked.

A few clicks of the keyboard. "Charles Rangely. Booked for one night. Checked in yesterday," said the clerk.

Leilani thanked him and turned away. The last stop was the security office, deep in the building's concrete underbelly. The head of security, Peter Chang, had the look of a man who'd run out of panic an hour ago and now wanted to get to sunrise alive. He wore a suit jacket over his uniform, and his hands never stopped twisting the paper cup.

"He was here three months," Chang said, meaning John. "But you could tell right away he was a pro. Not like the others. He always had a plan, always checked the logs twice."

"Any friction?" Torres asked.

Chang stared at his cup. "Some of the old guard resented him. He wanted to change things. Tighter patrols, more drills, stuff like that. But he was never disrespectful."

Leilani watched the man's eyes. They didn't meet

hers. Instead, they flicked towards the CCTV monitors, now running a stuttering playback of empty hallways. She followed his gaze and noticed the main camera feed outside suite 1208 was still dark, looping the last clean frame before the blackout.

"Who else has access to the footage?" she asked.

"Me," Chang said, "and the IT consultant. But I don't even know how the drives were swapped. I checked them myself before the shift started."

Torres jotted that on his notepad. "Who's your IT?"

"Guy named Nawaz," said Chang. "Works for the contractor. He's good. Nobody ever had a problem until tonight."

Leilani looked at Chang. "Do you provide portable gun safes to your guests?"

Chang looked surprised and stuttered. "No. We have some high rollers stay with us, and some of them bring their own. Why?"

"There was an empty gun safe in 1204. Any idea what the guest was involved with?" asked Leilani.

Chang's face paled. Leilani leaned closer. "He was delivering a valuable necklace to a resident of the island. I don't know who, and I have no idea whom he worked for. We had a casual conversation last night when I ran into him at the bar and he asked me about crime in the area and if the hotel was safe. I told him it was. That's when he mentioned the necklace. He was some kind of courier."

"Any idea where he is now?" asked Torres.

"No idea. Last I saw him, he was heading for his room. That was around ten."

They left Chang to his coffee, Torres flipping the business card in his fingers.

In the hallway, Torres said, "Nawaz, again. Second hotel he's involved with. We might need to visit him. You think the clerk was hiding something?"

"They all are," Leilani replied. "But he's scared, not complicit. The Mastermind was in and out before anyone even noticed."

"Unless Charles Rangely noticed," said Torres. "I'll put out a BOLO on him and see if I can track down rental car info. His car might still be in the lot."

They compared timelines, filling in blanks, arguing in low voices as they walked to the suite. With every answer, two more questions unfurled.

Sunrise came in a rush of gold, slicing through the cloud line and pouring into the upper floors like liquid heat. Leilani and Torres stepped outside. The sky was blood orange, and the sea dotted with outriggers and fishing boats.

They stood side by side, the two people in the hotel not rushing anywhere. Leilani pulled her hair up, squinting into the light.

"Remember when cases were about catching the bad guy?" she said.

Torres didn't smile, but his eyes crinkled. "Now, it's about catching the one who catches all the others."

"Yeah." She dug her heel into the balcony rail.

"We're not dealing with a simple thief anymore."

Torres turned and set his hand gently on her shoulder. The touch was quick, a pulse, but it cut through the tired like a shot of caffeine.

"No," he said. "This case has grown, and the mayor will not be happy."

They both knew what that meant. No more shortcuts, no more rivalry. From here on out, they would need every tool in the kit, and each other.

# Chapter Six

## Family Insights

If there was any place in the world that could comfort or wound Detective Leilani Kealoha in the same breath, it was her mother's kitchen. The air inside was a microclimate, ten degrees hotter than outside, charged with the steam off twin pots on the battered gas stove and a baseline of salt that clung to every surface. The fridge door hung crooked on its hinges; the Formica table bowed with the weight of a half-completed jigsaw and, tonight, a parade of ingredients lined up for inspection. There were slabs of taro, wild ginger root and a pile of avocado that had already started browning at the cut.

Leilani stepped in, blinked through a stinging fog of onion and steam. Her mother was there, Naalei, kumu hula, matriarch and master of the domestic offensive, stationed at the counter, wrist-deep in a bowl of dark, viscous marinade.

She barely looked up. "You're early, Lei," she said, using the old name as if Leilani was eight and trailing mud across the kitchen tile.

Leilani hung her bag on a chair, took the open seat, and pressed her hands flat to the cool tabletop. She exhaled, realizing she'd been holding her breath since the parking lot. "It's after six," she managed, her voice so thin she barely recognized it.

Naalei's hands didn't pause, but the angle of her shoulders shifted, a change a child would notice.

"Something happen at work?"

That was the trouble with mothers. They never let you bleed in peace.

"Yeah," said Leilani, rolling her eyes upward, the movement almost too much. "Lost a friend." She left it hanging there, an unfinished sentence.

Naalei rinsed her hands, wiped them on her apron, then set a cut of fish on a broad ti leaf. She worked silently; the knife moving in practiced, rhythmic strokes, each cut a precise and perfect line. The kitchen filled with the sharp green snap of lū'au leaves, the brine of fermented shrimp paste, the sweet-bitter edge of caramelizing onions. Somewhere outside, a mynah bird warbled, and the wind slammed the back door shut, making the windowpanes tremble.

"Was it bad?" Naalei asked, her tone unreadable.

"It was ugly." Leilani saw the spiral again, smeared and drying, the wound already going to crust along the edges. "At first it was those cute little petroglyphs in chalk I showed you, but they're getting more complex and tonight, he drew one in blood."

This time the knife stopped, for a heartbeat. Naalei resumed, now with a heavier, slower chop.

"Show me the newest symbols," she said.

Leilani reached for her phone, thumbed through the gallery, and set the device between them. The close-up was a study in violence, lines traced with a steady hand, the arc, and spiral so deliberate it seemed premeditated. She watched her mother's face and saw the recognition before the words came.

"Kaulu," Naalei said.

Leilani blinked. "Who?"

Her mother pinched the bridge of her nose, looking older than Leilani remembered. "Kaulu was a trickster in the old chants. Not the clever Maui kind, worse. He made his enemies see things. Messed with their minds before the battle ever started. The spiral when it's drawn this way is not a map. It's a warning."

Leilani splayed her fingers and thumb, unconsciously finding the faint scar at her palm's base, the one thing her body kept as a souvenir from a childhood full of climbing and falling and learning where not to step. "What kind of warning?" she asked.

"That someone's coming for you," Naalei said, soft enough that it barely survived the crackle of the rice cooker.

In the silence that followed, Leilani tuned into the kitchen's details: the high-pitched whine of a mosquito circling the pantry light, the slow drip of the faucet over an avocado pit in the sink, the ghosted fingerprint smudges along the fridge. Every part of the room was vital, like a crime scene in miniature, every mess a clue.

She watched her mother dice ulu before moving on to mashing steamed kalo with a stone pestle. Each motion was both practical and ceremonial. The preparation of food was a language, and tonight, Naalei was speaking in code.

"Mom," said Leilani, suddenly feeling like a child who'd stayed too long at the adult table. "You know the old stories. Do you really think someone could use that stuff today? Mess with people's heads?"

The question sounded childish even as it left her mouth.

But Naalei didn't smirk, didn't dismiss. She looked up, her gaze meeting Leilani's with the force of an undertow. "The old things never left. Some people know how to use them. It's not the symbol that scares you, Lei. It's that someone remembered how to use it."

Leilani pressed her hands tighter to the table, feeling the damp from a recent wipe-down, the faint grittiness where salt had been ground in. "It's a game, then," she said. "He wants us to see it. Wants me to see it."

"That's what Kaulu did. Got into the enemy's mind before they even picked up a spear. This isn't just misdirection." Naalei leaned in, voice dropping to a near-whisper. "Whoever's doing this knows what keeps us up at night."

A creak from the hall told Leilani they weren't alone. She glanced over her shoulder to see Kai, her son, peeking through the bead curtain, one eye magnified to the size of a grape by the fisheye effect. He shrank back as soon as she locked eyes with him, but not far enough to be out of range for a cop's senses.

Naalei saw him, too, and her face softened. "You want to come help?" she called out, and in a flash he was at the counter, elbowing for space like he'd been standing there all along.

Kai had a streak of rice flour across his cheek and wore a T-shirt with a pattern that looked like it had been chewed on by a wild animal. He eyed the cuts of fish, then glanced at the phone still glowing.

"Are you talking about the case?" he asked slyly.

Leilani side-eyed him. "Don't you have homework?"

"Did it," he said. "Math and reading."

"Really."

He nodded with solemn intensity, then reached for a sliver of raw fish. "What's the symbol mean, Grandma?"

"Depends on who draws it, nani," said Naalei, brushing Kai's hair back with a floury hand. "But tonight, I think it means trouble."

Kai chewed, considered, then asked, "Is it like the ones at the heiau, the old stone places?"

"A little," said Leilani. "But this one was made in blood. Not marker or paint." She regretted the words even as they escaped her, but Kai widened his eyes, hungry for detail.

"Like a warning?" he whispered.

"Exactly like a warning," Leilani answered.

Naalei pressed a mound of mashed taro into a bowl. "Lei, help me wrap these." She slid the ti leaves, the marinated fish, the pile of lūʻau, all within reach.

They worked together, fingers moving in sync, the years of shared habit turning food prep into a low-key symphony. The leaves were glossy, pliant, sticky with brine. Each packet, once folded, looked like a little green grenade.

Kai watched, fascinated, then tried to fold his own. His first attempt unraveled instantly, and the fish plopped out onto the table. He laughed, tried again, this time getting halfway before the filling leaked. "Squeeze it tight," he said, watching his mother's and grandmother's hands with laser focus.

Outside, the last rays of sun turned the kitchen window into a mirror. Leilani caught her own reflection, eyes red-rimmed, hair tangled, face caught between exhaustion and determination. She wondered, if she was built for this kind of war.

When all the packets were wrapped, Naalei stacked them in a bamboo steamer and clamped the lid tight. "Hour and a half," she said. "Just enough time to set the table, maybe do your homework again," she added, with a wink at Kai.

Kai made a face, then grabbed a notebook from his backpack and slunk off toward the living room, but not before pausing at the door, one foot dragging on the tile. "Are you gonna catch the bad guy?" he asked, not looking back.

"I'll try," Leilani said.

He nodded, as if satisfied, then vanished.

Naalei set the kitchen to rights, clearing the counter with a practiced sweep. She turned to face her daughter, hands folded, every line of her posture radiating concern.

"Don't let it get in your head, Lei. The symbol has power if you give it that."

Leilani smiled. "I'm more worried about the person who drew it. He's out there, watching us. Knowing exactly which buttons to push."

Naalei gave a little huff, a sound halfway between a laugh and a sigh. "Don't give him what he wants. Don't play his game."

They stood together in the thickening kitchen air, waiting for the rice to finish, for the lū'au to steam through. Somewhere in the house, Kai hummed to himself, probably building another elaborate crime board with crayons and tape.

For now, the spiral on the bathroom wall was far away, and the world shrank to the boundaries of a home. A mother, a daughter, and the quiet in between, and the lull before another day's hunt.

But even here, Leilani could sense the tension like a thread pulled taut through the heart of the island, ready to snap at the next hard tug.

Dinner at Naalei's was always more than a meal; it was an event, a half-magic act of repair after a day that tried too hard to break you. Now, as the kitchen steamed up and the last bands of sunset bled into the walls, Naalei turned her attention to the finishing rituals. She took down the fat glass jar of alaea salt from the windowsill, red as volcanic clay, dug up from a secret beach somewhere on the North Shore, and pinched it into her palm.

With the care of a jeweler setting a final stone, she circled the pot and scattered the salt in, whispering a chant so soft it braided with the sound of the rolling boil. The syllables were old, vowels melting into each other, carrying a weight that predated every history book on the island. Even Leilani, who considered herself allergic to ritual, noticed the pull of it, like the shift in air when a storm is near.

Kai, caught in the half-shadow of the hall, tracked the scene with bug-eyed intensity. Leilani pretended she hadn't seen him, but he was a terrible spy. His breathing alone would have given him away. She kept her voice low, not wanting to fracture the quiet. "Kai, you wanna set the table or stand there and absorb everything?"

Kai darted forward, nearly tripping over the threshold. "Sorry. You were doing the chant," he said, awed. "Does that make the food better?"

"It keeps the evil spirits out of the house," said Naalei matter-of-factly. "And it makes the fish taste like the ocean."

Kai looked unconvinced, but eager to believe.

Leilani plucked three bowls off the drying rack and stacked them in Kai's arms. "Careful, don't drop." She glanced at her mother, dropping her voice further. "You think he's too young to know what's happening?"

"He already knows," Naalei replied, never breaking eye contact with the simmering pot. "He listens to everything. Like a little coconut wireless."

"I can hear you," Kai said, grinning. He set the bowls down and sensing the license to ask more, added, "Are you really working on a murder? Like, a real one?"

Leilani felt the old ache in her ribs, the guilt that came with bringing death home in her jacket pocket. "It's my job, Kaimana. But I don't want you worrying about it."

"But if you catch the guy, will you get your picture in the news?" he asked, almost trembling with excitement.

"Probably not," said Leilani. "That's not the kind of detective I am. The fewer people know my name, the better."

Kai looked briefly disappointed. "But you get to figure out all the clues, right? Like Sherlock?"

Leilani smiled. "Sort of. But actual detective work is mostly paperwork and chasing leads that go nowhere." She didn't add that the job was also about burying things, and not the dead.

Kai slid into his chair, face scrunched with thought. "I bet I could help," he said. "I found the missing Xbox remote when no one else could. I'm good at finding things."

"True," said Leilani, softening. "But this is a little different than the remote."

Kai accepted the rebuff because he could smell the food now, his nose twitching like a puppy's. "What's for dinner, Grandma?"

"Laulau," Naalei said, lifting the steamer basket and letting a plume of vapor curl up like incense. "Old style. But you have to say thank you to the fish first, or it'll give you bad dreams."

Kai pressed his palms together, eyes closed tight,

mumbling something that sounded suspiciously like, "Thank you, fish, for giving your life so I can get big muscles and also finish my homework."

Naalei laughed, the sound round and bright. She plated the laulau, then spooned a heap of rice onto each plate. The kitchen was just a kitchen again, the violence of the world kept at bay by a locked screen door and three generations at a table.

But as soon as they sat, Kai circled back. "Was the murder scary?" he asked, looking at Leilani.

She hesitated, then nodded. "It was, a little. But I've seen scary things before. I know how to deal with them."

"Did you find clues?" he pressed.

"Yeah," she said, trading a look with her mother. "The killer left a message. A symbol."

Kai's eyes were dinner-plate wide. "Like a secret code?"

"More like a warning," Naalei said, cutting in. "In the old days, chiefs, and warriors would draw marks on enemy land to show they were coming. Sometimes the marks told the truth. Sometimes they lied to make the other side panic and mess up."

"That's cheating," said Kai, scandalized.

"No," said Naalei. "That's called psychological warfare. Sometimes you win by making your enemy afraid to fight at all."

Leilani watched Kai chew on this, spoon halfway to his mouth, the thought as heavy as poi.

"So the guy you're after," said Kai, "he's trying to scare you?"

"Yes," said Leilani. "And other people, too. But I don't think he knows who he's up against."

Kai beamed, reassured. He took a big bite, then winced as he chewed. "Hot," he said, mouth full, fanning his tongue.

They ate in silence; the lull punctuated by the metallic scrape of spoons against bowls and the hiss of the rice cooker as it powered down. Outside, the streetlamps kicked on, turning the windows into a black mirror. In the glass, Leilani caught the outlines of the three of them, her mother's unyielding back, her son's wild hair, her own profile caught mid thought. The image seemed almost ceremonial, a family locked in the still point of the present, knowing tomorrow could bring anything.

When Kai reached for seconds, he paused, serious again. "Will you tell me if you catch him?" he asked, not meeting her eyes.

"Of course," said Leilani, her voice almost gentle.

He grinned. "Cool."

Afterward, while Naalei stacked dishes and Kai vanished to construct an obstacle course out of laundry baskets, Leilani stayed behind, letting the kitchen noise settle her nerves. She watched her mother work, hands moving with the confidence of a woman who'd outlasted more than her fair share of trouble.

"Thanks for the help tonight," said Leilani. "And for dinner."

Naalei shrugged, the motion dismissing decades of pain and love in one smooth arc. "It's what we do. Feed the living, honor the dead."

"Even when the dead leave blood on your walls?"

Naalei met her gaze, eyes as sharp as the knife she wielded. "Especially then, Lei. Otherwise, the dead win."

They let that hang, the knowledge as real as the food cooling on their plates.

Later, as Leilani put on her jacket to leave, she called for Kai, ready for the nightly struggle to get him home and into bed. But this time, he stood at the door, shoes on, backpack slung and zipped, waiting.

"Ready, Detective?" he asked.

"Ready," she said, and meant it.

They walked into the dark together, the memory of salt and song trailing after them, a thin shield against whatever the island's old gods, and its new monsters, had planned for tomorrow.

By midnight, the house had fallen into the deep silence that came when every obligation had been met. Even the refrigerator had given up its humming, and the surf, two blocks off, was the one thing still in motion. Leilani sat alone at the kitchen table, the cheap laminate pitted with years of use. The light overhead dimmed to a glow that softened the edges of every shadow. The night was sticky. Humidity glued the curtains to the window frame and left her forearms tacky as she leafed through Kai's homework.

Most nights, she checked his work because she

strived to be the kind of parent who checked. Tonight, it was an excuse to stay awake, to keep the world at arm's length a little longer. The division facts were neat, the spelling words a mess of corrections, but the last sheet, a detective story for English, made her pause. He'd written four pages about an action figure who solved the theft of a lunchbox by fingerprinting the suspects with cocoa powder and tape. After reading it twice, she signed the bottom, her hand shaking a little.

The house was as secure as she could make it, with deadbolts thrown, blinds drawn, porch light left burning. Her service weapon, cleaned and reassembled, sat on the kitchen counter in its holster, along with the two extra mags she carried. She ought to have been safe. Instead, she felt exposed, like every wall in the place was made of tissue paper.

She rinsed her mug, refilled it with black tea, and stood by the window, looking out over the sleepy street. A single car idled two blocks down, its headlights angling into the empty playground at the corner. She watched it for a long time, waiting for the driver to step out, to start something, but the car finally reversed, turned, and disappeared. She trembled with relief and anger.

When the phone buzzed, three quick pulses, the kind she'd set for the department, she nearly fumbled it into the sink.

It was an email, sent to her work account and forwarded to her personal account, the subject line a string of Unicode gibberish. The body of the email was blank.

She recognized the format. Encrypted message, double-hash, not standard PD issue. Someone had gone to a lot of trouble to mask it, but the headers were still visible. She copied the payload onto her work laptop, opened the department's forensic toolkit, and saw the script run. A few seconds of loud fan noise from the laptop preceded the appearance of high-resolution image files, all GPS tagged and time stamped.

Her heart slammed against her ribs as she clicked through.

The first photo was from the Aloha Shores crime scene, the safe room. The angle was one she hadn't seen before, taken from above, or with a GoPro on the ceiling. The spiral, bright turquoise, was dead center in the frame.

The next image, from the Makai Grand, the admin wing. The spiral, larger now, chalk lines sharp, flecks of dust still hovering in the air. The camera that took it was so good she observed the edges of a shoe print she'd missed in the original investigation.

Third, Honu Bay Resort, the suite where John Maka'ala bled out. But this time, the photo caught not only the bathroom wall, but the entire room, door ajar, crime techs in bunny suits frozen mid-sweep, and John's body, face up, arm flung toward the vanity as if reaching for help that wouldn't come.

There was a final image, out of sequence. This one showed a laptop screen, her own, from the kitchen, seconds ago. She recognized the mug, the phone, her own hand hovering above the mouse.

There was a message. A single line of text.

*YOU'RE LOOKING IN ALL THE WRONG PLACES, DETECTIVE. THE SYMBOLS AREN'T THE MESSAGE, THEY'RE THE MEDIUM. HOW MUCH MORE BLOOD BEFORE YOU UNDERSTAND?*

The air in the kitchen vanished, replaced by a roaring static. She checked the house again. Every lock, every window, the sliding glass door to the lanai, then double-checked Kai's bedroom, where he lay star-fished under a tangle of blankets, mouth open, hair wild across the pillow. His notebook was clutched to his chest.

She returned to the kitchen, checked the timestamps. The surveillance photo of her right now was less than two minutes old. She sensed an icy wind at her back and turned but found her own distorted reflection in the black window, the yellow porch light a garish halo around her head.

Her hands shook as she typed a response, forwarding the message to the department's cyber unit, tagging it URGENT, before smashing the phone's screen down until the world steadied. She poured the tea, but it tasted like nothing.

It took her ten minutes to gather herself enough to read the message again, to parse it like a clue instead of a threat. Symbols as medium, not messages. What did that mean? She hoped to call her mother, but the hour was too late, and besides, she already knew what Naalei would say.

The old stories were never about the symbols themselves. They were about who carried them, who wielded them. It was a game of power, of fear, of owning the air before the fight ever started.

She glanced at the hallway, at the gap under Kai's door, at the safe glow of his nightlight. She allowed herself a single, shaky breath, then squared her shoulders and powered up her work phone, ready to map the new moves.

The war had come home, and the enemy knew her better than she'd dared to admit. She allowed the fear to settle. She felt the chill in her teeth, then got to work.

# Chapter Seven

## Uneasy Alliance

HPD's fifth-floor conference center looked like the nerve center for a lunar mission gone slightly off-book. Rows of folding tables replaced desks, each surface covered by laptops, voice recorders, police radios and the brown stains of yesterday's coffee rings. Whiteboards rimmed three walls, a detritus of scribbled case numbers, arrows in different colors, and headshots scowling under the blue painter's tape. Someone hung a string of plastic leis over the precinct logo, and beneath it, the morning's haul of Leonard's malasadas slowly turned to paste in their pink box.

Leilani found her assigned seat by the window but hovered a beat before sitting. The view offered a sliver of downtown, rain-blurred and streaked with city grime. She took it in, then turned to the chaos.

Across the room, Torres was already in full operational mode. He'd commandeered the end table, arranging folders by color code. Blue for witness statements, red for forensic reports, and green for financials. Every folder bore his precise, slanted handwriting. He straightened them with a ruler, the line as crisp as a parade formation. He wore the same suit from the day before, but the tie had changed, a shade of slate that echoed the clouds outside. He worked fast, but never frantically, and seemed immune to the restless shuffling of the local detectives trickling in behind him.

Leilani's phone buzzed with a fresh barrage of departmental notifications, each one more frantic than the last. She silenced it, then started pinning up the new set of crime scene photos: Honu Bay, Makai Grand, Aloha Shores and Pacific Haven. Four resorts, four clean jobs, all now linked by the blood spiral left behind at Honu. She didn't bother with the expected order; instead; she mapped them by her gut, pinning shots in a constellation that made sense in her head.

She knew Torres was watching her. She didn't look over. "Have you ever heard of abductive logic?"

He replied without missing a beat. "Sure. Sherlock Holmes and Charles Peirce. Notoriously unreliable in peer review."

Leilani pinned up a blown up detail of the most recent spiral, the blood gone russet in the printout. "Lucky for us, the streets don't care about peer review."

Torres joined her at the whiteboard, legal pad in hand. His body language, military at rest, arms crossed, one foot exactly at twelve o'clock, jaw tight as a clinched knot. He scanned the photos but spoke to her.

"I'd like to start with a structured evidence review. Go linear. Time of entry, method, exit, signature." He stabbed his notepad with a capped pen, as if underlining an invisible line. "If we build a tight protocol, we might find the hole."

Leilani balanced against the table with one hip, hands in her pockets. "With respect, Special Agent, this guy eats protocols for breakfast. Every job is designed to slip through what you expect."

He didn't sigh, but his next words came slower. "We're dealing with a team, not a lone wolf. They escalate at predictable intervals. Last time it was a property crime. Now it's homicide. What's the next escalation?"

She eyed the wall, letting the question hang. The other detectives, Bautista, the downtown liaison; Yamamoto, out of Vice; and Choi, borrowed from financial crimes, sat at their stations, watching the back and forth like spectators at a tennis match.

Choi broke the silence. "Can't you two pool your brains and tell us who's next before they do?"

Torres's expression didn't shift, but he flipped to a new page on his legal pad. "Fine. Let's do both. Kealoha, what's your gut tell you?"

She waited a moment before indicating the printout from Aloha Shores. "Look at the petroglyph at Aloha versus Honu. First is perfect. Second, you can see the moment the killer's finger stutters. They weren't planning to kill at Honu, but something happened. I'd bet my pension the victim interrupted them."

Bautista squinted at the photo. "So, wrong place, wrong time?"

"No," said Leilani. "More like someone needed to be made an example of. That's why the spiral was bigger. Bolder."

Torres rapped his pen on the table. "That's a deviation. Deviations mean opportunity."

Yamamoto leaned in. "What kind of opportunity?"

"Someone got messy," said Torres. "Messy means

trace. Trace means we have a shot."

Leilani tapped the Honu Bay scene. "My gut tells me the killer is the same as the prior break-ins, or at least the same planner. The technique is identical. Entry is never forced; systems are always neutralized with custom tech. And the symbol? It's not a calling card. It's a dare."

Bautista arched an eyebrow. "A dare to whom?"

Leilani shrugged. "To us."

The room was silent, excluding the scratch of Choi's pen and the faint hum of the window AC. Outside, rain hammered the glass like it was trying to claw its way in.

Torres stepped up to the whiteboard, pen in hand, and drew a timeline between the four resorts. "Every heist is seventy-two hours apart. Each target is at maximum occupancy the day of. And in every case, the physical evidence vanishes within ten minutes of the alarm. This is precision engineering. Not a local amateur."

Leilani grinned. "Did you check the secondary crime scenes?"

He met her eyes, and there it was, a flicker of respect.

"After the primary, the perps always dump a fake trail, maintenance carts, service uniforms, sometimes a tip left at a bar." She circled a face on the bottom right of the board. "At Aloha, a contractor was seen on the service elevator at the exact moment of the break-in. He left no name, but used a badge number from another resort. That's not luck. That's design."

Yamamoto nodded, slow. "You think it's an inside job?"

"Closer to a ghost in the system," said Leilani. "I don't think any resort knows they're compromised until it's too late."

Torres put a dot on the timeline three days ahead. "So, the next hit should be—"

Leilani finished his sentence. "This Friday. Probably between one and four a.m. And if the pattern holds, there will be another body."

Choi, who'd been silent until now, asked, "Why Friday?"

Leilani gestured to the flow of activity at each site. "It's the day with the most cash and valuables in play. Honeymooners, whales, and wedding parties. More loot, more chaos, fewer questions."

Torres leaned in. "If you're right, then we must get ahead of it. Full surveillance at every likely target. Find the vulnerability before they do."

She grinned, this time wide enough to show teeth. "You'd better hope they're not counting on us to do exactly that."

For a few heartbeats, the two of them stood shoulder to shoulder, mapping invisible lines on the whiteboard. Bautista and Yamamoto exchanged a glance, and in it was a mutual question. Were these two going to save the city, or burn it down?

Choi summed up the room. "Either way, it's not

going to be boring."

At noon, the Chief of Detectives stalked in with his usual air of impending audit. He surveyed the wall, Torres's neat timeline, Leilani's scattershot constellation, and the thickening mess of theories crowding the room.

"Progress?" he barked, already scanning his phone.

Torres gave a tight nod. "We're building a unified case structure, sir. The next likely target is within seventy-two hours."

The Chief shot a look at Leilani. "You concur?"

She shrugged. "I trust his math. But I trust my gut more. I think we're being set up."

The Chief snorted. "Well, if you're both right, we're about to have a very busy Friday. You'll brief the mayor's office at sixteen hundred."

He left as quickly as he'd come, the scent of Old Spice lingering in his wake.

Torres stared after him, then turned to Leilani. "You know what I don't get?"

"What's that?"

He pointed at the spiral on the wall, the one done in blood. "If this is about money, why up the stakes? Why kill?"

Leilani thought about it. "Because the next job isn't about the money at all. It's about the show."

The team was quiet, watching her.

She uncapped a marker and, with a quick, looping

hand, drew a new spiral between the four sites. This one overlapped the others, radiating outward, the lines growing thicker, darker, until the board almost groaned under the weight of ink.

Torres stared at it and laughed a little.

"What?" asked Choi, nervous.

He said it out loud. "It's not a pattern. It's a story."

Leilani nodded. "And we're already on the last chapter."

The rain stopped before the shift change. Outside, the clouds peeled back, and the wet city blazed in the light, every street polished, every edge razor bright. Inside, the room stayed tense, the air thick with possibility.

Leilani thought they were finally moving forward, two steps ahead instead of five behind. She looked at Torres, and for a second, both grinned at the same time. There it was, she thought. Not trust exactly, but the next best thing. Respect.

The makeshift AV lab in the bowels of HPD headquarters was all shadows, save for the ice-blue illumination leaking from four wall-mounted monitors. The air was a two-stroke blend of burned popcorn and overworked CPU fans. A box of abandoned Hawaiian pizza perched precariously on the server rack, its top greased translucent and curling at the corners.

Leilani and Torres settled in for what would be a marathon viewing session. The chairs were stolen from Evidence, one too tall, the other missing a wheel, both likely to exacerbate pre-existing injuries. They scooted closer together than necessary, each with a laptop balanced on a thigh and a spiral-bound logbook at the ready. The only sounds were the shifting of denim, the tap-tap of keys, and the crackle from the outdated fluorescent tube overhead.

Torres worked the computer with a surgeon's restraint, pausing every fifteen seconds to log time stamps, camera angles and subject descriptions. His fingers, Leilani noticed, never changed no matter how fast he typed. Even his caffeine intake seemed optimized, taking one measured sip of black coffee every three minutes, then recovered the cup with the precision of a clockmaker.

Leilani ran the video at two times speed, toggling back and forth between different feeds, scanning for the smallest deviations. Her notes were a mess of underlines, exclamation points and cross-references. She kept her sneakers propped on the rung of Torres's chair, a minor act of rebellion that he either ignored or accepted as part of the cost of their partnership.

At 1:14 a.m. in the Makai Grand footage, a blur of motion caught her eye. She thumbed the spacebar, scrubbed backward, and watched the frame by frame.

"There," she said, voice low.

Torres looked up, not impatient but skeptical. "Maintenance guy?"

She let it play. The worker in question wore the resort's standard-issue coveralls, navy with reflective piping, pushing a rolling cart of tools past the elevator bank. What snagged Leilani's attention was the hesitation, a half-beat pause at the camera's edge, as if waiting for an unseen cue.

"See the patch?" she said, zooming in. "That's a temp badge. Green lanyard. Not on the payroll, probably contract."

Torres made a note, then pulled the guest access log from the time of the incident. "No maintenance tickets in this wing that night."

"Could be a ghost badge," Leilani mused. "Or someone cloned a real one."

Torres snapped a still, fed it into the facial recognition stub he'd set up earlier. The result came back blank, but he cross-referenced the uniform against the cleaning contractor's database. "I'll run it against the other nights."

They kept on, eyes burning from the screen's relentless glow. At Pacific Haven, the same worker appeared again, slightly different build, same uniform, same cart. Once again, he paused before the camera's line of sight, then disappeared for thirteen minutes before re-emerging by the loading dock, moving twice as fast.

Torres started lining the videos side by side. "Movement's too deliberate to be random. He knows exactly where every camera is."

"And he's using the same hardware each time," said Leilani, voice growing tight with excitement. "See how he turns the corner? Hugs the wall and keeps the cap low. He's casing as he goes."

Torres logged the minutes, until he rotated the

screen so she saw the data stack he'd built. "Watch the clock. It's always at shift change. That's when cameras get their auto-reset, when coverage is weakest."

She grinned. "Now we're cooking."

They pored through three more hours of footage. At each resort, the maintenance worker followed the same routine. He entered during shift change, slipped into staff areas, never doubled back, and always exits before the crime was reported. His face was never fully visible, but the posture, the gait, the rhythm, Leilani's detective brain filed them under a single, familiar category: predator.

Torres found the first overlap. "Look at this, Makai Grand, Aloha Shores and Pacific Haven all had a run on the same cleaning solution, ordered from the same supplier, delivered within forty-eight hours of the hits."

Leilani cackled. "That's logistics. He's building redundancy in the supply chain."

Torres glanced at her, with reluctant admiration shading his eyes. "Not bad."

They pressed on, hours telescoping into minutes, the world shrinking to the dance of a single figure across too many screens.

Sometime around three a.m., Torres reached for the communal coffee and, not watching, grabbed the mug at the same moment as Leilani. Their hands collided, each gripping the handle, neither willing to yield first. The world paused on that brief, absurd intimacy. Leilani looked up, eyebrow cocked, and said, "Didn't figure you for a hand-holder, Special Agent."

He didn't blush, but the line of his jaw softened, and she thought he might smile. "I could let go, but it's my cup."

She released first, a tactical retreat, and pulled up the next camera feed. "Fine. I'll suffer through dehydration. For the case."

They watched in silence, but the distance between their chairs shrank another fraction.

Near dawn, Leilani hit the jackpot. A maintenance worker, this time at Aloha Shores, swiping an RFID card at a secure door. She froze the frame, zoomed in, and found the detail they'd been missing.

"There." She pointed, her finger leaving a crescent smudge on the screen. "See the badge? The sticker is a month out of date."

Torres leaned in, nearly shoulder to shoulder. "So he's not cycling through new credentials. He's using throwaways."

"Or printing his own." She leaned back, satisfied.

Torres started a new page. "That means there's an equipment cache somewhere on the island. You don't print that kind of stuff without infrastructure."

They both sat, the adrenaline ratcheting up. For a few minutes, they ran wild, chasing the rabbit holes together, mapping badge access, timing staff routes, even drafting up a list of suppliers within fifty miles.

It was Yamamoto, coming off his own graveyard shift, who finally noticed them. He stepped in, saw the avalanche of stills and notes, and whistled.

"Somebody's making the rest of us look bad," he said.

Leilani held up a mug, her own this time, and saluted. "It's all Torres. He's a machine."

"Tell that to my doctor," said Torres, not breaking focus.

When the sun finally wormed through the basement windows, they had a suspect: the ghost maintenance worker. A dozen partial stills, four timelines, three fake badge IDs, and a half-page of predictions for the next hit.

Torres printed the key frames and put them in a folder so he could pin them to the case board in the main conference room, eyes blazing with the high of a breakthrough.

Leilani watched him and saw past the Bureau polish. Underneath was another detective hungry for a win, for the simple truth of finding the right line at the right time.

He finished with a flourish. "Breakfast?"

She arched an eyebrow. "Is that Bureau speak for good job?"

He gave her the faintest of grins. "Something like that."

They left the AV cave together, the scent of stale pizza and cold coffee trailing after, but for once, it didn't seem like failure. It seemed like hope.

With luck and perseverance, this time they'd get the

bastard.

As noon burned off the night's rain, HPD headquarters was a nest of bad tempers, over-brewed coffee, and increasingly desperate emails. Torres set up shop in the operations bullpen, laptop anchored dead center of a battered conference table, flanked by several burner phones and a stack of subpoenas printed in Bureau blue. He barked into the phone and requested payroll data from the last four years for every cleaning and facilities contract on Oahu. He ran a side-by-side comparison against the badge numbers they'd lifted from the footage.

Leilani bounced from phone to phone, her tone swinging from fake casual to shy of an interrogatory. She started with Aloha Shores. The HR specialist answered on the first ring. A miracle.

"Do you ever hire outside maintenance at odd hours?" she asked.

"Sometimes for emergencies," said the specialist, "but it needs a manager sign-off. We use approved personnel, and they always have a contract badge, not a sticker."

Leilani played dumb, asked about a particular night, and described the suspect from the video. The line went silent. The HR specialist said, "That's not one of ours. Never seen him. Who is he?"

"We're still figuring that out," Leilani said, and hung up.

At Makai Grand, she got the head of security, a voice that tried to sound authoritative but barely camouflaged the nerves.

"If you have a badge number, I can run it," the man said. She gave him the one from the video, heard him tap it into a system, and hesitate. "That's… that badge was deactivated a year ago. We recycle the numbers every quarter."

"Do you keep old photos?" she pressed.

A pause. "For three months. After that, they're wiped."

"Convenient," said Leilani, too flat for sarcasm.

Between calls, she scoured the suspect's stills for more clues. She zoomed in on the shoes, a faded pair of New Balance 608s. At one site, the soles were tagged with black gaffer's tape. At another, white paint on the left heel. Cheap, effective disguise and none of the shoes matched the in-house uniform standards.

When she brought her findings back to Torres, he was already six layers deep in a spreadsheet.

"Nothing on the Bureau side," he said. "I pulled the entire badge request log for the island for the last six months. Sixteen unique names. Five are dead, three moved off-island, and the rest are still local but not working this month. Every application was clean, tax ID, home address, references. No flags."

Leilani paged through the records. "The signatures match the same hand. See the way the R loops? And here, at the H in Holani."

Torres flipped to another tab. "There's more. All the resumes are built on the same template. And each had a different phone number, but the numbers were sequential. Burners, most likely."

"So, he's a ghost," Leilani said, tossing the printout onto the desk. "Doesn't exist except for the footprint he wants us to see."

Torres closed the file. "Which means we have to catch him in person. If we know where he lives."

"We can set up surveillance," she finished.

They both eyed the last known address on the badge log. It wasn't far. Leilani grabbed her keys, and Torres was already packing up his case files.

The address led them to a flat-faced apartment building in lower Kalihi, the kind that hadn't been painted since the statehood. Each unit was bracketed by a rusted AC unit, the hallway floor coated in a film of old rain and mop water. A kid in a T-shirt and mismatched shorts watched them from behind a half-open door, then vanished when Leilani smiled.

Apartment 2B was supposed to be the suspect, but it looked like nobody had lived there in months. The lock was new, keypad entry, not standard for the neighborhood. They waited in the hall until the building manager shuffled up, a heavyset man in knockoff Crocs and a Dodgers hat.

"FBI," said Torres, flashing his badge.

The manager looked at it, unimpressed, then at Leilani, who'd already lined up her questions.

"When did the tenant last pick up his mail?" she asked.

The man scratched his chin. "Couple weeks? He

always paid rent on time. In cash. Six months up front.”

Torres pointed at the lock. “Who installed this?”

“The tenant,” said the manager. “He said he worked in maintenance at the Sheraton. Didn’t want his tools stolen.”

Leilani hid a smirk. “Do you have a key code?”

“Sure.” The manager punched in four digits, and the door beeped open.

Inside, the unit was airless; the shades drawn tight, and the furniture consisted of a battered card table and a camping chair. No clothes in the closet, no sheets on the mattress, not even a coffee mug on the counter. Leilani swept the place in under a minute, running her finger along the windowsill, then crouching to eye the baseboards. Torres moved slower, checking the bathroom, then opening every drawer and cabinet with the deliberate patience of someone who believed in the process.

“He never cooked here,” Torres called from the kitchenette. “Not even a takeout box in the trash.”

“Look at this,” said Leilani, from the corner of the room. She pointed to a faint indentation in the carpet, a rectangular outline about the size of a banker’s box. The edge was pressed deeper near the front, as if someone had rested a heavy briefcase there for a long time.

“Sat and watched the door,” Torres said, noting the angle. “Possibly waiting for a tail.”

“He was expecting company,” Leilani agreed.

She checked under the mattress and found nothing but factory tags. In the bathroom trash, Torres found three crumpled envelopes, all addressed to different names, each at this address.

He showed her. "He used this as a mail drop. Every month, a new name."

Leilani's pulse spiked. "He's never going to come back."

"Not unless he needs something," said Torres. "Which he doesn't, now that he's burned it."

They closed up, locking the door behind. In the hallway, Torres leaned against the rail and looked out at the cloud-streaked sky. He seemed tired.

"Ever get the feeling you're one step behind no matter how fast you run?" he asked.

Leilani snorted. "Story of my life, Agent."

They walked the outside stairs to street level. The manager was back by the mailbox, sorting through an avalanche of junk. He saw them and shrugged, as if to say, hope you found what you were looking for.

They hadn't.

In the parking lot, Leilani scrolled through her emails, looking for a miracle. Her phone buzzed. A new text from dispatch.

*HONU BAY RESORT. MALE BODY FOUND AT QUEEN'S BEACH. REQ LEAD DETECTIVE IMMEDIATE.*

Torres saw her go still. "What is it?"

"Body three blocks from Honu. Male. Might be our missing guest."

He nodded, already moving.

They made it in under twelve minutes; the siren cutting through the afternoon as if slicing the humidity itself. Queen's Beach was empty except for two patrol cars and a small crowd gathered by the picnic tables. The officers parted for Leilani and Torres, who ducked under the yellow tape and headed straight for the blue tarp.

The dead man was maybe forty, pale under the blood. Shirtless, chest bruised and streaked with two gunshot wounds, close together like someone had aimed for the same spot twice. But it was the spiral that stopped them. Someone had carved it into the skin around the wounds, clean, almost ceremonial, the edges still oozing.

"Charles Rangely," said one officer, checking the wallet on the ground. "Registered guest at Honu Bay."

Torres crouched, eyes level with the wounds. "The message," he muttered. "It's for us."

Leilani watched the spiral, feeling its pull. She remembered what her mother had said about the old symbols, about the line between warning and curse.

Torres stood. "He chased the thief," he said. "Walked in on the job, followed the suspect, got himself killed."

"Or he was meant to find him," said Leilani. "This is the escalation."

They traded a look, equal parts dread and resolve.

"I'll call the lab," Torres said. "We'll run every surface for DNA."

Leilani nodded, but her mind was already running, assembling the timeline, replaying every missed clue. She kneeled by the body, careful not to disturb the sand, and looked out to the horizon. The sky was flat and iron-colored, the sun nothing but a hot smudge at the edge.

The world seemed to shrink, the circle closing tighter. She stood, took a breath, and allowed the air to burn through her.

"Okay," she said. "Let's see what happens when you chase a ghost into the daylight."

Torres heard her, and for once, said nothing. The spiral was closing. But Leilani was ready to push back.

# Chapter Eight

## The Hacker's Trail

There was a temperature gradient in HPD's digital forensics suite that rivaled a jet engine at takeoff. The room squatted in the windowless heart of the building, insulated from sun and humanity, lined wall to wall with humming towers and a dozen vertical screens. Everything glowed faint blue, like the inside of a saltwater fish tank. The carpet had been original issue in the mid-eighties, Leilani guessed and now curled at the corners under the heat of rolling server racks.

Akira sat hunched in the middle of it all, barely visible over the wall of monitors, cords, and half-crushed cans of Monster. Her hair, short and scalped up one side, had streaks of electric purple, and her ears glittered with a constellation of steel. She wore the universal costume of the tech tribe, threadbare tank top, cargo shorts and bare feet propped on the power strip, her toes drumming to a tempo she heard in her head. She didn't acknowledge Leilani, didn't even twitch when the door creaked behind.

On the central screen, a web of nodes blinked in erratic pulses. Each orb carried a tiny headshot, the kind ripped from LinkedIn or department files, linked by scarlet lines that snaked into thicker cables toward the corners of the map.

Leilani edged into the room, pulling the door shut to mute the building's buzz. "You planning on blinking out the power for the entire block, Akira?"

"Not my fault your hardware's last-gen trash," Akira said, not missing a beat on her typing. "Also, your password is laughably bad."

Leilani's mouth twitched. "You needed me?"

Akira finally looked up, eyes sharp and sleepless. "I needed your brain, not your meat space. But if you're offering coffee…" Her hand flailed towards the uncluttered surface, which held an insulated carafe and two mismatched mugs. "Pour and observe."

Leilani poured, then circled around the tangle of wires to read over Akira's shoulder. The heat from the bank of CPUs was intense, making the cheap instant coffee taste even more like campfire and old ash. "What am I looking at?"

"The future of organized crime," said Akira, savoring the line. She pointed with a neon pink fingernail. "This is your spiral. Not the literal one; nobody in cyber cares about blood and walls, but the digital pattern. Each of these," she tapped a blinking green node, "is an access point. Hotel badge systems, employee emails, even one medical record server. All connected by a single hidden process. And every three days, the thing resets itself, buries a new entry code, and starts over."

Leilani sipped. The taste was miserable, but it forced her awake. "So, it's a botnet."

Akira rolled her eyes. "Please, that's the boomer version. This is more like a command chain for very smart, dangerous people. I found references to encrypted drop boxes in Switzerland, Moscow, and Singapore. Someone is using the resort's security system to route instructions for every job."

Leilani leaned in, reading the tiny font on the left screen. "That's why none of the badge entries show up after three days."

"Bingo. And every outgoing message from the nodes is triple encoded, but I've started breaking it. Check this out." Akira clicked on a log file and scrolled fast, highlighting a string of numbers and symbols. "That's a Bitcoin address. Last night, it got a transfer of fifty grand, probably a payment to one contractor. But look here." She highlighted another. "This is from the safe room job at Makai Grand. Same pattern, different time. The money moves through seven wallets, and then poof! It ends up in a shell company in the Caymans."

Leilani watched the diagrams tracking the red lines from node to node. Some faces she recognized from resort interviews: the head of security at Makai Grand, a janitor at Pacific Haven, even a front desk kid she'd met that morning. Others she didn't know, but the lines converged on one point, a node at the center, pulsing black.

"Did you get anything on the hub?" she asked, tapping it.

Akira's lips pulled into a grim smile. "Not a face, not a fingerprint. Just a code name: HOST. And the server that runs it? Relays through four darknet sites before it ever touches a local address. I traced it as far as Kaka'ako, but after that it's vapor."

Leilani let that hang, then pointed to a name on the side cluster. "Why is Rafiq Nawaz on this list? He's

IT, not security."

Akira nodded. "Yeah. Except he logged in to the Makai Grand guest network at the exact minute the access badge was cloned. And he's got a whole digital life outside of Oahu. He played in three online chess tournaments the week of the last two jobs, always at weird hours. I'm betting he uses it as an alibi for physical movements."

"Can you tie him to the network, not just the jobs?"

Akira cracked her knuckles and grinned. "That's why you're here. If you can shake him hard enough to get a password, or a thumb drive, I'll crack the rest in a day. Otherwise, it's slow and painful."

Leilani took a slow lap around the desk, trying to catch every piece of the puzzle. The diagrams were mesmerizing, but she forced herself to look at Akira. "What about the Russians? Torres said two of the early break-ins hit guests under FBI surveillance."

Akira flicked to another screen, this one all Cyrillic and gray scale mugshots. "There's chatter on the forums that suggests someone is using resort guest lists as a menu. The top tier, the big fish, and always with an eye toward financial leverage. The Russians are scared, but not of the FBI, of whoever's running the show. Rumor is, they lost money on the last job, and now someone's buying their debts cheap."

Leilani sipped again, then set down her mug. "And you're sure it's not an inside job at the resorts?"

Akira made a noise like a laugh. "It's both. The inside people are hired as pawns, but the Host runs everything remotely. They even rotate crews, with no one working more than once per job. There's a new player for each hit."

Leilani studied the whiteboard beside the desk, which was littered with sticky notes and Sharpie equations. Half the notes were in shorthand, but a few stood out in block letters.

TRUST IS THE HOLE

PAYLOAD = LEVERAGE

BLACKMAIL MONEY

"Whoever's behind this, they're building toward something," Leilani said, half to herself. "It's not about the heists."

"Right," said Akira. "They're not stealing, they're recruiting. Every time someone cracks under pressure, they get absorbed, blackmailed, or replaced."

Leilani looked again at the center node, the black one. "Can you get me an address, or at least a location?"

Akira hesitated. "I can try. But you have to promise not to let Torres screw up my server access again. The last time he tried to VPN in from the field, I almost got flagged by three different botnets."

Leilani smiled, tired but real. "Deal. You feed me the good stuff. I'll handle the fieldwork."

She stood but paused at the door. "Hey, Akira. Get some sleep. The city needs you alive, not in the ICU with caffeine poisoning."

Akira smirked, already diving back into the code.

"I'll sleep when the Host is dead."

Leilani closed the door behind her, letting the cool dead air of the hallway soak in. For the first time since John Maka'ala's murder, she saw the outline of the monster they were chasing. Not a myth, not a phantom, but a person, or something close enough to bleed.

She noted the faces she'd seen on the network. Tomorrow, she'll start with Nawaz. And after that, whoever else popped up on the pulse.

Somewhere inside the blue glow of that basement, a new war was brewing. And Leilani was ready to bring it topside.

Kaimuki at dusk was nothing like downtown; the air was thicker, the light older. Every block bore the scars of a different ambition. Some houses were razor straight and painted with suburban optimism; others hunched behind jungle growth, battered cars baking under mango trees. The Maka'ala house sat in the crease between two worlds, its vinyl siding clean but patched, a double stroller tucked behind a hedgerow and a chain link gate strung with plastic leis from some long ago birthday.

Leilani pulled up to the curb, the engine ticking in the heat. Her arrival triggered the usual perimeter scan. Two bored teens playing mobile games on the neighbor's porch, a cat darting across the driveway, and the heavy thump of a bass line leaking out from a passing car. Nothing dangerous, nothing even notable, except maybe the silence inside the house itself.

She made her way up the walk, dodging a pile of sidewalk chalk and a tumble of waterlogged Nerf darts.

At the door, she hesitated, the badge already out of her pocket but held low, not wanting to make this anymore official than it already was.

The woman who answered was half the size of her husband and built from different stuff altogether. Where John was broad and easy, she was compact, all shoulders, and cheekbones, with black hair chopped into a no-nonsense bob. Her eyes were red, but dry; whatever tears she'd had, she'd run out before Leilani arrived.

"Detective?" she said, voice steady as a rock slab.

Leilani nodded. "Mrs. Maka'ala. I'm sorry for coming so late."

She shrugged, gesturing Leilani inside. "I was up anyway."

The living room was brighter than expected. The walls were crowded with family photos. John in HPD blues, medals askew on the wrong side of his jacket; kids in birthday hats; everyone grinning with the genuine foolishness you never get in posed shots. The furniture was nothing special. Big overstuffed sofa, battered Ikea coffee table, a kid's beanbag chair cowering in the corner, but the air smelled like lavender and Murphy's oil, as if someone had blitzed through trying to make things right.

They sat at opposite ends of the couch. The television was on mute, stuck on a YouTube kids' playlist, the rainbow thumbnails chasing each other in endless auto play.

Mrs. Maka'ala folded her hands and let them rest in

her lap. "I can't help you," she said, flat. "I already told the other detectives everything."

Leilani nodded, letting the pause grow. "I know this is hard. But I need to ask again. You were with your husband before his last shift?"

She nodded, jaw working. "He left for work at eight. He took the new badge, the one with the black lanyard. He hated it, called it the dog collar. Said the old ones were better."

"Did he seem nervous? Anything unusual in his routine?"

Her eyes narrowed as if weighing whether to answer. "He was different in the last couple of weeks. Wound up. Not angry, but more alive. He'd stay up after the kids said goodnight, watching YouTubes on lock picking and safecracking. At first I thought it was for work, but …" She hesitated. "He started getting calls. Late. Sometimes he'd go out and walk around the block while he talked."

Leilani scribbled, careful to keep her expression blank. "Did you ever hear what he said? Or who was calling?"

"Never," she said. "But the area code was from the mainland. He'd get quiet after, like he was chewing on something."

She ran a thumb over the seam of her jeans, worrying about a loose thread. "I asked him about it, but he said not to worry. That it would all be okay soon."

A mug sat on the coffee table, half full of congealed

coffee, the rim smudged with coffee lipstick or years of dishwasher fade. It looked like it belonged to John, the mug a man never let go of even after a dozen birthdays. The sight of it abandoned, made Leilani's throat catch.

"Did he mention a specific job?" she asked.

Mrs. Maka'ala's face creased, and she seemed ancient, worn hollow by what she'd lost. "He said there was a score. That if he helped one time, we wouldn't have to worry about the kids' college. He didn't say how, except that he'd be a hero. He joked he'd finally get to retire in style."

"Did he seem scared?"

"Sometimes. Mostly, he was proud. But that night, he kissed the kids before he left, told them they were his 'ohana and they'd always be safe. He'd never said that before." She bit her lip. "I thought it was sweet."

Leilani wanted to say she understood. But cops weren't allowed that kind of confession.

"Is there anything else? Anything small? Sometimes it's the little things that help."

Mrs. Maka'ala glanced up at the photo wall, at the generations stitched together by Polaroids and digital prints. "He left his wedding ring in the medicine cabinet. I found it this morning." She held up her hand, showing the band on her own finger. "Said he couldn't wear it to work, not with the new badge. But he never took it off, not in seventeen years."

Leilani wrote it down, heart pounding. That was a tell, even if she didn't know what it meant yet.

A door creaked at the back of the house. A small boy, seven or eight, shuffled into the hallway, hair wild and sticking up like he'd been shaken awake. He didn't see Leilani at first but climbed onto the sofa next to his mother and curled into her side, eyes already drooping closed again. Mrs. Maka'ala ran her hand over his head. She smiled at Leilani, equal parts apology and warning not to wake him.

"I'll let you go," said Leilani, quietly. "Thank you."

Mrs. Maka'ala stood, smoothing her jeans, face calm again. "Will you catch the person who did it?"

Leilani hesitated. "I'll try."

At the door, Mrs. Maka'ala paused. "He wasn't a bad man. Whatever he did, he did for us."

Leilani nodded, the words stuck somewhere behind her teeth. "I know."

The screen door banged shut behind her, the evening air sucking the heat off her skin. She walked to her car, sat behind the wheel with her hands at ten and two, unmoving.

Inside the house, a woman made breakfast for tomorrow's kids, picked up after yesterday's husband, lived in the hollow between promise and fear. The world kept spinning. Leilani wondered what her own son would remember if she didn't come home one night. If a spiral drawn in blood was the total of her life's math.

She called dispatch. "Kealoha," she said. "I need a background run on John Maka'ala's recent finances and flag any out-of-state calls to his cell over the last six months. Also, can we get a subpoena for hotel key card access from the Honu Bay security system? Ask Choi to handle it. He's better with the admin."

The dispatcher grumbled, but Leilani knew it would be done.

Leilani always trusted her gut more than her brain. Half the time, her head would logic away the threat, but her back, her nerves, her skin, those never lied. As she hit the sidewalk outside Maka'ala's place, the base of her neck was buzzing like a live wire.

Across the street, a black sedan idled at the curb, windows smoked so dark you couldn't see the driver. It was a single car not battered or personalized or even remotely lived in. A blank, high-gloss surface, the color of wet oil on asphalt. It wasn't there when she arrived.

She unlocked her Explorer with a single beep, kept her pace lazy, a hand inside her bag. The sedan didn't move, but she knew it was watching, if you could call it that. A car like that didn't watch; it recorded. It absorbed.

Leilani didn't hurry. She got in, closed the door, and let the old engine rattle to life. On instinct, she flicked on the dash cam she'd installed last spring, part of a half-abandoned project to document officer safety scenarios. She fished her sunglasses from the glove box and put them on, a signal to anyone watching that she wasn't interested in games.

She rolled out, signal on, left hand casual on the wheel. The sedan waited three seconds, then ghosted after her, silent as a rumor.

For the first mile, she played it cool. No sudden moves, nothing to alert a neighbor or give a patrol car a reason to call it in. She drove down Waialae, merging with the early evening traffic, the sedan holding three lengths back in a way that almost made her respect the professionalism. Almost.

At the stoplight near St. Louis Heights, she looked in the rearview, caught a flash of a shape in the driver's seat. Male, she thought, but the silhouette was too generic to be useful. The sedan's plates were mud-splattered, but she committed the first three digits to memory. TLB.

At 8th Avenue, she eased into the left lane and waited. The sedan stayed back, with one car between them now. She wondered if they'd hired mainland muscle, or dipped into the local bench of silent, steady creeps. Her money was on neither. The city had plenty of its own ghosts.

She hit the gas at the next green, not enough to make a scene, but enough to catch the tail off guard. The sedan compensated. On a straightaway, she braked, checked her mirror. It slowed, never losing its cool. Fine.

She punched the next right, a narrow cross street clogged with parked cars. The houses here were tight together, driveways short, every lawn divided by cinder block or ancient plumeria. The sedan followed, a silent black shark in a sea of mismatched minivans.

She tested the driver, ran a rolling stop, turned into a blind alley, and doubled back on herself. The sedan never wavered. Whoever was behind the wheel, they were drilled for this.

She picked up the pace, skipped a turn signal, and took a sudden left onto the sloped drive behind an old Safeway. She cut through the delivery lot, dust and gravel pinging the undercarriage, coming out the other side, straight into the open pulse of Kapahulu. Now the chase was real.

She floored it, the Explorer shuddering as she hit sixty, blasting past a line of taxis and a half-asleep bus driver. The sedan matched her speed, always three cars behind, never more, never less.

Down the stretch past the Rainbow Drive-In, she saw her opening. A pocket of empty street, four blocks of nothing. She swung hard, accelerating up Monsarrat, using the incline to gain a second or two. At the crest, she checked the rearview. The sedan had closed the gap.

The city blurred at the edges. The tight clench of her knuckles on the wheel, the taste of adrenaline crawling up her tongue, and the faint sound of her own breathing in the dead air of the cab. The world outside was noise and hazard.

She made another turn into the night market, a chaos of closing up stands and lingering teens. She used the foot traffic as cover, slowing suddenly, faking a right into a loading zone before doubling left, straight down a one-way the wrong way. The sedan hesitated, a beat and barreled in after her.

She laughed. "Okay," she said to the empty cab.

She took them through a few more tourist traps,

threading narrow lanes, cutting along the Ala Wai, where the canal glimmered under floodlights and the banks were alive with strolling couples. The sedan was closer now, almost reckless. It wanted her to know it wasn't going away.

She remembered a checkpoint the department was running tonight, a DUI trap on McCully. She looped around, merged into traffic, and headed straight for it.

Halfway there, the sedan tried to pass her. She swerved, blocking the move, then braked hard as a red light trapped them both. The sedan idled alongside, windows still up, the engine vibrating the entire frame.

Leilani stared dead ahead, one hand on the gearshift, the other hovering near the emergency brake. Her mind spun through options, calculating the odds. The longer she waited, the more she wanted to see who was in the car.

The light changed. She took off with the sedan right there, running neck and neck. The checkpoint loomed ahead, with strobing lights and a line of flares.

She kept her pace steady, slowing when she was two cars out.

The sedan saw the trap but didn't blink. It kept even with her all the way to the roadblock, then, at the last possible second, made a screaming left across two lanes of traffic and vanished into the dark.

Leilani allowed the relief to sink in. Her pulse jackhammered, but her hands were steady now.

An officer waved her to the checkpoint. "Ma'am, license, and registration?"

She flashed her badge and gave a tight smile. "Detective Kealoha, 1068. Pursuing a suspicious vehicle, black four-door, partial plate TLB."

The officer nodded, his radio squawking. "You want backup?"

She rolled forward. "No, keep your eyes out."

She eased through the checkpoint, pulled into a parking lot, and cut the engine. She sat there, sweat chilling her neck, the afterimage of the sedan burning through her skull.

Her phone buzzed. Unknown number.

She hesitated before answering.

A voice, flat and electric, said, "You're very good, Detective. But we see you, too."

The call ended.

Leilani laughed, low and fierce. She looked in the mirror at her own reflection, jaw set like it would never soften. Bring it, she thought. She pulled back onto the street, this time watching the rearview, and every shadow. Every reflection. She was being hunted, but hunting back was always her favorite part. Somewhere out there, the Host was watching.

She hoped he was taking notes.

# Chapter Nine

## Kai in the Crosshairs

Recess at Kahala Elementary was Kai's favorite thirty minutes in the whole day, not counting midnight crime TV reruns with his mom, and he meant every minute. On Tuesdays, the fifth graders ruled the far soccer field, and the kindergartners got the swings, but the cracked blacktop beside the gym, the asphalt jungle, according to Kai's partner Sam, was reserved for detectives.

Today, Kai wore his lucky red hoodie and double-knotted shoes, both mandatory for good surveillance. He and Sam had ditched the usual basketball game in favor of a mission. To solve the Case of the Mysterious Backpack, which, technically, was a moldy old pack left under a shrub, but Sam insisted on calling it evidence. They took turns poking it with a stick, as if it might explode with clues.

"Probably some teacher's lunch from, like, a thousand years ago," Sam said, squinting at the torn mesh pocket.

"Or it's got secret documents," said Kai, voice low and dramatic. "Like plans for a robbery, or a ransom note." He could make up half the crime in his head, but the universe was always generous enough to supply the rest.

He kneeled beside the bag, scanning the perimeter. The playground was loud and bright, the sky that sharp, blinding blue you get after a rainstorm. Kids roared around the monkey bars and shrieked in the four-square courts, but Kai's ears tuned out everything except his own mission.

Sam, his self-declared Watson, nudged Kai with the stick. "Okay, what's your verdict, Detective?"

Kai grinned, rolling his eyes for effect. "Elementary, my dear Watson. The owner of the bag is left-handed; see, the shoulder strap is more frayed on the left, and they probably lost it on purpose because of the spilled milk smell." He sniffed theatrically. "Plus, it's full of sand, so they were on the beach before school."

Sam looked impressed despite himself. "How do you do that?"

Kai shrugged. "Pay attention. It's a superpower."

He zipped the bag, careful not to get his finger stuck like last time, and, returning the bag to the bench, noticed something at the chain link fence.

Two men stood beyond the playground border, past the sagging hibiscus hedge. Not parents, not teachers, and not groundskeepers. Both wore dark clothes, jackets even though it was hot, and hats pulled low, like they wanted to be invisible but didn't know how. They were far enough away to be ignored by the grown-ups, but Kai had watched enough episodes of Crime Scene, Honolulu, to know a stakeout when he saw one.

Sam followed Kai's stare. "Who're those guys?"

"Shhh," said Kai, grabbing Sam's sleeve and dragging him behind a battered recycling bin. "Don't look. They'll know you're onto them."

Sam whispered, "It looks like they're waiting for someone."

Kai watched the way the two men pointed at the Coral Reef Casino across the street. He leaned close, talking too fast to be normal. "Nobody waits on the playground in a wool jacket unless they're up to something. Trust me."

He peeked again, heart thumping. If his mom were here, she'd tell him to mind his own business, but Leilani wasn't here, and besides, this was the thing she'd want to know. He pulled a chewed pencil stub from his pocket and started writing what he saw on his hand, using shorthand so Sam couldn't read it.

"Okay, new plan," Kai whispered. "You keep an eye on the backpack in case the suspect circles back. I'm gonna get closer to the fence and see what those two are up to."

Sam made a face. "What if they see you?"

"They won't," said Kai, brimming with the confidence of the one kid in class to escape detention twice in one week. "I'll pretend I'm looking for a lost ball."

He left Sam and slipped along the playground fence, keeping to the shade where the trees grew in a half-ruined line. He watched the adults, cataloguing everything. The shorter guy had a limp, an old sports injury, maybe, or something worse. The shorter one kept checking a thick silver watch, like he was timing something, or someone.

Kai slowed near the hopscotch grid, careful not to make a show of looking. He squatted and picked up a stray kickball, then angled his head to catch a few words from the men's conversation.

"…shift change at midnight. That's when the guards rotate. The security office is here." The tall one tapped a hand-drawn map, unfolded enough for Kai to see the blue ink scribbles.

"Boss says we go in through the employee entrance. If we time it with the fire alarm, no one's gonna be looking at the vault," said the short one.

Kai's mind spun. Vault? Security? He'd overheard enough grown-up talk to know the Coral Reef Casino had a real safe, plus more alarms than a missile silo. He pressed his ear against the wire fence, fighting the urge to shout out.

The tall man lowered his voice. "Don't get sloppy. Last job almost went sideways 'cause your buddy got cute with the cameras. This time, we do it right. In and out, nobody even knows."

The short one grumbled, "Hope it pays better than last time."

Kai bit his lip to keep from grinning. He'd never heard a real heist plan before, not even on his shows. He focused hard, soaking up every word, every gesture. He could almost hear his mom's voice in his head, asking, "What did you notice first? What was out of place?" It felt like a test, and he was acing it.

"Tournament's in two days," said the tall one. "Nobody's going to care about a couple of missing chips. Long as you get the code from your friend."

Shorty spat. "He'll talk. Everybody does."

As Kai was about to back away and tell Sam, the tall man glanced over his shoulder. His eyes glanced straight at the fence, straight to Kai, who tried to duck but was too late. The man's stare landed like a baseball to the ribs.

"Hey, kid!" the man called, voice sharp enough to cut through the noise of the whole playground.

Kai froze, part of his brain still insisting he could play it cool. "Uh, hi?"

The tall man's mouth curled. "You lose something, little man?"

Kai didn't let go of the fence. "No, sir. Looking for my baseball."

The men exchanged a look. Kai thought they'd let him go, but the shorter one stepped forward and jerked his chin. "What did you hear, kid? This is grown-up business."

"Sorry, I heard nothing." said Kai, and backed away, not running but not slow enough to look casual.

Behind him, Sam waved frantically, signaling "Abort!" but also, "Come back!" which didn't help.

Kai made it to the blacktop, adrenaline still fizzing in his chest. He ducked behind the bin, heart pounding. Sam stared at him, wide-eyed.

"What happened?" Sam hissed. "Did they catch you?"

Kai nodded, a little proud, a little scared. "They're gonna rob the casino. I heard them. Friday night, when the tournament's on. They have a map. They're gonna use the fire alarm and sneak in while the guards are busy."

Sam's jaw dropped. "That's… that's insane. What do we do?"

Kai glanced at the men already walking away, muttering to each other, the map tucked out of sight. "I gotta tell my mom," he said, decision already made. "She's a detective. She'll know what to do."

Sam, didn't argue. "Should I come too?"

"Yeah," said Kai. "But we gotta stay invisible until then. If they see us again…"

He didn't finish. He didn't have to.

Kai hadn't even made it to the blacktop before the eyes were on him again, hard, drilling, like searchlights through a window. He risked a peek and saw the two men moving fast along the outside of the fence, cutting around the basketball court in a dead sprint. For a split second, the world seemed to slow: the rubbery whap of a dodgeball hitting pavement, the caw of mynah birds in the monkeypod, the sharp, nervous laugh from someone on the swings.

The men didn't look like they were going to stop for anything.

Kai ran, bare legs pumping, shoes scraping up clouds of hot dust. He swung his head back in time to see the taller man barrel straight through the open gate, sending the chain link rattling. There was an old security guard posted there, Uncle Henry, who never said no to popsicles and always handed out gold stars for good citizenship. Uncle Henry stepped forward, arms wide in a no passing gesture, but the man slammed into him, shoving the old guy sideways like he weighed nothing. Uncle Henry staggered, his foot caught on a sprinkler head, and he fell hard. His head cracked on the sidewalk with a sound Kai would hear again that night, and for years after.

Kai's throat restricted.

He yelled, "Help!" but the word barely made it past his lips before he was flying past the jump ropes and jungle gym, heading for the big red doors that marked the entrance to the main building. Behind him, the shorter man had cleared the gate too, and his breath whistled as he ran, wild and loud.

Teachers noticed. Mrs. Mapu, whistle always at the ready, shrieked a series of blasts that pierced the playground noise. "Everyone inside! Move!" she shouted, grabbing kids off swings and shoving them toward the nearest wall. Sam disappeared into the crowd, arms windmilling, his face pinched with terror.

Kai dove through the red doors as the taller man's fingers brushed his hoodie. Inside, the hallways yawned with fluorescent light and echo; the floors were waxed so bright you could almost see your own panic in the reflection.

Kai ran, not sure where to go but sure it couldn't be back. He ducked into the first side hall and made a beeline for the cafeteria. The men thundered in behind, their steps out of sync and monstrous. He heard the man curse, the word strange and ugly in the sanitized air. Two short alarm bells rang followed by the dreaded announcement they had heard dozens of times in drills.

"Intruders in the school. This is not a drill. Immediate lockdown." Now the siren wailed.

Down the second hall, past the lockers, some slammed shut by scared hands, others standing open like mouths, Kai zigzagged, changing direction whenever he saw a teacher or another kid. He wanted witnesses, people, chaos. Safety in numbers. Everyone was running. It was chaos.

He rounded the corner at the nurse's office and nearly plowed into a group of second graders, who screamed and pressed themselves to the wall, eyes huge. Kai didn't stop to apologize but used their confusion as cover.

He could hear the men talking now, voices sharp and close.

"Split up," said the tall one.

"Go right," snapped the short one, breathless but mean.

Kai knew the building better than anyone. He took the janitor's shortcut, under the broken drinking fountain, left at the lost and found cart and past the staff bathroom with the weird purple air freshener. His lungs were burning, but he kept running.

At the end of the hall, he saw the heavy oak door to Room 212, which always smelled like vanilla and old highlighters. Ms. Patel's room.

He skidded on the floor, sneakers squealing, and

burst through the door.

Ms. Patel and Mr. Domingo were gathering the kids out of the hall and pushing them into a corner. Ms. Patel ran back to lock the classroom door. Both turned, startled, when Kai tumbled in, slamming the door behind him.

"Kai?" Ms. Patel's voice moved up an octave. "What are you?"

"They're coming," panted Kai, "Bad guys. Please lock the door."

Ms. Patel and Mr. Domingo stared. The handle rattled, and the tall man's face appeared in the wired glass, eyes wild, sweat plastering his hair to his forehead.

Mr. Domingo, who used to play linebacker for UH, stepped to the door. "Who are you?" he barked.

The man didn't answer. He threw his weight against the door, but it was reinforced, one of those "active shooter upgrade" things from a year back. The frame groaned but held. Mr. Domingo braced both arms against it.

Kai darted under a desk, hands over his head, wishing he'd never left the playground.

The shorter man arrived next, and the two men shouted at each other, too muffled for Kai to catch. The tall one pulled something from his pocket: a long screwdriver, not a knife, but scary enough. He jabbed it between the door and the frame, twisting, trying to jimmy the lock. The shrieking alarm continued. The school's automatic system, a wailing, rising pitch that told everyone to shelter in place.

Ms. Patel grabbed her phone, dialing, eyes never leaving the intruders. "I'm calling the police," she said, voice shaky but determined.

"Already coming," Mr. Domingo grunted. "Part of the protocol when the alarm goes off."

The screwdriver slipped. The tall man banged on the door with his fist. "Open up, or we're coming in any way!"

Kai peeked out from under the desk, heart doing gymnastics. He wanted to help, but he was ten and unarmed, and everything was suddenly more dangerous than any episode of his detective shows.

Somewhere outside, there was a different siren. Kai recognized the police sirens as they sounded from several directions, closing in on the school.

The two men froze. The tall one glared through the glass, locking eyes with Kai, who wished he could shrink into the floor.

"This isn't over, kid," the man mouthed, lips twisting.

Both men turned and bolted back.

Kai shivered so hard he rattled the desk. Ms. Patel slid in next to him, wrapping her arms tight. He smelled of vanilla and chalk dust.

"It's okay," she whispered, even though it really, really wasn't.

Within a minute, patrol officers rushed into the school, walkie-talkies squawking, weapons drawn. Mr.

Domingo stood at the window, watching as the two men sprinted across the soccer field, out the back fence, and into the neighborhood beyond.

When the danger passed, Ms. Patel helped Kai up and checked him for injuries, her hands shaking.

"What happened?" she asked, brushing dust from his cheek.

"They… they wanted to hurt me," Kai said, the truth heavy and thick.

She hugged him tighter, and he let her.

A few minutes later, the principal and two actual police officers, badges gleaming, faces tight, arrived to take statements. Uncle Henry, who'd opened his eyes and was being attended to by the school nurse, his head, and shirt were covered in blood, his gold stars scattered on his shirt like confetti.

When they asked for details, Kai told them everything. He didn't leave out a single clue. But even as the grown-ups praised him for his bravery, and the police scribbled notes, Kai kept hearing the last thing the tall man had said. This isn't over, kid.

He believed it.

Leilani got the call after lunch, before the message even hit her official phone. Ten minutes and fifteen seconds later, she was parking outside Kahala Elementary, barely missing the ambulance still idling in the bus lane. The sky was sharp enough to slice you, and the sun bounced off every badge and windshield and fresh roll of police tape. Even from the curb, she spotted two news vans already jockeying for the best angle on the red front doors. Parents were lining the fence, waiting for the kids to be released from lockdown. It was a scary time for everyone, and they all wanted answers.

Leilani ducked under the tape, flashed her badge at a rookie with an overzealous jawline, and pushed through the gate. She stopped next to a gurney and recognized Uncle Henry lying on his back, covered in blood, while two paramedics worked on his head. She placed her hand on Henry's shoulder, and he smiled up at her. She did not let herself imagine anything beyond this moment. Anything before or after. It was a trick she'd learned on patrol. Move, don't think, or you'll freeze. She pushed through the crowd and into the school.

The scene inside was more hospital waiting room than school. There was a cluster of paramedics working on some children that had been knocked down during the rush to find shelter. Three teachers huddled near the front desk, trying to pretend they weren't all crying. They were lining up the children with the help of Honolulu SWAT officers, so they could be released to their parents outside. The principal, a solid woman with an ironic "PEACE, LOVE, LEARNING" T-shirt, intercepted Leilani before she made it ten steps.

"Detective Kealoha?" Her voice was this close to shaking.

"Where's Kai?" asked Leilani, already scanning the hall.

"In my office," said the principal. "He's, uh, he's okay. Little shaken. We gave him some water. He wouldn't let go of the cup, so we left it with him."

"Thank you," said Leilani, already walking.

The principal caught her arm, gentle but firm. "The men who chased him, they're gone. Police are canvassing. I didn't want you to think." She trailed off.

Leilani wanted to say something comforting, but couldn't. She squeezed the principal's hand and strode straight for the office door; the window painted with a peeling rainbow.

She opened it and found her son in a plastic chair, both feet on the rung, a silver space blanket draped over his shoulders. He was the smallest she'd seen him in years, jaw clenched, hands shaking, but when he spotted her, the tremble stopped. Neither of them moved. She nodded to the patrol officer standing next to him.

Kai grinned, the crooked, defiant grin that always made her heart hurt, and held up the water cup in a toast. "Hi, Mom."

She sat beside him and checked every visible inch for injury, even though she'd done this a thousand times in her head. "Are you okay?"

"I didn't cry," said Kai, voice proud and unsteady. "I remembered what you said about witnesses. I saw everything."

Leilani laughed. "Bet you did." She put her hand over his, squeezing it so tight she could feel the pulse in his palm.

There was a minute of silence, save for the hum of the window AC and the muted walkie-talkies. Kai's cheeks were streaked, his nose red, but he sat tall. "They hurt Uncle Henry," he said. "He tried to stop them, but." The next word stuck.

Leilani brushed his hair back, the way she did when he was two, and let him finish in his own time.

"I ran," Kai said, almost in a whisper. "I ran, and I got away, and Ms. Patel and Mr. Domingo saved me."

She saw the weight on his shoulders. Not the scare, but that he'd been hunted, marked like prey.

Kai took a breath. "Mom, I heard them talking. Before they saw me. They're going to rob the Coral Reef Casino. Friday night during the tournament. They have a map. They said the vault's open during the cash count, like, at midnight."

Leilani almost smiled at the way his voice changed gears, from kid to cop, like that. She smiled, knowing he had a vivid imagination. "Are you sure that's what they said?" she asked.

He stared at her. "Yes. I'm not kidding. They looked like they were casing the place. That's why I noticed them."

"What else did you hear?" she asked.

"They're gonna set off the fire alarm. That's when the guards rotate. One guy knew the combo or had a friend on the inside. The tall one was like the boss. He got mad when the other guy messed up last time. He said, if this doesn't work, he'd burn down the entire island."

Leilani wrote the phrases on her notepad in blue ink. A surge of pride and something much darker washed over her.

"You did good, Kai. You did good." She yearned to hug him, to hide him under her jacket and never let go, but that wasn't how things worked. Not for either of them.

He nodded, lips pressed together. "I wasn't scared until after. Is that bad?"

"No," she said. "That's how it goes."

There was a knock on the door. The principal again, with a police officer at her elbow, a big guy, new to the district, name tag reading TAO. He looked nervous, like he might break the furniture if he sat down.

"Detective," said the officer. "Can we get his statement to help us coordinate with your department?"

"Of course," she said. "Give me two minutes." The cop nodded.

She turned to Kai. "Let's get you somewhere safe. Nana's, probably. You okay with that?"

Kai hesitated. "Will I see you?"

"Every night. I'll pick you up after work. No more after-school programs for a bit, though."

He shrugged. "Can I watch TV?"

"As much as you want, but no cop shows for a while. Right now, I need you to tell Officer Tao everything you told me, okay? I'll be right here next to you."

He smiled and said, "Mom?"

"Yeah?"

"You'll catch them, right?"

She didn't promise, but she didn't look away, either. "I'll try."

Officer Tao, for as big as he was had a soft voice and gentle manner. He walked Kai through the event several times and thanked him for being a stand up citizen. He shook his hand and nodded to Leilani as he left the room.

Kai and Leilani walked out together, past the admin desk, past the teachers, past the paramedics gently lifting Uncle Henry into the ambulance. He raised two fingers in a hang loose gesture as they passed, and Kai did it back, his face brightening.

Outside, the news vans had multiplied. Leilani kept her arm around Kai, head down, weaving through the crowd with the precision of someone who never wanted to be seen again.

She got him buckled in the passenger seat, shut the door, and leaned against the car, letting the tension drain away.

Her phone rang. It was Isaac.

She answered before the first ring finished. "Torres."

"I heard. He okay?"

"Yeah," she said. "He's okay. Scared, but okay."

Silence on the line. "The two men, any ID?"

"Nothing yet," said Leilani. "But we've got a new

lead. The Coral Reef Casino, Friday at midnight. Fire alarm, inside job, two-man crew. One tall, one short, both pros. Kai got a look at both."

"We'll get a sketch artist."

"I want a protection detail at my mom's house tonight. And at the school, too."

"You got it," said Isaac, voice clipped and clean.

She hung up and got into the car. Kai had already found the glove compartment gummies and was dividing them into color-coded piles on the dash.

"Mom?"

"Yeah?"

"Did you ever have to run from bad guys when you were a kid?"

She started the engine, watched the traffic part in the rearview, and smiled, for him. "All the time."

She put the car in gear and peeled off the curb as the city closed in behind them. Tomorrow, the war started again. But tonight, she had Kai, and the world had not taken him from her.

Not yet.

# Chapter Ten

## The Money Trail

By 5:50 a.m., the joint HPD-FBI task force office looked like a hedge fund after a midnight raid, monitors blinking, legal pads bristling with angry arrows, empty Red Bull cans outnumbering clean coffee mugs. Isaac Torres had been there for two hours, teeth vibrating with caffeine, still in his dress shirt from the day before, collar open and tie hanging like a dead man's tongue. He stood at a hurricane of paper, cross-referencing bank statements and subpoenaed resort payrolls with the grim focus of someone who'd once considered applying to the IRS out of spite.

The new evidence board, real estate office surplus, bought off Craigslist for twenty bucks, groaned under the weight of printouts. Four central columns, one for each resort, hit in the last three weeks, Aloha Shores, Makai Grand, Pacific Haven and Honu Bay. Each was a skyscraper of highlighter, sticky notes and red-twine connections, so overbuilt it looked like the world's saddest game of Connect Four.

Torres was midway through his third re-read of the Makai Grand's LLC structure when a scuff of footsteps broke his tunnel vision. He didn't look up. There was one person on the island who wore that brand of beat-up New Balance sneakers and insisted on stomping even at dawn.

"Good morning, Detective Kealoha," he said, eyes

still on the spreadsheet.

Leilani yawned, stretching in the doorway. Her hair was pulled back with an HPD evidence clip, and the dark circles under her eyes suggested she hadn't slept more than a few hours. "If I answer honestly, you'll report me to Internal Affairs."

He gestured at the board, then at the single chair that hadn't yet been colonized by binders. "You need to see this."

She flopped into the seat, arms crossed, face set in that skeptical stone he respected. "Let me guess. The big breakthrough is that every resort on Oahu is run by the same three sleazeballs and their in-laws?"

He grinned, half pride, half caffeine tremor. "Worse. Look." He flicked a laser pointer, circling a cluster of names that, in any other context, might have been lost in the weeds. "Every robbed resort is owned, not directly, but through a shell company. The shells are all managed by different lawyers, but the trust beneficiary is always the same, Polynesia Capitol Holdings."

Leilani frowned. "That's not possible. PCH is an umbrella. They don't run the day-to-day."

"That's what I thought. So, I checked with the SEC. Turns out, PCH's largest stakeholder is registered through a double-blind trust in Nassau. Want to guess the name on the Articles of Incorporation?"

She laughed. "Don't say it. I don't want to know."

Torres leaned in, pointing with the laser: "Makani'olu Development Group."

Her mouth twitched. "No. No way."

"Makani'olu. As in, Makani'olu Heiau. As in the place where the old ali'i buried their enemies upright so they could never rest." He lowered the pointer, gaze direct. "You see where I'm going with this?"

Leilani nodded, her jaw ticking. "It's a warning. The shell company names are not random. They're all ancient sites. Sacred places."

"Right. Someone's flagging these jobs with the old language." He started pacing, wound up now. "But the money is newer than you think. The accounts all end in Zurich. I've got a buddy at FinCEN flagging the wires. But here's the twist. Every time a job goes off, the insurance payout doesn't just get laundered; half of it's funneled right back into buying beachfront property. Usually, the day after the heist."

Leilani rocked back, letting it sink in. "So, it's not merely theft. It's a hostile land grab."

"Yeah," said Torres, "but with less blood and more contracts."

She scanned the board, eyes narrowing as she mapped the timeline in her head. "Whoever's behind this is doing more than robbing resorts. They're orchestrating the collapse. Buy low, torch the value, then buy the ashes for half price." She pinched the bridge of her nose, fighting off a headache. "Classic colonial playbook."

Torres nodded, something like admiration flickering in his eyes. "You see it, too."

"Always have." She glanced at the names, the

colored lines, the ocean of fake signatures. "You get anything on who actually signs the checks? Who's running Makani'olu?"

He shrugged. "All the directors are dead ends. Retired, moved to the mainland, and a couple have terminal cancer. And the listed CEO? A man named Gerald Nakoa."

Leilani snorted. "You know who that is?"

Torres shook his head.

"He's the nephew of the State Tourism Board's chair. Used to run scams out of Manoa, fake time shares, Ponzi stuff. Last I heard, he bought into a coconut water startup and declared bankruptcy twice."

"Well," said Torres, "He's back in the game. He's laundering money through properties that should be bankrupt, but never quite are."

They sat in silence; the implication settled like silt. Leilani scanned the board again, then dug a phone from her jacket.

"Who are you calling?" Torres asked.

"My cousin. She's a paralegal at the State Real Estate Office. If anyone can give us dirt on Makani'olu, it's her. She owes me a favor." She dialed, voice dropping into a husky whisper. "Lili, it's Lei. Yeah. Do you know anything about Makani'olu Development? Uh-huh. Shit. What about their next project? North Shore, casino? Are you serious? No, I'll hold."

She turned to Torres, covering the phone with her hand. "Rumor is, Makani'olu is building a casino at

Kaena Point. Under the radar. But the land deals are getting dicey, with locals refusing to sell and lawsuits everywhere. And they're not stopping. They keep buying, lawsuit or no."

Torres started writing furiously in his notebook. "Every heist destabilizes another chunk of real estate. They devalue it, buy it up, and launder more cash. It's not about the score. It's about flipping the island, piece by piece."

Leilani nodded, pressing the phone to her ear. "Yeah, Lili, I'm still here. Can you get me a list of recent property transfers around Kaena? I'll pick it up in an hour. Same place. Yeah, I owe you malasadas. Done." She hung up and looked at Torres. "We have to map every shell, every property, and cross-check it against unsolved cases in the last year."

Torres grinned, handing her a mug of what passed for coffee. "Way ahead of you."

She sipped, grimacing. "God, this is horrible."

He shrugged. "It's not for taste. It's for fuel."

They stood there, shoulder to shoulder, tracing the web of theft, money and ancient names. Leilani sensed the case was less about the next job, and more about unmasking the architect behind it.

Torres reached for the red string, about to loop it around a new name, then paused.

"You're good at this," he said. "You see the whole picture, outside of the crime."

Leilani smiled. "Someone has to before they finish the job."

Together, they started filling in the gaps, a pair of predators running down the line, pulling the monster out of hiding by force of will and stubborn faith, and they wouldn't let go.

Leilani arrived at the pier-side café ten minutes early and used all ten of those minutes to case the joint. The crowd was shift workers and off-duty charter captains, loud in their trucker hats and sun-peeled skin, but nobody paid attention to the corner booth except her. She ordered a coffee, black, no sugar, then positioned herself with a view of both the street and the kitchen door.

Her contact, a woman in her late twenties with hard acrylic nails and an even harder stare, slipped in wearing oversize sunglasses and a windbreaker, despite the thick humidity. She didn't take off the glasses or the jacket, but slid into the booth and hunched low, palms flat on the Formica.

"You're early," said Leilani.

The woman shot her a look over the rims. "And you're a cop. Let's keep this fast."

"Relax, Lili," Leilani said, not unkindly. "I need the folder."

Lili nodded toward her own bag, lips pressed tight. "You didn't say you were looking into Makani'olu. You said nothing about Nakoa. I have a kid, Lei. I can't get burned for this."

"Nakoa doesn't even know you exist," Leilani said, though she doubted it was true. "This is between us."

The harbor wind and the odor of diesel and frying

eggs were the things moving.

Lili reached into her bag and brought out a manila folder, thick with color-coded pages. She pushed it across the table as if it were laced with cyanide. "That's every land transaction in the last six months. Not Kaena, but anything with a shell company signature. You'll see the same names pop up repeatedly." She leaned in, voice down to a tremble. "They're buying around the resorts, Lei. Not after the jobs, sometimes before. The price drops, a company no one's heard of scoops up the deed, and two weeks later it flips to Makani'olu."

Leilani opened the folder. The paperwork was a blizzard of deeds, notarized signatures, property maps and sticky notes in Lili's tight, angry handwriting. She scanned, closed the folder, and pushed it back.

Lili shook her head. "No. You keep it. I never saw it." She pulled her jacket tighter. "If they ask, you forged my name."

"Thank you," said Leilani, and meant it.

Lili stood to leave but hesitated. "If you're going to poke this, do it quickly. My boss says Nakoa's got a councilman and at least two guys at the permit office in his pocket. Everyone else who tried to slow him down…either took a vacation or took a payout." She hesitated. "One thing you ought to know. Nakoa's not at the top. There's someone above him."

Lili bolted, vanishing into a tangle of tourists in less than a heartbeat.

Leilani waited another five minutes, then paid for

the coffee and walked back to her car, every instinct on high alert.

The task force room was quieter than usual when she returned, but Isaac was there. Maps and satellite images already spread across the table. He was so focused on a laptop that he didn't notice her until she tossed the manila folder onto the paper snowdrift.

He looked up, eyes shadowed with exhaustion. "Anything?"

She grinned, a little feral. "Everything." She dumped the contents onto the table, sorting them into piles by hand. "Here. Here. Here." She tapped each property. "All within a mile of the robbery sites. And every time, the price is below market. Sellers are desperate."

He started pinning pages to the wall, connecting dots with red push pins and sticky string. "That's not all," he said, handing her a stack of receipts. "Every one of these 'shell companies' uses the same notary service. The owner is a guy named Joaquin Atoa. Guess what? He used to run security at the Makai Grand."

"Inside job," said Leilani, almost to herself.

"Worse," said Isaac. "It's an ecosystem. They rob, they tank the price, they buy, they flip, then the new resort gets built with clean money." He turned, hands splayed on the desk. "They're not thieves. They're city planners with no rules."

They worked in sync, taping and scribbling and highlighting, until the board resembled a battle plan.

Leilani pointed to the northernmost pin.

"That's where they're going next," she said. "Kaena. There's nothing up there but a couple of decaying condos and the old military installation. Why would they want it?"

Isaac scanned the latest press release from Makani'olu, then blinked. "They want to build a casino. Not any casino, a casino, and a private airstrip. With direct flights from Macau, Singapore, and, get this, Moscow."

"High rollers," said Leilani. "No locals allowed."

"Of course," said Isaac. "It'll be the biggest, most exclusive money laundering operation in the Pacific."

They stepped back from the board, neither needing to say it out loud.

"It's never about the jewels," said Leilani, almost gentle. "It's about the dirt underneath."

Isaac let out a slow breath. "And whoever's doing this, they're ten steps ahead."

She smiled, but there was no humor in it. "Not for long."

They stood shoulder to shoulder, maps and memos fluttering in the office AC, the whole rotten blueprint finally in view.

This time, they'd play the Mastermind's game to the last move.

Once Leilani and Isaac hit city hall, the morning air had already transformed into a wall of wet wool. The old pineapple-shaped lobby had three lines, one for traffic fines, one for zoning, and one for records and permits. The last was ten people deep, half of them retirees holding battered folders or watermarked envelopes. A sign above the plexiglass partition read: SERVICE WITH ALOHA. The woman behind the desk looked like she'd run out of aloha before sunrise.

"Next," she called, not glancing up.

Leilani and Isaac flashed their badges, HPD and FBI.

"We're looking for access to the latest property transfer records, specifically, anything related to Makani'olu Development or shell companies with similar PO boxes," Isaac said, keeping his tone as bland as the décor.

The receptionist's smile was as fixed as a carnival doll's. "Oh, those records are… currently being audited. No public access until the review is complete."

"When will that be?" asked Leilani, hand on the counter.

The woman pursed her lips. "Indeterminate. A week, possibly a month. Sometimes the files are lost in transition." She slid a business card through the slot. "If you have questions, email this address. They'll answer within seventy-two business hours."

Isaac pocketed the card, noting the generic cityinfo@honolulu.gov. He tried a different angle. "Can we speak to whoever is heading the audit?"

She checked her screen, making a show of squinting. "There's no supervisor listed. Sorry."

"Who requested the audit?" Leilani pressed.

She shrugged, the movement almost invisible. "Couldn't say. Might be council, might be state level."

They tried the next window over, Zoning. Same faces, same deflection. This time, a security guard in a polyester blazer hovered close, making sure the line moved.

After half an hour, what they got was a single sticky note: Try the Department of Land and Natural Resources.

The DLNR's suite was on the sixth floor, in a corridor that smelled faintly of mildew and floor wax. Their meeting had been confirmed at 10:30, but the office door was locked, and a sign read: CLOSED FOR TEAM BUILDING. Through the frosted glass, Leilani heard laughter and the tinny sound of a ukulele.

Isaac knocked anyway.

Silence.

He dialed the extension on the sign. Voicemail. The same number was taped above the phone on the wall, but with an out-of-office notation in Sharpie: Back next Tuesday.

They gave up and tried the State Tourism Authority, in a high-rise so new the walls still reeked of fresh paint. Here, the appointment was double-booked and canceled. "Sorry, the boss just stepped out," chirped the receptionist, who eyed their badges and then promptly shut the glass partition with a soft click.

The situation continued this way all day, one door after another, one smiling assistant after another, all promising a callback, a follow-up, a file transfer that never materialized.

As the day came to a close, they found themselves in the outer office of a city councilman whose name appeared on half the permitting signatures for the North Shore. The lobby was sterile, decorated with faded campaign photos and a plastic bowl of stale M&M's.

An aide, thin and nervous, sat at a desk overflowing with papers. He was typing furiously when they entered, and when he saw the badges, he closed his laptop with a snap.

"Can I help you?" he asked, voice high with anxiety.

Leilani leaned in, voice low and even. "We would like to speak with Councilman Nakoa. It's urgent."

The aide didn't even pretend to check a calendar. "Councilman Nakoa is unavailable."

"For how long?" Isaac pressed, not blinking.

The aide glanced at the door to the private office, then back at them. "Indefinitely."

A beat of silence.

Leilani smiled, all teeth. "Is he in trouble?"

The aide's face twitched. "No, of course not. He's, uh, very busy with… constituent matters. If you want to schedule an appointment, you'll have to go through media relations."

Isaac pushed a business card across the desk so hard it slid and landed on the keyboard. "If Councilman

Nakoa wants to avoid a media circus, tell him to call us."

The aide nodded, scooping up the card and immediately hiding it.

Back in the hallway, the hush was absolute. Leilani glanced up and down, making sure they weren't being watched, but she knew better than to expect privacy.

They left City Hall and walked a block to her Explorer. They got in, shut the doors, and sat in the hum of recycled AC.

For a while, neither spoke.

Leilani slammed her palm on the dash. "I fucking hate this town sometimes."

Isaac looked over, the corner of his mouth tugging upward. "You know what this means, right?"

She wiped sweat from her forehead. "Yeah. We rattled the cage. They're scared."

"Which means we're right over the target," Isaac said.

They sat side by side, breathing the same stale air, both grinning now, a little wild, a little angry. The next move, they knew, wouldn't happen in an office. It would be in the field, and soon.

Leilani pulled into her driveway at half-past nine, the sun long gone and the street awash in sodium vapor and the blue TV glow leaking from other people's lives. She looked in the rearview out of habit, sat with her hand on the ignition, then killed the engine and listened, two dogs barking, distant, and the dull hiss of tide on sand. No sign of the black sedan from two days ago, or any car that didn't belong.

She grabbed her jacket and the brown paper grocery bag from the passenger seat, careful not to spill the takeout containers stacked inside. She stopped at her mailbox; she thumbed through bills, a court summons for a neighbor, and a glossy flier for a Polynesian dinner show she'd never attend. All junk, no threat. She crossed the lawn, shoes silent on the grass.

Inside, she locked the deadbolt, dropped the mail on the kitchen counter, and allowed the cool dark to wrap around her. The air had that stale fridge-mustiness of a house shut too long. She exhaled, slipped out of her shoes, and turned on the overheads.

Everything looked in place. The TV, still on the same kids' channel Kai had left it; the couch, pillows askew; the table, sticky with last night's teriyaki sauce. But something wasn't right. Not the fear. She'd grown used to that, wore it like a badge under her shirt, but a shift in the space, a shadow pulled a quarter inch to the left.

She inspected the windows. Locked shades drawn. The glass slider to the lanai? She tested it. Secure. She walked through the house in a slow circuit, every step deliberate. Nothing. Kitchen cupboards closed, no footprints on the tile. She put the groceries away, then opened the fridge to get a soda.

That's when she noticed it, a breeze. Faint, like someone exhaling. It came from the hallway at the back of the house.

Leilani closed the fridge, opened the silverware

drawer and palmed her service weapon from its felt-lined nook. The grip steadied her. She held her breath, padded down the hallway, soft as a reef eel.

Kai's room was empty, his model cars parked in a formation he insisted was an evidence grid. Nothing out of place. In the bathroom she found the clean towel damp from the morning. The master bedroom door stood ajar, about two inches. Leilani nudged it open with her toe, the gun held in front. The room was empty. The window on the far side was open two inches. Enough to let in the damp air and the drone of night insects. She scanned for movement, listened for breathing. Nothing.

She turned toward her dresser mirror and froze. Drawn on the glass, in a looping, deliberate spiral, was a mark she knew too well. The petroglyph, the same symbol left at the crime scenes. This one was red. Not blood this time, but the oily swipe of a wax marker. It dripped slightly, a bead trailing toward the base. The sight made her vision tunnel, with a static roar in her ears.

She checked the closet, empty, and the space under the bed, then double-checked the window. The screen had been popped; the latch forced and set gently back so it looked unbroken. Whoever did this was a pro, or at least wanted her to think so.

She holstered her weapon, pulled out her phone, and snapped five fast photos of the spiral, getting the angle from the bed, from the door, from her own pillow.

With her thumb, she dialed Isaac.

He answered on the first ring. "Yeah?"

"They were in my house," she said. Her voice was flat. "The Mastermind. He left the spiral on my bedroom mirror."

A pause. "I'll call the detail at your mom's house and make sure they're okay. Anyone else in the house?"

"No."

"Secure the scene," Isaac said. His voice was cool, but she heard the panic in the way he clipped the words. "Don't touch anything. I'll get Choi and bring a team."

Leilani hung up, checked every room again, this time slower, letting her senses reach. The intruder hadn't taken anything, no computer, no evidence, not even the backup gun from her lockbox. This was a message, pure and simple.

She sat on the bed; the spiral reflected twice over in the mirrored closet doors, like a sequence of warnings. She steadied her hands, wiped the sweat off her neck. This was how the game changed, not with a bullet or a bomb, but with a mark drawn in the color of rage.

She thought of Kai, of the smile he'd worn this morning, of the old stories her mother told about trickster gods who could slip into a home without leaving a footprint. She'd let her guard down. Once. She stood, backed out of the room, and closed the door. She'd clean it up when the forensics team finished. For now, she left it as it was, a warning. A dare.

Tomorrow, she would call her mother, making sure she was locking her doors and windows. She would also call in some favors from the old patrol crew. But tonight, she stood in the heart of her small, violated house, the gun in her hand and plotting the next move. She was done playing defense.

And in the dark, the spiral on the glass seemed to burn.

# Chapter Eleven

## Undercover Operations

The employee locker room at the Coral Reef Casino was two steps above a city jail cell and three below the staff room at a Jamba Juice. Molded benches bolted to the floor, a coffee vending machine stuck permanently on "warm," and a string of metal lockers so new the warranty stickers still flaked off when you scraped a fingernail. Leilani stood near the sole uncracked mirror, arms folded, back tense, watching her own reflection do nothing to make the uniform less humiliating.

She took in her reflection. The uniform, what there was of it, was all sharp lines and indigo, miniskirt cut for eye level with a barstool and halter top tight enough to wring out a heartbeat. There was a bowtie, too, a clip-on, and a pin-on name tag with HALEY laser-etched in cursive. She'd practiced pinning it on with a left-handed move, like she'd seen from the real servers. The casino had issued her a company-standard makeup kit, and now her lips were outlined a little too perfect, her lashes spiked with some off-brand mascara that stung the first half hour and then settled into place.

She checked her earpiece, a skin-colored bud that barely bulged under a curtain of hair. It wasn't much. A modified bluetooth wired to an encrypted channel, but she liked the way it felt, snug and secret. A quick tap, and Isaac's voice hummed in, low and clear.

"You set?" he asked.

Leilani didn't answer, not with two servers gossiping three lockers down, so she squeezed her shoulder against her ear, hoping the gesture would carry. She heard Torres exhale, a tiny hiss, then a pause as he realized she was surrounded.

The other two servers, both off-shift but milking the free break room coffee, eyed Leilani's legs with bored admiration.

"You've got some legs, girl," said one server. "The customers are gonna love you."

"You got a dinner shift, hun?" asked the tall one, a narrow blonde with a spiderweb tattoo crawling up her wrist.

"Yeah," said Leilani, pitching her voice a half-step higher, making herself softer at the edges. "First night. They told me to shadow?"

The short one, Filipino, not older than nineteen, flashed a gap-toothed grin. "Don't worry. Keep the whales wet and keep your hands to yourself. The old dudes try to tip you in chips, but it's all scanned, anyway. If you need a smoke, I'll show you the fire exit with the alarm turned off."

Leilani laughed, like it was a joke and not a low-level shakedown for loyalty. "Thanks. I'll probably need it."

She watched how they moved, how they peeled their uniforms from street clothes and back, how they threw their phones into the cheap lockers, kept their lipsticks in a pocket of the casino-issue aprons. She caught the rhythm, fast and unbothered. When the tall one left, she did it with a snap of gum and a one-handed text, already halfway back into the zone.

Leilani finished buttoning her top, ran a quick check on the earpiece, tied back her hair loose enough to frame her jaw and tight enough to stay out of her face. She closed her locker, spun the dial, and walked out into the service corridor, following the painted arrows toward the main floor.

She checked herself in the mirror one last time. What looked out was not her, not anyone. Hair sprayed up and off her neck, cheekbones sharper than usual, eyes ringed with drama, chin set at a party-girl angle. It was the face she used in high school to steal cigarettes from the ABC Store, or to talk her way past the front desk at a Waikiki dive bar when she was fifteen. She wasn't sure she even knew the woman in the mirror, but she nodded at her anyway, as if to say. This is your gig. Don't blow it.

She breathed in slowly and reviewed the plan, because routine was the armor against nerves. Isaac was working the main floor, at the high-stakes poker table, suit tailored perfectly, Miami tan on loan from the tanning salon in a strip mall. She would run the grid, float the cocktail lanes, use the mirrored columns to ping the faces and patterns while waiting for the mark to appear. They had five hours until the rumored handoff; ten, if things ran slow. No backup, only each other, which was how she liked it.

Time to move. She stepped out into the service hallway and followed the yellow tape arrow that led to the staff entrance.

The service hallway ran parallel to the gaming floor, walls done in the same over bright maroon and brass as the casino itself, though here the art was all stock prints of palm trees instead of the priceless originals hanging near the whale rooms. Every fifteen feet, a black dome camera bulged from the ceiling. But tonight, Leilani was as legitimate as the next wage slave. The pass card clipped to her skirt worked on every door from the break room to the freight elevator, and her biometric had already been entered by HR that morning.

The world shifted as soon as she breached the threshold. On this side of the swinging double doors, the casino's heart thudded at max volume. Slot machines whined and chittered, their digital brains vomiting fake coins and blips in a pattern that could make you insane if you listened too long. Every third step, a server in a dress like hers weaved past, tray up, eyes dead. The air vibrated with the double rhythm of piped-in jazz and the thousand voices of men yelling, cursing, celebrating at the tables.

She fell in behind a few of the regulars, retired military by the haircuts. Probably here to nurse a rolling comp tab and leer at anyone younger than their own daughters, and she let herself slide into the current. Her feet found the same high-heeled walk as the other servers, chin tilted, the posture halfway between fuck you and please tip well. She made it three tables before the first grabby uncle tried to snag her wrist, and she shook it off with a smile she stole from a toothpaste commercial.

She felt the pulse in the earpiece. "Bravo one,

status?" Isaac, never more than five minutes from checking.

"On the grid," she said. "Nothing unusual. Running base scans now."

Leilani caught sight of Isaac.

He was sitting at the big poker table, high stakes, set apart from the crowd by a half-moon of velvet rope and the attention of three different servers. Torres had gone full native, hair slicked, suit sharp enough to draw a double-take from the dealers. He wore a pinky ring, which she knew for a fact he'd bought at a flea market that morning, and a Rolex that was too heavy to be real. He sipped a tumbler of Macallan, barely touching it, and kept one hand flat on the table.

The game was down to four. A tanned tech bro with hair like a bottlebrush, an older woman in pearls who could have played anyone's grandmother on TV, a stone-faced Korean man, and Torres. He played slow and loose, folding half the time, betting big to lose, like he wanted to give off the musk of easy meat. But Leilani knew the signals, each flick of a chip, each tap on the rail, a code she'd memorized.

At the dealer change, she approached the table. The head server intercepted her. A tight blonde with the walk of someone who'd danced through tipsy bachelorette parties since high school.

"You can take the rail," the blonde said. "But don't step over the line."

Leilani flashed her best I'm-new-here smile. "Sorry, I'm shadowing. Training night."

The blonde, satisfied with her own authority, moved off. Leilani glanced at Torres, caught the barest tilt of his head, then moved on.

She made her first drop at the corner bar, handing off two vodkas and a sticky shot glass to a bachelorette party in matching neon sashes. They didn't look twice at her. She cased the bar for a few seconds. No mark, no security, only the bartender's tight nod and a tilt of his chin that said, keep it moving. She did.

Next, the slots. Here the lights were lower, colors deeper, a sunken cave made for hiding both shame and fortune. She let her eyes sweep from left to right, pretending to search for a specific customer, but noting every face, every movement. A woman with a bucket of nickels muttered to herself, shoving her luck into the machine one slug at a time. Two men in ill-fitting suits hunched over video poker, one hand on the cards, the other on their phones. Nobody glanced at her, which was the best sign possible.

Next, the pit. She entered through the baccarat tables, where a pair of dealers worked the room with the slow, smug confidence of magicians running a birthday show for idiots. At table four, she spotted the shift manager, tie loose, knuckles white on the rail as he leaned in to whisper to a high roller. She watched his movements, the way he scanned the exits every third glance and the subtle pat of the pocket where the pass cards lived.

She kept moving. The mark would show, or not, but in the meantime, her job was to blend and to never be out of step.

At the next bar, a tray of eight Long Islands for a group of flight attendants in layover mode. She loaded them fast, balanced the tray on her palm, and cut across the blackjack lanes, keeping the path as straight as the shoes would allow. At the last second, the tray wobbled. She felt it, that rush of oh-fuck panic, but she righted it, letting the gesture read as clumsy and cute. The man at the table, a vacation dad with sunburned shoulders, winked at her. She smiled back, dropped a napkin and moved on.

Halfway to the service station, she felt eyes on her. Not the usual creep stare, but the chill-up-the-neck, someone-who-matters-is-watching kind. She rolled her head, scanning the mirrored ceiling in her periphery. There. Across the room, visible in the reflection, Isaac sat at the high stakes poker, elbows wide, chip stack fat, sunglasses perched low on his nose. He looked so perfectly at home that it hurt a little.

She tuned the earpiece with a casual touch to her earlobe. "Bravo one, status?"

"Pit is clean. Mark is not on the floor. You?" he replied.

"Confirmed. Doing another pass. Watch the shift manager. He's jumpy tonight."

A pause. "Copy that. He's probably waiting for a guest list update. I'll keep an eye."

She smiled, a flash, and drifted past the roulette table. Here, the mood was wilder; the table packed with a blend of frat boys and aunties betting on birthdays, anniversaries and the magic of even numbers. Leilani felt the energy, the stutter of hope and disaster, and realized she was enjoying the work. Not the uniform, not the shoes, but the art of being unseen while seeing everything. It was the best kind of magic.

On her way to the locker room for a fake break, she cut through the corridor behind the main bar. She passed two real servers, both with trays stacked and complaints already loaded, but neither paid her more than a grunt. In the employee washroom, she checked her face in the mirror again. Still there, but different now: cheeks flushed, eyes a little harder, the makeup blurring at the corners.

She patted her lips with a napkin, checked the line of her hair, then took three deep breaths, each one sharper than the last. The plan was simple: move, watch, wait. When the mark appeared, she would signal Isaac, who would get the manager to react, which would trigger the chain of events. All she had to do was be in the right place at the right time.

She checked the earpiece again. "Bravo one, anything?"

Isaac's voice, this time with a twist of humor: "I'm ahead by seven grand and got comped a steak dinner. You're slacking, Kealoha."

She laughed, letting it ring out, but caught herself and remembered the role. "I'll catch up."

"Always do," he said, soft now, and it felt like a hand on her back.

Leilani stepped back into the corridor, and the noise swallowed her up. The spiral was closing, and tonight, she was ready to twist it tight.

As midnight crawled up on the casino, the Coral Reef's main floor was halfway between apocalypse and revival tent. Slot reels still spun, the regulars still fumed and cursed, but the faces changed every hour. Tourists sucked dry, before being replaced by bolder ones, while the true addicts orbited the same machines with grim religious intent. Leilani blended, floated, made her drops, all the while watching for that ghost on the grid, the casino manager, never stationary, always restless, always in the orbit of high-value trouble.

At one a.m., the pattern broke. The manager, thin, nose like a switchblade, hair slicked flat and parted with a ruler, stopped scanning the floor and instead melted down a back corridor, eyes on his feet, hands clutching something inside his blazer. He walked with the too casual speed of a man on a mission, but also one hoping nobody would notice he was up to his neck in it.

Leilani noted the move. She signaled a fake trip to the bar, before curving behind a row of slot machines, ditching her tray by the waste bin. She followed the path to the staff-only door but slowed before reaching the entrance, letting herself lag far enough to avoid notice. She bent to rearrange the straws and napkins on a nearby tray, hunched, spine bent, invisible. The manager didn't look back. He slipped through the door, a soft click and vanished.

She waited fifteen seconds before continuing. The service hallway was a different planet, all soundproofed beige and spongy floor tile, the lights over bright and motion triggered. She noticed the hush of a voice ahead, then a second, lower and more dangerous.

She eased up to the bend, stopping short of being seen.

The manager stood with his back to her, shoulders tight. Across from him was the shadow figure, tall, built, his face obscured by the angle of his hooded jacket, and hands gloved black. Even in the ugly halogen, the man seemed to suck light out of the air. A presence, not a person.

She angled herself so she could watch the reflection off a chrome fire extinguisher.

"Next shift change," said the shadow. The words were so low they were almost a purr. "Zero three hundred. Security will be on cash movement. You have ten minutes max."

The manager made a sound halfway between a whimper and a laugh. "And what about the floor? There are new protocols. Audits. Eyes on all cages, not just the vault."

"Already handled," said the shadow. He made a flicking motion with two fingers, a gesture meant to erase problems. "The drop will happen as always. All you need to do is walk it out."

The manager wiped a hand down his face, visibly trembling. "This… this isn't like last time."

The shadow figure leaned in. "Of course it isn't. That's why you're paid triple. If you want to renegotiate, be my guest."

The manager grew silent. "No. No renegotiation. I."

He hesitated. "I want to get through tonight. No more phone calls. No more notes."

Shadow shrugged, as if he'd already stopped listening. "Okay, stick to the script. Move the package on time. And keep your mouth shut."

She heard footsteps. She tensed, ready to bolt, but the pair didn't exit toward her—they turned and disappeared through a secondary door, one labeled LAUNDRY with a handwritten sign. The moment they were out of sight, Leilani exhaled so slowly she thought her own lungs might rebel.

She stood, adjusted her skirt, and rolled her shoulders. The adrenaline surge left her buzzing, fingertips tingling, jaw locked tight with the effort not to sprint to the nearest phone and blow the operation. She needed to report it, but she also needed to stay on the mark, keep the story straight, act like nothing mattered.

She headed towards the main floor, picked up the abandoned tray, and swept a circuit around the bar, searching for Isaac. He was still at the high roller table, his chip stack even fatter, sunglasses now propped on his head. He looked bored as a monk in meditation, but the moment she came into line of sight, she ran the signal. Right hand up to earring, slow, deliberate, followed by a half second tilt of her head. It was the sign for the target in play.

He didn't look her way. Not directly. But he reached for his whiskey, and in the slow drag of his fingers across the glass, he tapped the bar twice, loud enough that it could be heard by someone listening for it.

"Bravo two, status?" she whispered, keeping her lips almost still.

Isaac's voice, calm: "Saw your signal. We're a go for shift change. SWATs already staged. You okay?"

She swallowed. "Adrenaline high. But yeah. Keeping eyes on. Shadow man confirmed. Package is the play."

"Copy. Stay clear. Don't get cute."

"Wouldn't dream of it," she said, and meant it.

She did another slow lap around the bar, fingers icy, spine locked straight. The casino crowd was thicker now. More animated. She made her drops, scanned the staff area, and caught the manager slipping back onto the floor, face paler than before, hands wringing the fabric of his jacket like a dishrag.

She would keep him in her periphery. That was the job. Watch, wait, then move when the moment came. She'd done harder things, but never with this much on the line. Her hands didn't shake as she poured a gin and tonic for the next customer. Outwardly, she was the perfect server, never missing a step, never letting the mask slip.

Inside, her heart banged against her ribs, counting down to three a.m.

At 2:58 a.m., the casino floor was a living beast, its pulse slow and thick, everything stretched out by exhaustion and adrenaline. Leilani kept one eye on the pit, the other on her target. The manager paced in circles near the back office, sweat dotting his collar, lips working over a silent monologue of self-doubt and dread. Every three minutes, he would check his watch, glance at the exit, then double back. The rest of the world didn't care—dealers kept dealing, uncles kept drinking, the endless hunger for one more hand, one more spin.

She made her final pass with the tray, rolling the weighted silver across her palm, eyes fixed on the clock above the cashier's cage. Two minutes. She adjusted her earring and saw in the reflection, Isaac setting his whiskey down and standing up, moving in slow motion toward the pit. The room seemed to inhale, waiting.

The first note of the fire alarm was almost musical, a pure, high-pitched sine wave that for a heartbeat ran through the casino with the clarity of a songbird. But as the next note hit, the sound doubled, trebled, and warped into a siren so punishing it rattled the stemware and stabbed her skull. Instantly, the world ruptured. Every screen and light panel in the casino erupted into warning red, flashing in a strobe that sent shadows leaping like panicked animals across the floor.

Leilani was moving before her mind caught up. Years of academy training and fieldwork had programmed her body for this. Tray to the nearest table, duck low, eyes up for exits and hazards. She scanned for Isaac, but he was gone, washed out in the flood of fleeing patrons. The crowd split and surged in slow motion, then crashed back together, a crush of limbs and voices and perfume. Glass shattered somewhere, and chips ricocheted off felt, spinning in wild arcs as desperate hands grabbed for whatever could be carried. Drinks spilled and ran in greasy ribbons toward the floor drains.

Sprinkler heads snapped on, a cold mist beading on her bare arms and then soaking the shirt she wore. She blinked through the spray, her eyes burning, but the pain brought the world into harsh, high-definition focus.

The pit bosses were already on the move, their voices amplified by the bullhorns they snatched from behind the security desks. "PLEASE EVACUATE IN AN ORDERLY FASHION," one blared, his words shredded by feedback and the high drone of the alarm. "DO NOT STOP TO GATHER BELONGINGS— EXIT IMMEDIATELY—THIS IS NOT A DRILL."

Security guards, blue-jacketed and newly energized, formed a moving wall, shunting people toward the main entrance. But even in the panic, the casino's natural hierarchy asserted itself. High rollers barked orders; the regulars followed, grumbling and elbowing but never truly running.

Leilani was carried by the first wave. Her head ducked, one hand over her ear to muffle the shriek. But even as she moved, her eyes hunted. Not for the manager, not even for Isaac, but for the seam in the chaos, the weak point where the actual play would surface. The package, the shift change, the window.

She spotted him near the keno section, the maintenance worker, the one from every piece of surveillance, walking with a bag slung low on his hip and a yellow vest over his street clothes. He wasn't running. In fact, he was moving with total composure, navigating the stampede as if he were invisible.

That's the move, she thought. Blend in, disappear, but keep your path. Every instinct screamed to intercept, but she had to stay in character, to not draw heat. So, she trailed him at a distance, letting herself be jostled by the crowd, every nerve stretched so thin it hummed.

The maintenance worker passed the main security cluster and doubled back through a dead end slot row, ducked behind a bank of old quarter machines. The area was briefly shielded from the cameras, and Leilani saw him key open a side panel, slip something black and shiny into a pocket, then pivot out and head straight for the emergency exit. He moved with the certainty of a man who knew every blind spot, every inch of the blueprint.

Leilani checked her six. Nobody was watching her except a grandma with a bucket of chips and terror in her eyes. She gave the woman a we're in this together smile, then followed the worker through the narrow corridor. The further she got from the main floor, the more the noise softened, the fire alarm dulling to a heartbeat-thud in the walls.

The worker slipped his badge through the mag lock on a steel door labeled AUTHORIZED PERSONNEL ONLY, and it popped open. He paused inside, adjusting his vest, and Leilani caught the flash of a gunmetal object tucked at his waistband. She had no weapon, no backup, but the adrenaline was purer than any she'd felt in years.

She glanced back once. Still clear. She stepped through the door after him. The corridor behind was all concrete and flickering fluorescent, with the scent of bleach and overcooked wiring hanging in the air. The worker was fifty feet ahead, his silhouette moving briskly but without hurry. Leilani softened her step, kept to the left, passed a stack of plastic-wrapped casino chairs and a floor buffer humming in idle. On the walls, every ten feet, a red line ran towards LOADING DOCK, like a treasure map for the criminally impatient.

The worker reached a steel cage gate, swiped again, and vanished into the loading zone. Leilani closed the distance fast, flattening herself against the wall to peer in.

Inside, two men, both in the same maintenance livery, one already opening the rear of a delivery truck backed up to the dock. The package was not a package. It was a hard-shell roller case, larger than airline carry-on, the color of wet sand.

The first worker pulled a pistol from under the foam padding and handed it to the second man. The third, stocky and graying, kept his back to the door, scanning the corridor with small, sharp eyes. Leilani had no moves. She was unarmed, and her earpiece was acting up.

Leilani was a mess. Her hair was plastered down, and her mascara burned her eyes. The serving shirt appeared translucent in an instant, clinging to her like a second skin.

Halfway to the maintenance corridor, a shadow detached from the far wall, moving low and fast. It was him. Not the manager. The maintenance worker from the security footage, face half-shaved, blue jumpsuit, sneakers instead of boots. He clutched a duffel in both hands and slipped through a door marked AUTHORIZED PERSONNEL ONLY. He didn't see her, didn't even look back.

She made for the door, fighting the muscle memory that told her to wait for backup, to call it in, to not be an idiot. Instead, she touched her earpiece, praying the circuit would work.

"Bravo two, do you copy?" she hissed.

Static, then Isaac's voice, sharp and scared: "Where the hell are you? You're supposed to be outside."

"Pursuing a maintenance worker from the footage. Heading to." She squinted at the sign. "The loading dock."

A string of curse words, then, "I'm coming in. Wait for me at the main service stair."

She thought about it but didn't stop. The maintenance guy was already halfway down the hall. She sprinted, shoes forgotten, arms pumping. The duffel was heavy—he had to pause, set it down, hoist it again. It bought her seconds. She reached the next corner as he rounded it, ducking through a door with a slam.

"Fuck it," she said, and followed him through. The manager was talking to someone up ahead. She slowed and stepped softly.

"Let's get the boxes loaded before the cops and fire departments show up," said the manager.

A van in the distance started, and she the doors opened. She was trying to decide on her next move when she heard a noise behind her. Isaac came up behind her, his hair and suit soaked.

"We have to stop them," she said.

Isaac reached to his ankle and removed his backup pistol and handed it to her. He pulled his pistol and nodded. They stepped out onto the dock, pistols leading.

"Freeze, police," they yelled together and separated a few feet.

The maintenance workers on the dock stopped and stared. They had loaded one box into the van and had been reaching for the other. The worker standing on the dock pulled his pistol from his jumpsuit. Leilani fired twice, and he slammed into a crate and slid to the floor. The other two workers slammed the van doors, jumped into the seats and drove away from the dock.

Isaac pushed the manager against the wall, pulled his radio, and tossed it to Leilani. She keyed the mic.

"This is Kealoha, SWAT needed at the loading dock and have someone stop the white van heading around the building."

"SWAT, roger."

While Isaac cuffed the manager, Leilani checked the guy on the ground. He was wounded in the shoulder and the leg, but he would live. She moved to the box sitting on the dock, flipped the lock and opened the box. The manager, who was watching her, pushed past Isaac and stared.

"Those are old chips. They've been removed from the system. They have no value. What the hell?"

Leilani was about to speak when four SWAT officers arrived on the loading dock. She looked across the lot and spotted several more officers converging on the white van.

Leilani looked at Isaac and then at the manager. "You were expecting something else in the box?" she asked.

The SWAT team from the van led the two maintenance workers up onto the loading dock. Leilani stared at each man. "The maintenance guy from the pictures we have isn't here. What the hell?"

The manager paled, and his knees weakened. He held his ground. "Shit."

Leilani and Isaac stared at him. "What?" she asked.

"Let's check the accounts." His voice shaking.

Leilani looked up and noticed several of the SWAT officers staring at her and several snickering. She looked around to see what they were looking at when she looked down. Her wet cocktail blouse had turned translucent and was sticking to her body. She turned abruptly and faced Isaac., who was talking to the manager.

"Give me your jacket," she said and held out her hand.

Isaac turned towards her. "What?" he asked. He got distracted and looked down. "Oh," he said.

He peeled off his jacket and handed it to her. She slipped it on and buttoned the buttons. She turned towards the SWAT officers.

"Okay, folks. Shows over. Back to work."

As the SWAT officers walked away, she wondered how many of their body cams were on and how long it would take before her picture was all over the internet. She wouldn't have to wait long.

She reached down, slipped off her six-inch stilettos, threw them in a corner and followed Isaac and the manager to his office. This operation was royally screwed.

# Chapter Twelve

## The Double Cross

While Isaac worked with the Manager trying to figure out how much was missing, Leilani walked to the employee locker room, stripped out of her wet cocktail uniform and put on her jeans and T-shirt. She clipped her badge and gun to her belt and tossed the cocktail uniform in a nearby trash can. She was embarrassed and humiliated, but more than that, she was pissed. The operation at the loading dock was a decoy, while the maintenance man she had originally followed had disappeared at the dock, slipped back, and wiped out the account for the big poker tournament. Billed as the largest tournament in the world, the payout amount was fifteen million dollars. All gone. Wiped from the casino's accounts. The only thing remaining on the screen was the spiral that covered the account page.

Security had been tight in the card room where a million dollars had been sitting in the middle of the final table. Until it was needed, it was locked in a glass case. What Leilani found was that the true value of the pile of money was ten thousand. The rest of the money in the case was Hollywood play money. The thief never attempted to grab the money. He gravitated straight to the accounts.

Leilani needed to clear her head, so she walked towards the loading dock. She was trying to figure out when the maintenance worker she had been following had disappeared and was replaced by the three on the dock.

The casino's loading dock was empty, save for a cat hissing under a rusted dumpster and the metallic echo of the fire alarm and the stench of gunpowder from when she shot the one maintenance guy.

Leilani slipped through the exit, the heavy door thudding shut behind her and stood outside. She drew a deep breath when something in her peripheral vision caught her attention.

Down the ramp from the exhibit hall, forty feet ahead, a maintenance worker was walking quickly and looking around. He ducked his head and hugged the shadows, but Leilani could see the blue jumpsuit. She followed, shoes sliding a little in a puddle, her pace measured. She didn't need to sprint. She needed him to think he had a chance.

The alley wrapped the length of the casino, a straight line before it doglegged into the underbelly of the resort proper. He'd have to go there—there was nowhere else to hide. She trailed at a distance, silent except for the click of her service weapon coming out of its holster. The sound was soft, but the man's shoulders hitch at it, his gait stuttering for a heartbeat before he took off running.

She passed the dock's roll-up, kept her eyes on his back, tracked every move. At the dogleg, he veered left and vanished into a doorway marked EMPLOYEES ONLY; the door swinging wild on its hinges. She took it at a jog, braced with her left hand, as her right guided the muzzle of her SIG through the opening.

Inside, the world changed. The corridor was a

horror show of bad lighting and flaking white paint, the overhead fluorescents flickering with enough strobe to make her nauseous. The air hung damp, filled with the aroma of Pine-Sol and wet concrete. She moved along the cinderblock, eyes up, one foot at a time, clearing each bend before stepping through.

The maintenance worker was ahead, breath rasping, as he skittered past rows of stacked banquet chairs and racks of rolling tablecloth bins. She let him run, watched his silhouette and bided her time.

They passed the laundry. The sound of the machines was deafening, every washer rattling like a riot. She lost sight of him, caught a reflection in a window of him slowing, checking for pursuit, and thinking maybe he'd shaken her.

She advanced faster, Nikes swallowing the tile, then stopped dead as a housekeeping cart toppled into her path. It was an amateur move, more desperation than a tactic, but the crash was enough to make her curse and sidestep, giving him another half second head start.

"Stop! HPD! You're done, man. Don't make me run," she shouted, putting all the boredom and steel in her voice that years on patrol had trained into her.

The answer was more frantic footsteps, a thud as he clipped his shoulder on a corner, a muttered string of words. Sounded like English, but different. Leilani set her jaw and followed, keeping her weapon high. He was cornering himself. These corridors were a dead end.

She caught up at the receiving dock of the housekeeping wing, where the hall knotted into a T, one branch ending at a locked supply cage, the other at a mop closet. He hesitated, tried the supply cage, found it locked, doubled back and dove into the closet, slamming it shut behind him.

Leilani approached, pulse and flattened herself against the wall beside the door. She listened, scuffling, a low whimper. She waited until the panic settled. "Last chance. Open. Slow. Hands high."

A tremor, a click. The door creaked open. The maintenance worker's face was ghost white, eyes rolling in fear, sweat dripping down the tip of his nose. He held his hands high, palms up, fingers twitching. His name tag, KEALO, hung askew from a safety pin. The closet stank of ammonia and moldy rags.

She kept the SIG fixed on him, voice steady. "Step out, turn around. No sudden moves."

He obeyed, knees threatening to buckle as he did a shaky pirouette. "Please," he croaked, "I'm not a bad person, they."

"Who's they?" she asked. Her tone was all business, but she let her finger drift off the trigger, enough to show him she would not shoot him on a whim.

The man's hands shook. "I didn't want to. They have my wife. My daughter. Please." He sagged against the doorframe, half-crying, half-mumbling in a language she didn't know.

Leilani stepped in, keeping him at arm's length. "Who has them?"

"Don't know," he said. "I never met them. Only the phone calls, always a new number. They say do the job, or they'll send me pieces of." His voice died.

"What job?" She risked a glance to make sure no one was in the hall, then eased the SIG down, but not away.

He shook his head so violently his glasses slipped down his face. "All of them. The four resorts and the casino. I don't touch money. I deliver packages. They make me move it from the building to a van. I never open, I never look. They pay after delivery. It's always cash, always a dead drop."

Leilani's mind raced, matching this with the three jobs before. The ghost runner, the perfect inside man. Disposable.

"Why you?" she asked.

"I spent time in prison for theft, mostly high end jewelry. While I was in, I figured out I have a knack for computers, and I studied programming and security systems."

"Who pays you? You ever see a face?" she pressed.

He answered, eyes glassy. "Tonight, a man in a white suit, not from here, could be from Russia or Europe, somewhere. I gave him a USB drive with the account numbers of where I sent the money from the tournament. What happens after that I have no idea, but I assume the money has already been transferred to dark accounts. What's going to happen to my family? I need your help."

Leilani cuffed his hands behind his back, walked to the center of the T and turned.

A single gunshot shattered the air, impossibly loud

in the narrow space. Leilani hit the deck, gun up, scanning for a threat, but the maintenance man was already falling. Blood sprayed onto her arm, warm and bright, and his mouth froze in mid-scream as he collapsed. Leilani dropped behind the cleaning cart, waited a full beat for a follow-up shot. None came.

She popped her head up and scanned down the corridor. Forty feet away at the far end, a shadow ducked back, then bolted toward the emergency stairs. She memorized the stride, the black jacket, the limp in the right leg. Gone before she could give chase.

She looked down. The maintenance worker, Kealo, was dying fast. Blood soaked the tile, pooling in a cracked grout line. She pressed a rag against the wound, not bothering to call for EMS. It wouldn't matter.

He tried to talk, lips working around vowels, and she leaned in, catching one word before his gaze became blank.

"Host."

She waited until his chest stopped shuddering. She stood, holstered her weapon, and forced her hands to stop shaking. She scanned the hallway again, along with the ceiling, for a camera. None. But someone would have heard the shot. She pulled her phone out of her back pocket and dialed 911.

"This is Detective Kealoha, badge 1068. Shots fired in the laundry hallway of the Coral Reef Casino. One victim down. The suspect ran out of the exit. Short black jacket with a limp. Need backup and paramedics."

She closed her phone and put it back in her pocket. She stepped over the body and started after the shooter. But even as her Nikes slapped the tile, she knew he was gone.

She slowed at the stairwell, looked for blood, for prints, for anything, and found nothing. Whoever did this had planned for a clean getaway. She ran a hand through her hair, wiped the blood on her sleeve. The disappointment burned in her gut. She heard sirens in the distance.

The last thing she heard was the hiss of a closing door, way down the stairwell, echoing like a laugh

She ran the service corridor twice, checked every door, and found nothing but a ghost trail, possibly the whiff of aftershave, her brain inventing it. In the stairwell, there was no blood, no casings, no evidence except the sound of her own breath in the hollow concrete. She doubled back, the lump of guilt already forming in her gut, and stopped by the dead man.

She kneeled, checked the carotid again, knowing it was pointless. The bullet had torn through his sternum, punching a black hole above the "a" in Kealo. She closed his eyes with her thumb, then checked his pockets quickly and impersonally. A crumpled Polaroid fell out, a little girl, big front teeth, gap-toothed, throwing shaka at the camera while a woman, the wife, squinted into the sun. Leilani folded it and slid it into her pocket.

She stood, wiped the blood from her hands on her skirt, and kept moving.

The door down the hall opened, and several officers

raced in with guns drawn. She holstered her pistol and held up her badge.

"Kealoha," she yelled. "Down here. The hall is clear."

The first officer in the hall said something into his shoulder mic, and they moved slowly, followed by two paramedics. She stepped aside to let them pass and walked away, feeling alone in the world.

The casino floor was a whole different universe. Where the service halls were cave-dull and brown, the main gaming lounge was alive with color, light and hysteria. Security herded crowds toward the exits, a tide of gamblers in windbreakers and sequined dresses, the alarm still going off in the background. People yelled, cell phones held high, some live streaming, some trying to find their friends. Over it all, the house PA system blared a weirdly chipper evacuation warning, like a theme park ride gone wrong.

She nearly got trampled by a line of retirees shuffling toward the bus lot. She sidestepped, bounced off a cocktail server crying into her hands, and nearly collided with Torres, who barreled in from the bar side, shirt untucked and pistol low at his thigh.

"You good?" he barked, scanning her up and down for bullet holes.

She nodded. "We lost our guy. He was the mule."

Torres set his jaw, glanced around the melee. "Where?"

She jerked her head back toward the staff area. "Supply closet left off the housekeepers' corridor. He was gonna give us something, but."

"Someone cut him off," Torres finished. He spat the words out, not angry at her, but at the world for being so on the nose.

A manager in a mauve suit charged up, hairpiece askew. "This is a goddamn disaster! We still have high rollers in the VIP! And now my staff is quitting on me."

Torres put up his badge and addressed the patrol officers. "FBI. Everyone out but security, and if anyone tries to leave with a backpack, you tackle them."

The manager deflated, blinking, then scuttled away to bark into a walkie - talkie.

Leilani pulled him aside. "They left a body and vanished. Classic shell game."

Torres shrugged. "Not vanished. Perhaps they are still here. Waiting for the noise to die."

She glared at him, her anger obvious. "They're gone. They played us for fools," she muttered. "The fire alarm, the sprinklers, the chaos, even the maintenance guy. It was all fucking noise."

"What time were the accounts hit?" she asked.

"Right after the sprinklers let go," he said. "This whole thing was over before we even reacted to it."

Leilani looked at Torres, saw the flicker of admiration and annoyance that always came when they hit a wall together. "So, while we were running their decoy in the basement, they hit the main event."

"Yep," Torres said, mouth twisting. "Whoever was running the crew probably left in the first wave with everyone else."

Leilani scanned the exits, watching the casino security waving people through metal detectors, a last minute show of diligence. She grabbed the walkie from the downed pit boss, tuned to the staff channel.

They found the nearest exit and staked out the parade of tourists. People stumbled out, confused, a few trailing crimson streaks where they'd fallen or been pushed. Leilani watched a blonde woman in a sequined dress clutching a giant fake Prada, then a pair of college bros in matching team jerseys, faces red and loud with adrenaline. She scanned for the limp, the dark jacket. Nothing.

She turned to Torres. "We're not gonna find them now."

He grimaced, wiped sweat off his brow. "Let's get the surveillance footage and start matching up every exit time."

She nodded, then saw the red stain on her pants; blood, but not hers. "I've gotta get cleaned up."

Torres managed a half-smile, half-sigh. "Go. I'll handle this side."

She washed her hands, watched the water run red, and thought of the maintenance guy's last word, Host. She wondered if it was a warning, a plea or an echo of something bigger out there, waiting for her. "Who was this host character and how did he fit in with Mastermind?" she thought to herself. There must be a connection.

She dried off, checked her face in the mirror, and saw how tired she looked. She grinned anyway. This was the work. This was the game. And whoever was at the epicenter of the web, they weren't out of reach yet.

She stepped into the corridor, back toward the noise, already planning the next move.

The garage lights flickered overhead, washing the row of parked cars in a cold blue haze. Leilani sat in the battered Explorer, the driver's seat slung low, her left hand flat on the steering wheel and the right one pecking a report into her phone. The glow of the screen made her skin look radioactive. She typed the facts with her thumb, each entry a flat line on a crash monitor.

At 05:30, suspect deceased via gunshot wound to thorax. Witnessed by det. Kealoha. Shooter unknown. Investigation is ongoing.

She sipped from a can of Diet Coke that was already warm, stared out the windshield at the still-buzzing perimeter of the casino, then typed the next line.

At 05:35, HPD responded. Secured scene. Confirmed maintenance worker deceased. Casino surveillance collected.

She heard her own pulse in the hush, a rhythmic nudge behind the traffic and far-off sirens. Her body was crashing, nerves depleted and mind jittery, half from the rush and half from the sugar.

She started a new paragraph, reached for the seatbelt to prop her phone against, when the screen lit up. UNKNOWN CALLER.

She let it ring twice, then answered. "Detective Kealoha."

The voice was glass. Not a voice, really, but a synth echo, masked and sanded smooth, like a commercial for a robot overlord.

"You're getting closer, Detective. But not close enough."

She didn't move, didn't even blink, but let her thumb hover above the record button, then pressed it. "Who is this?"

A pause, as if the caller was smiling. "You already know."

"What do you want?"

He laughed. "Nothing you can give. But you keep me entertained."

Leilani set her jaw. "Why kill the maintenance worker?"

"He was a liability. You understand. He broke his contract. In the end, everyone does."

She heard an elevator door slide open somewhere in the garage, the hiss of the hydraulic coming through the air and the phone. She pressed herself further into the seat, eyes on the rearview mirror, and pulled her pistol. "You're here," she said, making it a dare.

"Always," the voice agreed. "But I prefer to keep my distance. It's safer."

"What about the girl in the photo?" she asked. "You

threaten kids now?"

The voice was silent, then said, "The girl and her mother will be safe. Her father paid the price. But you, Detective."

"Me?"

"You have a son, don't you? Kai. Bright boy. Reminds me of myself at that age." The voice softened, becoming almost parental. "He had quite the day at school."

Leilani's mouth became dry. "You stay away from him."

"I have no interest in harming children. I want you to be sharp and not distracted by grief. But I suggest you watch him closely. He's clever, but also very visible."

The line crackled.

The voice dropped low. "You should have left this alone. But you can't help yourself. It's the Kealoha way. The spiral never ends."

She inhaled a shaky breath, keeping her hand steady. "You want me scared?"

"I want you motivated. There's more coming. Tomorrow, next week, who knows? It will be spectacular."

The call disconnected. Leilani sat for a full minute, breath shallow, hand cramping around the phone. Her heart pounded so hard she thought the next car over could hear it.

She dialed her mother's number first.

Naalei answered on the second ring, voice low and annoyed. "Lei, it's late. I'm in bed. What is it?"

"Where's Kai?"

A pause, the rustle of sheets. "Sleeping. Dreaming about pizza and volcanoes, probably. Why?"

"Don't let him out of your sight. Not for anything. Lock the doors. I mean it."

Her mother, wise to the undertow of Leilani's voice, shifted instantly. "Is this about the thing?"

"Yes, I'll explain later. Keep him close."

"Always," Naalei said. "Are you okay?"

Leilani smiled but didn't mean it. "Yeah, Mom. I'm good."

She hung up and dialed Torres. He answered like he was still on the job, which he probably was. "Torres."

"We've got a problem," she said. "Mastermind called. He knows everything about Kai, my mother, and you."

Torres didn't even exhale. "That's the point, isn't it? To make it personal."

"I'm not gonna let them get near my family."

"I know," he said. "Neither will I. I'll call the protection detail and alert them."

She pictured him back at the hotel, head bent over a laptop, fingers already typing up an alert. She found it comforting.

The silence lingered. "You ever get scared,

Torres?"

He laughed, a real sound. "On Mondays."

She grinned, not looking at her own reflection in the rearview. "I'll see you tomorrow."

"We'll catch this bastard, Lei."

She ended the call, set the phone down, and gripped the wheel until her knuckles ached. The air outside was heavy, humid, but she cracked the window and let it in. She closed her eyes, counted backward from ten, and opened them again, scanning the garage.

No one was there. It was her, the dark, and the faint electronic ring of a threat she wasn't sure she could stop.

She started the engine, hands steady now. Tomorrow, it was back to the chase. The spiral was closing, and she had no intention of letting go.

She was going to go home to get a few hours of sleep, but her car headed towards headquarters. She was sitting at her desk as the first rays of the sun cleared the darkness from the island. A voice behind her boomed.

"Kealoha, my office, now!"

The chief of Ds did not look happy as she entered his office and took the seat. Over the next twenty minutes, everyone sitting in the bullpen heard the tirade.

"Fifteen million!" "How the fuck!" "Who the fuck!" What the fuck happened!" "The mayor is up my ass!"

The chief's voice was loud enough to shake the glass in the windows. The lucky few in the bullpen bowed their heads and focused on their laptops.

Leilani listened to the yelling without flinching. When he stopped to catch his breath and let his blood pressure come back to normal, she explained the entire night from start to finish. When she finished and he didn't say anything, she stood and walked towards the door.

"Just a minute," he said, so calm it scared the shit out of her. "What about this?"

She turned and stepped to the desk as he turned his laptop towards her. There she was filling the screen. The body camera image wasn't too bad. Not centerfold quality, but good enough. Her wet hair hung limp around her face, her makeup had run in streaks down her cheeks, and her soaking wet white cocktail shirt clinging to her body, leaving nothing to the imagination. She studied the picture for a few seconds, looked up and smiled.

"I look pretty damn good," she said.

She turned and walked out of the office. Her next stop was the IT department to see if they could scrub the picture from the network, but she wondered how many people with department laptops had already uploaded a new screen saver.

# Chapter Thirteen

## Family Under Siege

The call came at 8:12 a.m. She was halfway to IT, still muttering about perverts in the bullpen, when her phone buzzed with the little-used FBI code. She thumbed it open, and before she could speak, Isaac's voice dropped in like a depth charge: "They missed their morning check-in. Your mom's house. I'm sending units now."

She didn't answer but pivoted and ran. Her sneakers flashed up the waxed corridor, out the side door, and she barely remembered to badge through the sally port before sprinting to her car.

The key jammed in the ignition. The engine caught on the second try, with a cough and a stutter. The familiar rattle of her battered Explorer. She peeled out, hitting the lights and siren when she was clear of the station's parking lot. The sound rattled her teeth.

She took the H-1 at eighty, weaving through late traffic like a missile. The city blurred into bands of concrete, bougainvillea and old paint. Her radio warbled with chatter. The stolen millions, the murder at the casino, a missing councilman, and, rising over it, a CODE YELLOW officer down at the listed address in Palolo Valley. Naalei's address.

She cursed and hit the pedal. The world narrowed to a tunnel, the lines on the freeway pulling her forward and the steering wheel pressed white into her hands. She didn't dare let herself think about the last time she'd seen her mother, or the way she'd left things with Kai the night before. This was the job. This was what it looked like at the sharp end.

Palolo Valley climbed steeply with houses stacked against the ridge in a messy riot of architecture and desperation. Naalei's house was halfway up, tucked behind a stand of plumeria and a rusted out minivan held together with spit and bailing wire. She could see the flashing blue lights from four blocks away.

She skidded to a halt behind the first patrol cruiser, nearly clipping the mailbox. The air was already thick with the smell of burned coffee and the wet green that always followed rain in the valley. The yard was chaos. Two men on the grass, shirts dark with blood at the head and shoulder, neither moving. Both FBI, both meant to be the protection detail.

The front door of the house gaped wide, hanging on one hinge. Splinters haloed around the jamb.

She was halfway up the lawn when the HPD backup crunched to a stop behind her. Two uniforms bailed out, guns up, moving in a stacked line. Leilani flashed her badge and kept moving. "House has two more," she barked, voice lower than she meant. "Older woman, ten-year-old boy."

The first officer, a kid who'd probably idolized her from a distance, nodded and swept right. She headed straight in, SIG out, eyes up.

The living room seemed like a war zone. The couch overturned, pillows gutted. The TV lay smashed, glass spiked across the floor, a looping GIF of static playing on its ruined screen. Every shelf had been cleared. The family photos, the graduation plaque from Kamehameha, and the koa wood bowl Naalei always kept filled with origami cranes, scattered and stomped.

She moved fast, piecing together the narrative. Forced entry, quick. The agents outside probably never made it past the porch. The home invaders knew their job and didn't linger. From the pattern of overturned chairs and the ragged path down the hallway, Leilani saw it all in sequence. Her mother, outnumbered but defiant, put up a fight.

She called out, "HPD! Kai, Nana! Sound off!"

No answer.

She moved to the kitchen, which had been emptied onto the floor. The ceramic plates, half a box of li hing mui, the battered coffee percolator, and a rice cooker leaking starchy water across the linoleum. There were streaks in the mess, trails of something that could have been blood, or the bright red of chili sauce. She blinked, memory slicing in. Her mother always made the rice first thing in the morning. The percolator was a constant fixture in her life.

Her radio squawked, the exterior patrol reporting the scene secure outside. The HPD kid followed at her six, gun up, voice tight. "You clear the rooms?"

"Working it," said Leilani. She strode past the smashed family altar and the hula implements lining the wall. Every step was a study in restraint, her hands steady even as her nerves wanted to jump and bite.

She inspected the master bedroom. The bed was unmade, and the dresser drawers dumped out. It was a hasty, violent search. The bathroom was empty, with water still running in the sink. The back bedroom, where Kai always slept when he stayed over, was next. The door was half closed. She kicked it open and swept with the SIG.

Inside, the scene stuttered. The bed was empty, but the window was open, and a flutter of Star Wars sheets trailed onto the sill. No sign of a struggle, no blood. But something about the space felt wrong. Too clean, too intentional.

She stepped inside, holstered the SIG, and scanned the walls. Posters, model cars, the shelf where Kai kept his "detective kit", a magnifying glass, two sets of plastic cuffs, and a notebook filled with coded lists. She moved to the closet, found it empty except for two sets of school uniforms and an abandoned backpack. She crouched, scanned the floor and stopped.

There, along the baseboard, a barely visible seam. She felt it with her thumb, the outline of the panel. When she was a kid, she'd helped her mother install it, the secret crawlspace where they hid hurricane supplies and, in the old days, a stash of emergency cash and passports.

She pressed the latch, and the panel popped out a quarter inch. Inside, huddled in a ball, was Kai. He looked up at her, eyes red and wide, but he didn't make a sound. He clutched his own phone to his chest; the screen stuck on a photo of Leilani, from last year's Christmas.

She fell to her knees, pulled him into her arms, and held him, squeezing so hard his ribs creaked. He didn't fight, didn't cry, but pressed his face into her shoulder and shook.

She rocked him until the HPD kid peeked in. She made herself let go. She got Kai's face in both hands and forced herself to smile. "Hey, bud. Did you see where Nana went?"

His mouth opened, but no sound came. His voice became tiny. "They took her. Two men. Black van."

She hugged him again. "You did right, Kai. Exactly like I taught you."

His face was wet with tears he hadn't noticed, and he whispered, "I hid good. They didn't see me."

"Best I ever saw," she said. It was almost a laugh.

She carried him out of the crawlspace, up the hall and into the living room. The patrol officers had set up a perimeter outside, tape strung between the old mango tree and the mailbox. The two FBI agents on the lawn were stirring now, groggy and cursing. Leilani caught one agent's look and nodded her head. Not your fault.

She found a patch of grass under the eaves, removed from the chaos, and sat Kai down. She kneeled to his level, looked him over for bruises, smoothing his hair back the way her mother used to do for her. He shivered.

"Breathe, Kai. In, and out." She modeled the motion, waiting until he matched her.

He calmed a little. "They wanted Nana. Not me. She… she hit them, Mom. Like, hard." His voice was a raw edge, pride, and fear mixing.

"She always was a fighter," said Leilani.

He nodded. "They said they had to take her. Because of the…spiral. Nana told them they were cursed if they messed with the old stuff. They laughed at her. But they looked scared, too."

Leilani felt her stomach knot. "Did you see their faces?"

Kai nodded. "One had a tattoo here." He pointed to his neck, under the ear. "Big, blue-black, like a shark. The other one limped, and he kept touching his mouth. Like it was bleeding."

She memorized every word. "Anything else?"

"They called her kumu. And they said, the boss wants the real one, not a copy. I think they meant Nana."

A chill ran up Leilani's neck. She pulled out her phone, took a quick statement, and called Isaac who was three minutes out. "Ka Moana," she said to Isaac when he answered. "Blue shark tattoo, old school style. It's the enforcer crew for Makani'olu."

Isaac's voice was all steel. "We're on the way. Sit tight."

She didn't move. She kept Kai tucked against her side, watching the street, waiting for the next move. The cop in her wanted to rage and chase, but the mother in her wanted this, her son, alive, his head on her lap, the world burning at the edges for the moment.

More sirens drew closer, and Leilani closed her eyes. She let the sound wash over them, the song of a city that never stayed safe for long.

Leilani wanted to run. She was determined to tear across the city, to rip the world apart until she found her mother. But she had Kai, and right now he was a shaky mess of adrenaline and collapsed bravado. She walked him up the path, past the two groaning FBI agents, one clutching a makeshift ice pack to his temple, the other spitting blood and pride onto the grass, and steered her son through the front door like it was another bad day.

The inside was worse than she'd seen when she first entered. The light through the east window showed the whole range of violence: kitchen chairs shattered, refrigerator magnets shot-gunned across the floor, the family whiteboard, today's date, three chores, a doodle of a surfing gecko, smeared to blankness by a swipe of someone's arm. There was no place to sit that wasn't covered in splinters or glass, so she cleared a space on the kitchen table, swept up the debris with her bare hand, and sat Kai down.

She found his favorite cup in the mess, somehow unbroken, and filled it with water. He drank it in three nervous gulps. "Are you going to yell at me?" he said.

"No, Kai." Her voice was raw from the siren. "You did everything right. You did better than right."

He glanced at her sideways. "Nana told me to hide and not come out, no matter what."

Leilani crouched to his level. She noted the shine in his eyes, a tremor in his jaw that he fought to lock down. She kept her words soft, letting them float above the panic line. "We must go through what happened again. Like in a police interview. I need you to help me, buddy. Like you do on my cases. Tell me everything, all the little things, okay?" She opened the recording app on her phone and set it next to him.

Kai nodded, but when he spoke, it came out mechanical, like he was reading a report. "There were two. One was huge. He wore all black, no logo. He had a tattoo here." He tapped his own neck, the way he'd shown her outside. "It went up behind his ear and down under his collar. Not new, kind of faded."

"What kind of tattoo?" she asked, doing her best to stay neutral.

"Shark," said Kai, and now he was the detective. "Blue. Like navy blue. Not black. But with triangle teeth. The top was cut by a scar, a thin white one, like someone tried to erase it."

Leilani's mind noted it the way it always did. She let him keep going.

"The other one was shorter and stocky. Nana's height, but way wider. He limped on his left leg. When he walked, he put his hand on his hip, like it hurt. He had a scar here." Kai traced a finger down his left cheek. "His eye was a little droopy, and he had a bloody lip. He didn't talk much."

She ran the scene in her head, as vivid as a security video.

"What did they do when they came in?" she asked.

Kai squeezed the cup until his fingers blanched. "They didn't knock. They smashed the glass on the door with a hammer. Nana ran at them with the uh…with her hula stick, the heavy one, and hit the big guy in the knee." He made a motion, quick and fierce. "He dropped hard, but the short one tackled Nana from behind. They put tape on her mouth and zip-tied her wrists, before they dragged her into the living room. They kept saying they needed her alive."

Leilani felt something crack under her sternum.

"Did they say anything about why?" she asked.

Kai nodded, and his voice was almost proud. "They said the boss wanted her because she was the one who knew the real story. The short one called her kumu, but also witch and crazy old bat." He looked away. "They said if she didn't cooperate, they'd come back for me next."

She put a hand over his, absorbing the tremor. "Do you remember anything else, any numbers or names?"

Kai's brow furrowed. He scrunched his eyes, accessing the memory like it were a hard drive. "They talked about a place, the docks, and the word warehouse. The big guy was mad, said it was too public, but the short one said it didn't matter, the boss would make everyone disappear if he wanted."

He took a breath, steadier now. "They left in a black van, no windows, looked like an old Honda? The license started with RLG. I saw it through the side window before they turned the corner. The van was noisy, like it needed a new muffler."

Leilani smiled at him. "Anything else?"

He thought for a few beats. "Nana… she kept yelling, even with tape on her mouth. She tried to stomp their feet. She called them stupid men and told them they'd regret it if they hurt her family." His voice fell to a whisper. "She looked right at me, even though I was hiding. Like she wanted me to know it was going to be okay."

Leilani pulled him into her arms, her badge digging into her collarbone. But she didn't let go.

"Good job, Detective," she whispered. "You kept your head. You did everything right."

He breathed against her shoulder, and she felt the deep, animal sob that came from somewhere below language. She let him go until he was empty.

Her phone buzzed, a three-syllable tone she'd set for Isaac. She fished it out, eyes still on her son.

Two blocks over. Team en route.

She stood, hoisted Kai onto the counter where he used to steal cookies, and let him kick his feet while she found her father's old ankle holster and his backup pistol and checked the magazine. She eyed the hallway, every corner, every window, mapping out what she'd need to do next.

"Am I safe?" asked Kai.

"You're with me, aren't you?" she said, flashing him a smirk.

He managed a ghost of a smile, while he wiped his nose on his sleeve. "They will not get away, right?"

She ruffled his hair, like her mother used to do. "Not if I have anything to say about it."

A siren whooped outside. She heard car doors, a synchronized slam, then boots on the gravel. The house filled with movement, uniformed voices, the bristle, and snap of procedure.

She holstered the weapon, strapped it to her ankle under her pant leg and lifted Kai off the counter, lighter now that the fear had gone out of him. Together, they walked to the front door, the sun hot and blinding on the threshold.

Isaac met them on the step, his suit jacket already off, eyes tracking every inch of the scene. He crouched to Kai's level and managed a crooked smile. "Heard you were the hero of the day."

Kai hid his face in his mom's side.

Isaac rose, voice quiet for her alone. "You got anything for me?"

She handed over her phone, the recording app open to the facts as Kai gave them. "RLG. Docks. Ka Moana crew."

Isaac's face flattened. "This is going to get loud, fast."

"Good," said Leilani. "Loud means we flush them out."

The FBI team fanned through the house, snapping photos, dusting for prints, cataloging the mess. A paramedic checked Kai's pulse, and gave him a Popsicle, which he held like an artifact. Leilani watched as the world reassembled itself around her, the procedural dance of uniforms and authority. Another paramedic was checking over the two FBI agents, and another agent stood next to them, holding a notepad and a recorder.

The chaos rolled over them, her hand never leaving Kai's shoulder. Every instinct in her screamed to be moving, but she knew better than to run half-cocked.

She was going to get her mother back, or die trying. She pulled her phone and called Uncle Edward. She needed some place safe for Kai to stay. After she told him what happened, he told her he was on his way and not to worry. He was bringing help.

The day outside was too bright. But at least it was theirs.

The FBI ran hot and cold. The evidence crew, in black windbreakers and latex gloves, moved through the wreckage of Naalei's house like a colony of ants. Every object was bagged, tagged, photographed, and zipped into evidence lockers. Isaac stalked the perimeter, barking orders into a mic. A field general on caffeine and righteous anger. Leilani got Kai's hands wiped free of smudges and crumbs, as the front yard looked like a TV set with three SUVs, four marked cruisers, one ambulance, and a tactical van idling with its back doors open.

Isaac appeared on the porch with a clipboard and a face carved from stone, but when he caught sight of Kai, something thawed. He crouched low, balancing on the balls of his feet, and gave the kid a look that said, I see you, and I know what it's like.

She handed him her phone, with the recording app open, and he listened to the interview. "Ka Moana crew. Black van, RLG on the plate. The kidnapping was targeted at my Nana, not random."

Isaac took a minute, making notes on his pad as he

listened. "Nice work, Detective," he said, and she almost believed him.

Inside, the kitchen had been reassembled into a makeshift command post. A folding table was dragged in, maps spread out, mug shots printed in color, annotated with red pen. Someone had cleared the fridge magnets from the whiteboard and repurposed it for a lineup of gang associates and their last knowns. The entire scene was alive with purpose.

Leilani led Kai inside, set him at the table, and let him stare at the photos. He zeroed in on one, tapping it twice. "That's him," he said, pointing at a man with a mouth like a shark and a neck tattoo to match.

Isaac leaned in and checked the label. "Jesse Waimano. Enforcer, former local MMA, in and out of Halawa since he was a kid." He flicked through to the next one. "What about the other guy?"

Kai scanned. "Him. Older, but with a scar on his face."

Isaac logged it. He turned to Leilani. "You see what I see?"

She nodded. "Muscle. But the brains are somewhere else. This was a pickup."

"Agreed. We traced the van's plate to a chop shop out past Sand Island. No cameras, no traffic. It'll be a dead end."

She traced her finger across the map, following the most logical route from her mother's house to the docks. "They'll want to sit her somewhere quiet. Not a house, too much risk. Not the casino. Too much heat.

They'll go to ground and wait for orders."

Kai spoke up, his voice weirdly steady. "They said something about the docks. Take her to the yellow one. The boss is waiting."

Isaac's head snapped up. "You remember which dock?"

Kai thought. "It's near the old shrimp trucks. Nana always gets garlic shrimp for me when we go. There's a warehouse behind it with a fence."

Isaac grinned, and he looked less like an agent and more like someone you'd trust in a dark alley. "Nice job, man."

He turned to Leilani, voice low. "We've got a shot at this. But it'll be tight. If the boss thinks we're closing in, he'll cut and run."

She felt a shiver, not of fear but anticipation. "Okay, we move now."

He was already on the radio, calling the tactical team into position. The room filled with electric energy, all nerves and momentum.

Kai tugged at her sleeve. "Are you coming back?" he asked, softer now, like a kid who'd realized how delicate life was.

She bent down, pressed her forehead to his. "Count on it, bud."

Isaac touched her arm as she straightened. "He'll be safe here. I've got the best agents on the island watching him. No more slip-ups."

She kneeled next to Kai. "Uncle Edward will be

here soon. When the FBI lets you, grab your backpack and your school clothes and some of your toys. You're gonna stay with your uncle for a little while."

Isaac started to say something, but she cut him off. "Edward will keep him safe," she said with a little more bite than she expected.

Both Isaac and Kai nodded.

The tactical team assembled in the living room, helmets, vests, ARs slung low. Isaac ran the briefing before he pulled Leilani aside near the hallway.

"This isn't about the job anymore," he said, voice soft for her alone. "You know that, right?"

She nodded, the weight of everything in her eyes.

He took her hand, his fingers warm and dry. "We're going to get your mom back. I swear it."

She felt like laughing or crying, but all she could do was grip his hand and believe.

He brushed a strand of hair from her face, and the world shrank to the two of them, conspirators on the verge of something big and terrible and right.

She leaned in, and when she spoke, it was a whisper. "Let's go get these bastards."

His mouth flickered into a grin. "Attagirl."

They grabbed their gear, and together they walked out into the sunlight, the future already burning on the far side of the horizon.

# Chapter Fourteen

## The Mastermind's Lair

By 9 a.m., the grass around the old Puunene Sugar Mill was wet enough to soak a tactical boot through three layers of sock. The last time Leilani had been here, she was twelve and the field trips were for history, not war. Now the place looked like a set piece from an abandoned planet, concrete walls peeled open by decades of rain, stacks of rusted conveyors leaning in the shadows like broken bones. The mill was a ghost, but this morning it buzzed with real-life ghosts in tactical vests, the early shift of HPD's SWAT working side by side with the feds, and all of them, Leilani included, running on nothing but caffeine and an electric sense of dread.

Isaac ran the briefing with his back towards the sunrise, so the first edge of gold light rimmed his hair and gave him a halo that would've made for a good funeral photo if things went sideways. He'd drawn up a basic plan on the hood of the FBI command van, the dry erase markers rolling in a cluster next to three radios and an untouched box of malasadas. "We move on three fronts," he said, voice all gravel and clipped consonants. "Blue team circles from the left, breaches at the loading dock. Red team cuts up the service stairs, main entry is the admin office here. White team on the roll-up door." He tapped the hood, traced the arc of attack with his thumb. "First priority, the hostage. Second, evidence of the operation. We want bodies in cuffs, not bags."

The HPD sergeant, stocky, fifty, with a mustache that could have won prizes in the seventies, grunted approval and started handing out shotguns and radios from a battered Tacoma. "Channel four is ours. No chatter unless it's for blood." He offered the first vest to Leilani, who took it and double-checked the fit, more out of habit than worry. The sergeant winked. "Nice to see you back, Detective. Your kid's a damn hero."

Leilani smiled, quick and brittle. "He's grounded until he's thirty."

Isaac stepped in with her radio, the earpiece wrapped in tape. "Last minute from Akira, the security cams in the main mill are live but looped. She's in the feed. They'll see what we want them to see."

"You were uncertain when I talked to her earlier. You trust her now?" Leilani asked, adjusting the clip on her SIG.

"I trust she enjoys messing with bad guys more than she likes money," Isaac said. He leaned in, voice lower. "You ready?"

She thought of Kai, asleep two towns over, and Naalei somewhere inside this monster of a building. "Yeah," she said. "Let's do it."

The approach was pure textbook. Six officers fanned out along the western edge, steps muffled by the spongy grass. They heard the distant clang of metal and the occasional curse when someone hit a hidden patch of mud. The mill loomed overhead, a hundred and forty years of sugar dreams gone to weed and owl shit. Even now, in the soft light, you could see the place wasn't dead, not really. The windows were blown, but some had fresh tape over the edges, and the main admin door had new hinges, bright and oiled. There were two trucks in the lot, both with dust over the plates, but neither looking abandoned.

Leilani was on blue team, following Isaac up the old railroad track that once ferried cane from the fields to the refinery. The rail was a black snake in the dew, and they kept to its edge, hunched low. Isaac held his weapon tight to his chest, eyes on the target, but every ten steps he checked over his shoulder, a tic Leilani guessed he'd picked up after years of someone wanting him dead.

Halfway to the loading dock, they hit the first sign of new life. Fresh tire tracks, big ones, arched in a wide sweep past a mound of shattered cinderblock. Something heavy and recently moved. Isaac crouched, ran his finger along the mud. "Not older than a day," he said. "You ever see dirt this clean out here?"

Leilani shook her head. "Last I checked, the vehicles were government. That's not them."

They pressed on, every footstep measured. Leilani felt the adrenaline pool in her elbows and knees. She checked her earpiece, the volume low, and caught the crackle of red team cutting across the north end.

At the dock, the air was cold and filled with the tang of rust and something like burned plastic. Leilani peeked around the corner and scanned the entry. No movement, but inside the open bay, she heard the dull, lulling hum of a generator. Somewhere, lights were running.

Isaac signaled to hold, pointing up at the security camera perched above the door. It was new, slick black, nothing like the museum pieces dotted elsewhere on the property. She clicked her comm twice, confirmation. In the hush, she caught a flicker of movement, but enough to snap every nerve awake.

On the count of three, they moved. Isaac moved first, crossing the dock in a low sprint, shouldering to the left to cover the main entry. Leilani tracked right, SIG up, finger high on the trigger guard. They reached the door, flanked it, listened. The FBI tactical team moved with them.

Inside they heard the low whine of electronics, a chair scraping, a muffled voice in a language she almost recognized but couldn't place. It was a quick tap. Morse code, but not standard.

She nodded at Isaac, who counted down with his left hand.

The breach started at 9:57, right on the minute.

The tactical teams fanned out around the sugar mill, radio silence except for the whispered code: "Go." Three entry points: loading dock, office suite and a set of rusted garage doors on the south end. Every approach was a snapshot of motion. The crunch of boots on gravel, the low shuffle of Kevlar against polyester, the sharp, icy breath that always came before the storm.

Leilani and Isaac were at the loading dock again, this time with two of HPD's best, both built like brick walls and hungry for the rush. The battering ram hit the steel door with a whale's bellow, the echo rolling through the mill. The second strike caved it in, hinges screaming. The first wall of air inside was pure rot, yeast, and old chemicals, mixed with the sour edge of pizza and sweat. Light didn't so much fill the room as slice it into pieces, beams of white-hot LEDs scattering shadows like cockroaches.

The main floor was chaos. Tables overturned, rows of barrels stacked high as barricades, and a fog of dust kicked up by the sudden violence. Behind the barrels, several shots echoed; a pistol, automatic weapon fire and another pistol. The SWAT guys responded with a flanking rush, one laying down fire while the other leapfrogged forward in three long, low strides.

Leilani kept tight to the wall, her breath tight. Next to her, Isaac counted off the seconds on his hand, waiting for a break in the fire. When the first shooter paused to reload, he motioned her forward. They hustled past the threshold, weapons up. The mill's belly opened before them, a canyon of steel girders and puddles of water so black they reflected the world in negative.

Across the main floor, another squad breached the office space, the door splintering in a single blow. Yells went up, "Clear!" Followed by. "Hostile, north catwalk!" The echoes overlapped, making it impossible to tell where the threats were. The enemy had the high ground, shooting down through a jungle of old machinery. Someone lobbed a smoke grenade, and the room filled with ghost shapes, real, or imagined, or both.

In the first confusion, a gang member in a black hoodie tried to make a run for the loading ramp. Leilani saw him coming, counted the distance, and took a bead on his kneecap. The shot landed, and he folded with a howl, tumbling through a nest of pipes and landing hard.

Isaac kept moving, low and fast. He covered Leilani as she advanced, the two of them leapfrogging by inches. She counted the beats, marking the rhythm of the chaos, letting it become a kind of music.

Halfway to the back wall, a heavy sliding metal door caught her eye. It was newer than everything else, with no rust, no graffiti, not even a dent. That didn't make sense, not here. She pointed it out to Isaac with a sharp nod. He broke off, signaled the two HPD officers to join them.

The firefight raged on. Shouts and shots, but they peeled away, the sounds muffling as they closed in on the door. There was no obvious handle, only a thick keypad glowing a faint blue.

Isaac grinned, the adrenaline making him boyish for a flash. "I got this," he whispered. He yanked a pocket device from his vest, a tool the feds called the Skeleton Key, but which Akira had upgraded with a line of code that worked on ninety percent of commercial locks. He held it against the pad, pressed the button, and waited.

Ten seconds. A green light, and the door hissed open.

It was colder inside, a different climate. The corridor was lined with rows of bare bulb lamps, buzzing and flickering. The first stretch was empty, but farther down, another door, this one steel and set with a deadbolt. Leilani could hear voices beyond, muffled, urgent.

They kicked, and the door gave with a screech. Inside, the room was empty but for a bank of monitors, every one showing a different feed: the mill's perimeter, the loading dock and a drone shot of the parking lot. Isaac swept left, checked the adjacent space, and found nothing but old supply racks and a row of battered steel desks. "Clear," he hissed.

They moved through, boots crunching on glass and old rat droppings. The hum of the generator got louder, and Leilani realized it was powering all the cams and a server array tucked in a rack to the side. She shot a photo with her phone, then kept moving.

Down the hall, footsteps. Light, deliberate. Leilani angled off, took the right, and covered the main artery. The footsteps stopped. Another sound, higher. A squeal, but not human; metal on metal. Leilani pressed against the wall, heart knocking. A shape appeared in the hall. Not heavy, not the kind to fight.

This was a woman, thin, in a gray track jacket, arms full of boxes. She saw them, dropped the load, and ran. Isaac gave chase. Leilani moved after, quick and low. They hit the corridor, took a hard left, and found the woman scrambling for a back door. She reached it, fumbled the lock, and had pushed it open when Isaac wrapped her up from behind, pinning her arms in a textbook takedown.

"Don't fight," he growled, "breathe."

The woman collapsed to her knees, shoulders shaking. She wore latex gloves and running shoes, the kind you could get online. Leilani scanned her for weapons, found none, then patted down her jacket. Her pockets were stuffed with thumb drives.

"Feds," Leilani said, holding up her badge. "If you lie to me, I'm going to let him cuff you to the nearest broken window and you can wait for the rats."

The woman looked up, and her eyes were blank, flat, but familiar. Leilani had seen that look on more than one IT bust. The good hackers never lost control.

"What's your name?" Isaac asked.

"Marina," the woman said, a whiff of accent in the word. "They told me to run if anything happened. I am the monitor. I don't do violence."

"Who's inside?" Leilani asked.

"I don't know. I never go upstairs. I watch the feeds."

Leilani scanned the stairwell, the old iron railings pitted with rust.

"Upstairs?" Marina nodded. "Top floor, always top floor. He says it's safer. The Mastermind. The rest are muscle. You'll find them there, or they could be in the lab."

Isaac zip-tied Marina's wrists and eased her onto a crate. He pointed to one tactical agent. "You watch her." He looked at Leilani. "I'll sweep up."

"No," Leilani said, voice hard. "We go together."

He nodded, silent, and blue team moved up the stairs, every sense burning. They counted each tread, listening for the creak, for a shadow, for the telltale click of a hammer being drawn back.

They closed the distance, arriving at another door. Isaac listened.

"...She's leverage. If we don't get the signal, it's over."

"Doesn't matter. Mastermind said burn everything on exit."

Leilani's heart grew cold.

She counted down with her fingers—three, two, one—and they burst in.

The room was spare, but not empty. There were three men, two with guns, cheap pistols, but with the alert look of people who knew how to use them; and in the center, a figure hunched over a laptop, fingers dancing on the keys.

The room beyond was a storage vault, windowless, lined with gray shelving, but in the center was a folding chair and taped to it at the wrists and ankles was her mother.

Naalei looked up, eyes bright and fierce, hair wild around her face. She saw Leilani, and the tension snapped, a filament broken. The two men guarding her, both built for intimidation, spun at the breach. One reaching for a gun, the other held a knife to Naalei's throat.

Isaac didn't hesitate. He fired twice, both shots clean, one to the arm, the other to the man's thigh.

The other guy hesitated. "You come any closer," he said. "She dies."

Leilani's mind ran through every simulation. The

angle, the distance, the echo of Kai's face from yesterday.

"You don't want to do this," she said.

The guy at the computer never moved. "We're out of time," he said to the computer screen. He turned, and Leilani saw him not as a monster, but as a man. But It was the masked face on the screen that grabbed her with cold eyes she found somehow familiar. The computer guy pressed a key on his laptop, and the screen flashed. The computer guy bolted for a back door.

Downstairs, alarms exploded to life. A klaxon, the kind used in tsunamis, wailed out of every broken window.

Isaac barked, "Go!" and Leilani shot the man holding Naalei, a controlled double tap that caught him in the shoulder. He dropped the knife and stumbled back.

The computer guy was already at the fire escape, climbing down, moving with the urgency of someone who's lived in flight. Isaac tried a shot, missed, then hustled to the window, checking for more shooters.

Leilani crossed the space in a single bound, untaped her mother's mouth, and cut her hands free. Naalei's first word was "Kai?"

"Are you hurt?" she asked, barely hearing her own voice over the ringing in her ears.

Naalei managed a smile, a bloody one, but it was real. "Yeah, my pride," she whispered. "He never shuts up, you know."

Leilani cut her mother's wrists free, hands shaking. "Let's get you out."

Leilani hauled Naalei up, supporting her as they dashed down the stairs. Behind her, the alarms kept wailing, but above them, she heard the pop of smoke canisters and the shrill, angry shouts of red team clearing the lab.

Behind them, the two officers cuffed the wounded men. Isaac searched the shelves, grabbing anything that looked like a drive or folder. He handed a thick file to Leilani. "Evidence. Take it."

They hustled back through the corridor, up the metal steps, and into the sharp noise of the mill's main floor. The fight was almost over. Red team had three suspects face-down on the ground, hands zip-tied and heads pressed to the concrete. One SWAT guy was bleeding from a nick on his ear, but otherwise, it was a clean sweep.

They led Naalei into the daylight, the world outside brilliant with sunlight. No one said anything. Naalei pulled Leilani close, nails digging into her daughter's arm.

Outside, the scene was full of cops. Sirens. Shouting. HPD SWAT officers poured through every gap in the old mill, covering the perimeter, arresting anyone who moved.

They cleared the main yard and saw people running in every direction. Isaac's team covered the rear, and they reached the FBI's tactical assault vehicle, where the FBI was processing the hacker, Marina, and two other men in zip ties. More people were being tackled in the fields around the building by HPD SWAT.

Naalei collapsed onto the step of the vehicle, breath hitching. "You came," she said to Leilani, voice a whisper. Leilani nodded, unable to speak.

Isaac pulled Leilani aside, eyes locked on the chaos. "He got away. But we got most of them. And your mother's safe."

"The guy at the computer was a hacker, not Mastermind. Mastermind was on the laptop screen. He could have been talking from anywhere. Let's get your digital forensic team down here and tear the servers apart." Isaac nodded and stepped away.

Leilani watched as the morning light hit the wall of the mill, making the place look less haunted, more human. She hugged her mother hard. The trembling wasn't from fear. It was over.

At least for now.

She sat on the step next to her mother while a paramedic checked her blood pressure and butterfly taped a gash on her forehead. She leaned into Leilani.

"He knows everything about us, Leilani. Everything." Her voice was a dry scrape, terror and warning all in one.

Leilani nodded at Isaac, who had walked back and was flipping through the files they retrieved.

This wasn't over, not even close. But she felt like she was finally moving ahead of the spiral instead of getting dragged behind it.

She put her arm around her mother, and together,

they watched the mill empty. Every corridor and shadow was now claimed for the good guys, at least for a morning.

They brought Naalei to the ambulance; the paramedics worked her wrists with cool hands. Leilani watched her mother sit on the ambulance bumper, every muscle slack but for her jaw, which refused to let the world see an inch of weakness. She was hoping to stay, to take an inventory of every scrape and bruise, but Isaac touched her shoulder and nodded for her to follow.

"You need to see this," he said.

She followed, stepping over the splayed limbs of the last two suspects who had chosen surrender over suicide. At the mill's old boiler room, past the banks of gutted furnaces, there was a door Leilani didn't remember from the blueprints. It was set into the brick, seamless, the sort of thing you'd spot if you were looking for a hide. Isaac produced the skeleton key again, worked the lock, and they slipped inside.

The difference was immediate and violent. Gone were the rot and the dust and the stink of history. The floor here was tiled and scrubbed clean. The air ran crisp, filtered by something hidden in the walls. On the back side of the room, half a dozen monitors flickered with live feeds, beach cams, casino interiors, traffic at the airport, and a persistent, scrolling display of every tourist who'd checked in at a Waikiki hotel in the past twelve hours.

In the center, a single office chair, still spinning from a too fast exit. Next to it, two laptops, one closed, the other humming a silent boot-up routine. Isaac leaned over, scanning the logins.

"Whoever ran this," he muttered, "didn't do security for the operation. This is a command post for the entire island."

Leilani ignored the computers, drawn instead to the wall behind. Maps, but not the kind you found at the gas station. These were blown up aerials, layered with transparencies, red, and black lines marking property boundaries, shell companies and new construction permits. Every resort on Oahu was flagged, along with the names of their holding corporations. Some had yellow highlights; others were green. At the bottom of the map, there was a string of dates, and a handwritten note. All in play by August.

Leilani let her eyes move from the maps to the filing cabinet tucked beneath the table. She opened the top drawer, expecting more paperwork, but what she found was a folder marked KEALOHA. She opened it, her hands steady. Inside, surveillance shots of her, her mother, Kai at his school, even Edward in the old Chinatown market. There were phone records, emails and printouts of police reports she'd filed over the past year. Every move documented, cataloged, anticipated.

She handed it to Isaac, who whistled low. "They're not running a crime ring. They're running a shadow government."

"Or trying to," she said. "Look at this." She flicked to the last page, a table of shell companies, cross-referenced with bank transfers from the last month. It was all there, the robberies, the ransom, the laundering.

But the final step was always the same. Real estate purchased cheap after the public panic, then bundled into anonymous trusts.

"This is a land grab," she said, voice flat. "They use the hits to destabilize the resort. Market tanks, they buy it for pennies, clean the money and sell it to the mainland, tripling the profit."

Isaac grinned. "It's beautiful, in a psychotic way. And like we talked about."

She closed the folder, then bent to check the rest of the drawers. More dossiers, more blackmail, all the tools of empire built in the shadow of a dead industry.

When they finished, they swept the room for anything the techs would need. Isaac popped the hard drives out, bagged them for evidence. "You know what the best part is?" he said, hefting the bag. "This is half of it. The rest is still out there. Whoever ran this knew we were coming."

Leilani pictured the Mastermind, with those cold eyes peering over the mask, watching them from some bunker with a better view. The thought made her itch.

Back outside, the sun was climbing. Teams swept the perimeter, rounding up the last of the muscle. SWAT gave the all-clear, and the scene quieted. The noise was now the crunch of tires as the ambulance pulled away, Naalei safe inside with two HPD SWAT officers.

Leilani stood with Isaac, looking at the broken windows, the blue-white flash of police tape against the dark skeleton of the mill.

She opened the KEALOHA file again. On the last page, someone had written in a deliberate, angular hand, IT'S NEVER ABOUT THE MONEY.

Leilani tore the page out, folded it, and slipped it into her back pocket. She thought of Kai, of his nervous grin and stubborn faith that everything could be fixed if you were clever enough. She thought of her mother, who had spent a lifetime teaching her how to be strong and soft at the same time. She thought of Isaac typing up his report and hunting for a connection.

She felt the weight of the morning settle into her bones, cold knowledge that the spiral would never really end. But as she watched the good guys reclaim every corner of the mill, she knew she was right where she belonged. They would get the bastard next time. They'd have to. She started the engine, let the air blow hot, and believed in the possibility of winning, even for a sunrise.

She called her son and told him it was over, at least for today.

# Chapter Fifteen

## Betrayal in the Ranks

Leilani spent the night at headquarters, burning through old coffee and the new evidence. By dawn, the homicide floor looked less like an office and more like a pop-up crime lab, the conference table buried in stacks of folders, thumb drives, hard disks and Isaac's favorite prop, a red-and-white string board that mapped every double cross on the island.

She sat on the corner of the table, shoulder to shoulder with Isaac, her hands wrist-deep in a pile of legal pads. Every page was a tile in the floor of the puzzle. Resort contracts, wire transfers, phone logs, blackmail photos, evidence of the old and new criminal order colliding like tectonic plates.

The whole thing would have been satisfying if she didn't know that some of the people they were about to report to were on the take. In the hallway, a crew of janitors worked their way down the row of offices, buffing the floor with the slow rhythm of a pulse monitor. She drank it all in, trying to focus on the next step and not the fatigue nipping at her eyelids.

At 07:50, the summons came. The conference room. Top brass, full dress, all smiles for the press and razor blades for the people under their boots. Leilani wore her cleanest suit jacket and a tie she found in the lost and found box, figuring it would make her look less like the department's loose cannon and more like someone who belonged at the grown-ups' table.

Isaac led the way, his stride crisp, the morning sun catching in the shine of his new Oxfords. When they reached the conference room, it was already half full, two supervising lieutenants, one with a Band-Aid on his temple, another with a mustache so thick it belonged to a villain in a silent film. Three sergeants, each with a departmental laptop open. And at the head of the table, the Chief of Police, Chief Janet Higa, five feet three inches of contained volcanic rage, white shirt pressed and collar pins so bright they could blind a pigeon. Alongside her sat The Chief of Detectives on one side and on the other, Assistant Police Chief Mori.

Leilani noticed the chill as soon as she entered. The Chief's eyes never quite landed on her; instead, they slid over her, like she was another piece of disposable office furniture.

Isaac cleared his throat. "Thank you for making the time, Chief. I think we have something that needs your immediate attention."

Higa steepled her hands. "I'm sure you do, Agent Torres. Is this related to the situation at the old sugar mill?"

"Yes, ma'am," Isaac said. "And more. We believe the event last night was not an isolated incident, but the keystone in an organized conspiracy to destabilize Oahu's real estate market, and possibly the state government itself."

A soft scoff came from one lieutenant, but Higa didn't flinch.

Isaac handed out copies of his summary. Timeline of Events and Key Evidence. The pages landed with a steady rhythm, and each time, Leilani noticed the recipients scanning ahead, looking for their own names.

Isaac started the PowerPoint from his laptop, the first slide a blow-up of the string board — names, properties, arrows, and in the center, the Makani'olu logo with an X through it.

Higa waved a hand. "Skip the history, Agent. Go to the meat."

"Right," Isaac said. "This isn't a string of burglaries. Every heist in the past two months has resulted in a fire sale on affected property. The shell companies buying them up all lead to Makani'olu Development. But the money doesn't stop there." He clicked to the next slide, this one showing a web of bank accounts and wire transfers. The names started as LLCs, but by the third tier, real human names appeared. Some local, some not.

"We found evidence that several officials in city hall and even some law enforcement officers have been receiving laundered payments. Our source is a series of thumb drives recovered from a secure room at the Puunene Sugar Mill last night."

Higa's face never changed, but her right foot started tapping under the table. The mustached lieutenant scanned the folder, then up at Leilani, and then at the Chief, as if asking for permission to breathe.

Isaac moved ahead. "We have audio logs, too. Conversations in which a man known as the Mastermind gives instructions to mid-level muscle, including directions to avoid specific patrol units and to use friendly contacts in the permitting office."

Leilani watched the temperature drop as Torres moved on. Every cop in the building knew the legend of a mole somewhere in HPD, but hearing it spelled out in tidy bullet points made the threat real. Two of the sergeants whispered, not to each other but into their earpieces, probably relaying the news to whoever was waiting in the bullpen.

Isaac's next slide was the kill shot, a screenshot of an email. The sender, a Makani'olu address. The recipient, a private account registered to "Higa J." The Chief's personal Gmail.

Higa spoke before anyone else could. "You're accusing me of what, exactly, Agent Torres?"

Isaac kept his tone level, almost deferential. "I'm saying the money trail leads through your office, ma'am. But I'm not here to make accusations. I'm here to protect the integrity of this investigation. We wanted to bring this to your attention before taking it to the Feds in D.C."

Higa nodded. Her lips twitched. "Wise of you, Agent Torres. I appreciate your diligence." She leaned back, gave Leilani a once-over, and said, "Detective Kealoha, you've been on this for how long now?"

Leilani sensed the weight of every eye in the room. "Since the first resort break-in, ma'am."

Higa's smile was the kind you'd find on a shark, before it bit your foot off. "And in all that time, you never once thought to run this by Internal Affairs?"

"I did, ma'am," Leilani replied, keeping her voice

smooth. "But the case officer there was transferred to traffic duty the week after I filed my report. Since then, I've had trouble keeping my case files from going missing."

A beat of silence. The mustache guy coughed, but no one else moved.

Higa's smile collapsed. "I see."

Leilani thought it was going to be that easy. That the Chief would call for an immediate lockdown, detain everyone with a badge, and sweep the department clean in a single, surgical purge. Instead, Higa stood up, slow and precise.

"This is quite an accusation, Agent Torres," she said. Her voice was calm, but her hands trembled as she gathered the evidence packet. "And Detective Kealoha, I'm disappointed you didn't come to me directly."

Leilani blinked. "Ma'am?"

Higa's eyes glittered. "I run a tight ship, Detective. But every crew has barnacles. You should have trusted your own command."

She walked around the table, her heels making slow, deliberate clicks on the linoleum. "Here's what's going to happen. You and Agent Torres are going to step outside. Sergeant Liu will escort you to the break room, and you'll wait there while we review your material. If we have any questions, we'll call you back in."

Higa's words were vanilla, but the energy in the room was knife-edged.

Leilani glanced at Isaac, who had gone stony, all nerves and micro-movements.

Higa stopped next to Leilani and bent close. "You did good work, Detective. I don't want to see you caught in the crossfire." Her tone was oddly gentle, almost maternal. She stood straight, squared her shoulders, and gave a little flick of her wrist to the nearest sergeant.

The officers all stood at once, like a drill team. Two stepped to the back, closing off the exits. The rest fell in to gather the evidence.

"Sergeant Liu," Higa said, "escort Detective Kealoha and Agent Torres to the break room, and do not let them out of your sight."

Liu nodded. He was clean cut, mid-forties but with a face that looked twenty-five, the kind who still believed the job was about making the world better. He gestured toward the door, apologetic. "If you'd follow me?"

Leilani gave the room one last scan. Half of the officers had gone statue-still. The other half looked like they wanted to be anywhere but here.

Isaac packed up his laptop, keeping his voice cool. "Thank you for your time, Chief."

Higa ignored him, already in conference with the mustache. As Leilani walked out, she caught the Chief's eyes on her back, a hot, surgical stare that promised retribution, or a quick end.

In the hallway, the air was thin and hostile.

Isaac kept pace beside her, murmuring, "You see

the way she signaled? The little flick with her left hand?”

“I saw,” Leilani said, “and I saw the guns at the back.”

Liu led them down the corridor, away from the bullpen. “Sorry, Detective,” he said, voice low. “Chief’s orders.”

“Yeah,” Leilani said, “We get it.”

But as they passed the glass-walled side offices, she watched the ripple of commotion, hands gripping pistols, eyes watching through blinds, and every soul on this floor tensing for the next move.

She felt the trap close in; the jaws locking into place. The last thing she saw before the break room door swung shut was the smile on the Chief’s face, small, cold, and knowing. The game was on, and there were no rules left.

The break room had the chill and aroma of a walk-in morgue. Leilani clocked every inch, a microwave with a cracked display, the snack machine buzzing on its last life, two battered metal tables, one of which had a full view of the entrance and the hallway beyond. Isaac stood by the coffee urn, refilling his travel mug, while Sergeant Liu perched awkwardly at the table closest to the door, hands folded, eyes fixed at a spot somewhere over Leilani’s head.

“Want some?” Isaac offered, voice a shade too casual, but Liu didn’t even glance his way.

Leilani leaned back, listening. The walls here were thin as cardboard, cheap enough that you could hear every footstep, every cough, every cough-concealed radio squawk from the corridor outside. Something was off. She felt it in the way the building seemed to hush, like the air before a car crash.

She signaled to Isaac with a half tilt of her chin. Heads up.

Two minutes passed. Three. From the hall, a crash, no, a detonation. The boom shook the coffee in Isaac's mug, sending the vending machine into a fit of mechanical rage. Liu stood so fast he nearly toppled his chair.

"Wait here," he said, the order brittle, and yanked the door open.

Through the glass, Leilani watched as two uniformed officers hustled up. One had a shotgun. The other wore the haunted look of a rookie who knew the shit was about to fly.

She didn't wait for them to coordinate. She snapped to the window, sliding it open as far as the ancient frame would allow. Below, concrete, and a drop to the basement garage.

Isaac was at her side. "You wanna jump?"

"Not yet," she hissed, as a fresh concussion echoed along the walls. The first officer turned, shouted, "They're moving on the conference room!" and then Leilani knew the gunfight had started.

She barreled out of the break room, Isaac right on her hip. Liu, caught between panic and protocol, lunged for her, but she sidestepped and smashed her forearm into his solar plexus. He folded with a gasp, but not before grabbing her sleeve. The fabric tore, hot pain slashing through her bicep as Liu's nails raked flesh.

She ignored it and kept running, Isaac pulling Liu's weapon and tossing it across the room for distraction.

They hit the first corner as a shotgun blast took out the glass behind them. Pellets shredded the calendar and cascaded three months of optimistic vacation planning onto the floor. Leilani ducked, took a breath, and drew her SIG.

"We need the evidence," she said, her voice iron. "We don't walk out without it."

Isaac, already bleeding from a nick at his temple, nodded. "Follow me."

He led her back along the main corridor, doubling back toward the conference room. The nearer they got, the hotter the air. The next shotgun round ripped into the ceiling tiles, raining asbestos and dust.

Leilani and Isaac darted left, crouched low. As she passed a windowed side office, she spotted the Chief, flanked by two plainclothes with drawn Glocks, darting through a side door, clutching an evidence folder.

She had the binder. Not all of it, but enough.

Leilani signaled Isaac. "Intercept."

They split, Isaac taking the far hallway, Leilani cutting through the cubicle farm that ringed the conference room. For one beautiful, insane second, the crossfire parted, and she spied the Chief, calm as a shark, walking briskly, binder in hand.

"Hey!" Leilani called. "That doesn't belong to you."

The Chief didn't even break stride. The two plainclothes officers fired, sending rounds into the partitions, splintering particleboard and plexiglass. Leilani threw herself behind a copy machine and waited for the reload.

She moved, fast and low, angling around the outer edge. A bullet caught her sleeve, ripped across the muscle above the elbow, hot and wet. Inches below where she had been shot three weeks before. She screamed, but the sound was buried under the pop of gunfire.

"Torres!" she barked. "Now!"

Isaac crashed through the adjacent office door, tackled the first plainclothes officer to the ground. Leilani pressed her wound, squeezing until the stars faded from her vision, then took aim and double-tapped the second shooter in the kneecap.

The Chief hesitatcd. Leilani saw a glint of something. Regret? No calculation. Higa turned, leveled her weapon, but Leilani was already on her, SIG aimed square at the Chief's heart.

"Give it up," Leilani said, voice trembling from pain and adrenaline. "You can't outrun this."

Higa shook her head. "You should've kept your head down, Detective. You were the best. You know how hard it is to see you destroy everything we built?"

She meant it, Leilani realized, the hurt in her voice as real as the bullet in Leilani's arm.

"I don't want to shoot you," Leilani said, stepping closer.

"But you will," Higa replied. "Because you always finish the job."

Alarms sounded throughout the building. "There are other copies of the evidence binders," she said. "A copy was delivered this morning to the U.S. Attorney's office, and another is on its way electronically to the FBI in Washington."

The chief smiled and then she did something that stunned Leilani. She tossed the binder at her feet, yanked her badge, and threw it down too. A challenge.

The next moment was a blur. Someone fired, an old guard lieutenant, and Leilani dropped behind a table, dragging the binder with her. Isaac slammed the office door, barricading it with a chair.

"You hit?" Isaac said, breathless.

"Yeah," she spat, blood dripping down her sleeve, staining the pale blue blouse red. "A scratch."

"You got it?"

She lifted the binder, the prize heavy and slick with her blood.

Isaac grinned, wild. "Let's get the fuck out of here."

They used the table as a sled, pushing it down the hallway while keeping low. The next fusillade shattered the door behind them, wood chips spinning like shrapnel. Leilani fired back twice, aimed, enough to keep their pursuers down.

At the stairwell, she nearly collapsed, but Isaac

caught her, looping his arm under her good shoulder. "Come on. Not far now."

They opened the door and were surprised to see Assistant Chief Mori and four senior officers she had never seen before. They all had weapons drawn. Leilani stopped and raised her pistol. Mori raised her hands. "It's okay, Leilani. We're here to help." Behind them, coming up the stairs were several SWAT officers. Mori turned to the SWAT sergeant. "Todd, secure this floor and arrest the chief and the chief of detectives. Use whatever force necessary, but I want no more blood spilled unless absolutely necessary."

The sergeant nodded, and his men moved as one through the fire door and into the bullpen. Shots could still be heard. She studied Isaac and Leilani. "I'm here on the order of the governor. You walked into an ongoing investigation and broke it wide open. Now grab your evidence and get the hell out of here. I'll call you when it's safe to come in."

They had no desire to ask more questions, so they barreled down two flights. In the lobby, the glass doors had been locked, but someone had left a housekeeping cart wedged in the frame.

They broke through, out into the open.

They ran through the parking lot carrying the evidence binders, slid into Leilani's Explorer, and tore onto the street. In the rearview, Leilani watched the glass-fronted facade of HQ recede, the gunfight inside reduced to distant flashes, the old familiar rage replaced with a new terror. They had the evidence, but their entire world had come apart at the seams.

She glanced at Isaac, saw the blood on his collar, the way his hands shook on the wheel.

"Now what?" she asked, laughter and grief tangled in her throat.

Isaac stared at her, and she saw he was afraid.

"Now," he said. "We lie low until Mori gets things under control."

"I know the perfect place," she said.

Leilani pulled int an alley three blocks from the station, in the shadow of a sushi restaurant that never opened before noon. Isaac dragged her out of the front seat, where he ripped his sleeve off and tied it around her bleeding arm. The pain cleared her vision.

He wiped the sweat from his face. "How bad is it?"

"Another scratch to add to my collection," she lied, even though it felt like someone had stapled hot steel into her biceps. "Are they chasing?"

"Doesn't look like it," Isaac said, voice as tight as the knot he was tying. "We've gotta move."

They slid into the Explorer, and Leilani cut through the alley, out to the main road, every cell in her body on high alert. She kept the SIG stuffed between her thighs, her hand touching the black polymer. The evidence binders thudded with each turn, a brick of guilt and hope wrapped in blood-spattered plastic.

"You think they'll go after your Kai?" he whispered.

The question was a knife. "He's with Edward. The only way in is through hell."

Isaac nodded, approving. "We have one shot at this. Whoever's clean in the AG's office, or the Feds. If we go public, they'll shred us. Did you really forward the documents, or was that a bluff?"

She didn't respond, but smiled and kept one eye on the road and one on the rearview mirror.

Leilani observed him. The day before, he was smooth as glass. Now, his hands were raw, eyes red-rimmed, hair slicked to his skull with sweat and blood.

She squeezed his knee. "You good?"

He blinked, surprised. "What?"

She smiled, or tried to. "You look like a guy who saw his universe go sideways."

He coughed a laugh. "Yeah. Well. Not my first time, but definitely the loudest."

Leilani pushed a button on her phone and listened as it dialed.

"Lei, are you okay?" asked Uncle Edward.

"Not really. I guess you heard. We need a place to lie low for a while."

There was no hesitation. "You know where. I'll send some people over."

"I owe you," she said. "How's Kai?"

"If what I hear is true, you don't owe me anything. Kai's fine. I've got people on him at the school, so no one will bother him."

She disconnected the call

"You've got people everywhere?" he asked.

"Ohana," she said. "We're all family." She focused on the road.

She kept driving, and the city melted behind them as they drove up into the hills. After two hours, she turned off the highway onto a dirt road that wandered for a couple of miles until she came to a small farmhouse. She pulled up to the door and stopped. The front door opened, and two huge Polynesians stepped onto the porch.

Leilani pushed open her door, walked up to them and gave them a big hug, getting lost in their arms. Isaac slid out of the Explorer and stood behind them. She stepped back and looked at Isaac.

"These are my cousins, Tano, and Gabe," she said. Isaac reached out and shook hands. He glanced at Leilani and then at her two cousins. "You guys it?" she asked.

Tano, the larger of the two, with a dark braid down his back smiled. "Uncle said nobody gets through. We've got more coming. Let's get you inside and cleaned up."

They stepped onto the porch, and Isaac pulled her back. He held the binders in his arms, and his head was bleeding.

"This is all your uncles' doing?" he asked. "Edward."

Leilani laughed. "He hates cops," she said, "but he hates dirty ones more."

"What now?" he asked.

“We take down the house. And we never, ever look back.”

# Chapter Sixteen

## The Final Heist

The farmhouse wasn't much. Tin roof, walls so thin you could hear the feral pigs root through the avocado pits outside. It sat on a hill past the county road, where the city lights faded out and the stars cut like glass overhead. No one would look for them here, which was the point.

Inside, it felt like a fever dream of a police drama and a family garage sale. The kitchen table sagged under the weight of evidence bags, battered laptops, and half-eaten containers of poke and manapua. On the far wall, someone (probably Tano or another cousin, not Isaac) had hammered together a four-by-eight plywood board on a frame and covered it with a grid of tacks and red string, the classic conspiracy map, except with more tape and fewer straight lines.

Leilani worked the board in a loose T-shirt and sweats, arm bandaged above the elbow where the chief's bullet had clipped her, the rest of her still running on the aftershock of the last twenty-four hours. Isaac wearing a T-shirt, duct tape wrapped tight around his ribs, both arms streaked with dried blood. He moved with the coiled energy of a cat right before the jump.

The air hummed with caffeine and pure desperation.

Leilani scanned the photos, connecting lines. The break-ins at the four resorts, the theft at the casino, and the dockside shootout at the sugar mill. Each pinned in place, annotated in her blocky handwriting. But it was the middle of the board that drew her now, a parade of printouts and photos from the maintenance worker's apartment, the man who'd bled out at her feet in the hallway.

Isaac padded over, carrying a cup of gas station coffee. "You see something new?" he asked.

"Could be," she said, not looking at him. "You remember that stack of mail we pulled from Kealo's place?"

"The bills and the eviction notice? Yeah."

She pointed to a yellowing envelope taped beneath a blurry black and white scan. "Check this out."

He leaned in. The envelope was heavy cream, engraved in blue, the kind they used for fancy fundraisers or high end scams. The return address, Office of the Governor, Iolani Palace.

Leilani tapped the corner. "Postmarked six weeks before the break-in. Addressed to the guy personally. It's an invitation."

Isaac's eyebrows climbed. "You think it's real?"

She shrugged. "It's hard to fake the security watermark. If it's not real, it's a damn good copy."

He drained the cup, grimaced. "You think the Mastermind's after the gala?"

"Not the gala," she said, eyes narrowed. "What's scheduled for that night?"

He shrugged, then pushed off to the kitchen counter, where his laptop ran three monitors' worth of digital feeds. "Hold up. I'll check."

She watched him move, fast, deliberate, never hesitating on the keys. She'd always admired that, the way his hands never lost the thread.

He pulled up the palace website, and there it was, bold and obnoxious on the landing page.

GOVERNOR'S GALA. Benefitting the Historic Trust. Guest List. By invitation.

Isaac scrolled down, then glanced back at her. "There's a floor plan online. With security layouts."

She grinned. "Bless their over-sharing hearts."

He kept digging. "Wait, get this. They're displaying the royal collection for the first time in a decade. King Kalakaua's sword, the feather cloak, even the original Constitution." He looked up, eyes dark. "That's not only valuable. That's leverage against half the political elite in Hawaii."

Leilani perceived the chill starting in her teeth. "He's not after the cash. He wants to make a point. Or a mess."

She stepped up to the board, pulling down a separate cluster of crime scene photos. "It fits. Look, in each of these robberies, the actual target wasn't the money. It was the files. Access. Blackmail."

Isaac nodded, chewing on the rim of his cup. "So why steal the sword? What's the play?"

Leilani plucked a petroglyph printout from the cluster and slid it next to the gala invite. "Perhaps it's about the symbol. Remember the old Hawaiian legend? Whoever owns the king's sword has the right to rule. There's a whole conspiracy theory scene about it."

Isaac snorted. "People will believe anything if it's on the internet."

She let that one slide. "Okay, but say you're running a game on the governor and every connected politician in the state. You want to send a message, you pull it off at the party where everyone's watching."

"Humiliate them," he said, seeing the play now. "Shame them. Take their power away."

She nodded. "And then leak every secret you've stolen. Set the world on fire. A double whammy."

"You're sure this is the endgame?"

She exhaled, heavy. "It's the only thing that lines up."

He walked to the board, tracing the red string with a finger. "So, what's the next move?"

She glared at the board, every nerve raw, every cell vibrating. "We get inside. We get the drop on him. We end this before he does."

Isaac watched her, quiet. "You realize you're walking into a palace with half the island's cops and a hit out on your head, right?"

She flashed a hard smile. "Wouldn't be the first time."

He laughed. "Yeah. You like lost causes."

She was already back at the laptop, cross-referencing the guest list with every name from the corruption map. Half of the names overlapped. Judges, councilmen, developers, ex-cops. It was a murderer's row of Oahu's best and least bright.

As the sun burned down behind the hills, Leilani sat cross-legged on the dusty floor, index cards fanned out around her like a tarot reading. She pinned the last piece, an old photograph of the king's sword. The hilt worked with whalebone, the blade still sharp. Next to it, a scan of the petroglyph, spiral within spiral, the symbol she'd seen at every single scene.

She sat back, letting the chill settle into her bones and she knew it. The race wasn't about surviving anymore. It was about who wrote the story, and she was one page ahead.

Outside, the pigs screamed, fighting over scraps. But inside, it was quiet, the endless hum of a woman who would not stop.

The coffee shop was called Lava Java, but after midnight, the neon sign was unplugged and the windows were black. If you knew the owner, and Leilani did, you got in through the side door, down a corridor lined with mop buckets and crates of guava nectar, into the back room where the light was the blue flicker off the cold case and a single bulb taped to a desk lamp.

They met there in the hours when rats and cops were awake. Kaipo was first, a linebacker with a face like a busted lantern. He checked every window and door before he even sat down. Next came Flores and Matsumoto, partners, neither one taller than five-six, but together they made more felony arrests in a year than anyone in Vice. Last came Iosefa, one of the old guard, who still believed that the badge meant something. They were old friends of her father, were her friends and they were men Leilani knew she could trust, no matter what.

They gathered around a folding table cluttered with pizza boxes, laptops and enough caffeine to jump-start a dead patrol car. Isaac sat at the head, tapping burner phones out of a padded envelope and spreading them out.

"Take these," he said, voice low. "Never call your home numbers from them. Never mention where you are, even if you're ordering noodles."

Kaipo picked his up, turned it in his palm. "You expecting trouble?"

Isaac snorted. "The chief still has a lot of friends in the department, men and women who would do anything for her. You don't want to get caught with your pants down."

Leilani slid a stack of evidence across the table. Photos, some in color, some black and white, others blown up from surveillance stills. "This is what's at stake," she said. "Forget the money, forget the press. It's about power. They're not hitting the palace for a payday; they want to humiliate everyone at the top. And they won't stop until they have what they want."

Flores, ever the skeptic, looked up. "So why us?"

"Because you're clean," said Leilani. "Because you've got skin in the game, and because none of you owe the chief a damn thing. And more importantly. You are men I can trust like my father did."

They nodded.

Iosefa eyed her. "You're saying this goes higher than HPD?"

"I'm saying Higa was on the take, and so was the chief of Ds and at least one lieutenant on every shift." She didn't sugarcoat it. "If you want out, now's the time."

No one left. Kaipo even cracked a smile, then pinched it out like a cigarette.

Matsumoto asked, "How's this supposed to work? We crash the gala in our dress blues and play nice?"

"Akira is running point on tech," said Isaac. "We'll get you in as catering, valet, even security if needed. Leilani's face — and a lot more of her than she would prefer — is too well known, so she is going in as herself, invited by the governor. Hero cop and all. The rest of us, we blend in, we observe, and we act if Mastermind moves."

As if on cue, the door banged open and Akira, barefoot, in cargo shorts and a vintage Hello Kitty tee glided in. She set the laptop down and opened it with a flourish, filling the room with the soft glow of a dozen camera feeds.

"Hey, team," she said, grinning. "Sorry I'm late. Had to reset a few passwords on the palace firewall. They're not as dumb as they look, but they're not me."

She gestured to the laptop, where the entire surveillance grid of Iolani Palace now spun in a neat carousel. "They've been swapping out the cams every few hours. But watch." She tapped, and the feed split. "There's a back channel here. Looks like an admin account is monitoring more than usual. That means they're prepping for an inside job."

Flores whistled. "So, the enemy has access?"

Akira nodded. "They've left doors open all over. Physical and digital. The mainframe logs show ghost entries at midnight every night. Someone's rehearsing, testing response times."

Leilani nodded. "That fits. Mastermind never shows his hand until he's sure he can win."

Akira scrolled through the feeds, freezing on one showing a set of historic display cases. "This is where they'll make the play. The West Gallery during the toast. The old ceremonial sword and the feather cloak are both vulnerable. Security will be distracted by the dignitaries and donors. It's the perfect window."

Matsumoto leaned in, studying the layout. "If we want to catch them, we have to beat their time. Get in before they move, or we're cleaning up."

Iosefa grinned. "Or we bait them into a move and close the trap."

Isaac rapped the table, calling the huddle to order. "We prep tonight. Recon tomorrow. All comms through these burners. No social, no calls home. If you see a patrol car parked outside your house, call us first. You don't play hero. This is bigger than any of us."

Kaipo nodded, and pointed at Leilani. "What's your role?"

She met his gaze. "I'm the distraction. If things go bad, I take the heat. You get the perp."

Kaipo grunted. "Same as always."

They all laughed, but it was a nervous laugh, wound tight.

Akira clicked something and brought up the event staff list. "These are your covers. I've already inserted your names into the contractor's HR portal. You'll pick up uniforms at the service entrance by the archives. Try not to spill coffee on the first lady. She does not take it well."

Isaac laid out the rest in rapid fire. Ingress routes, escape plans, even a handoff protocol if the palace goes into lockdown. Each step mapped to the second. No room for improvisation aside from the part where everything always went to hell, anyway.

As the hour bled toward morning, the group gathered their things, each one stowing their new phone and burning the details of the plan into their memory. Akira stayed behind, cycling through the feeds with a hungry, shark-like focus.

When the last of them had gone, Leilani sat back, pinched the bridge of her nose, and breathed.

Isaac poured them both coffee from the battered thermos. "You think they'll stick?"

She nodded, tired. "They're the best we've got. The good ones left."

He sipped. "You ever get scared, Lei?"

"Every day," she said. "But the good ones never

admit it."

He let that settle, then passed her the cup.

As the first light crept through the slit in the blackout curtain, Leilani's burner buzzed. Unknown number.

She answered. "Yeah?"

Mori's voice came through, dry and calm, as always. "Word is the Chief, and the old guard have gone underground. They're spooked. That means they might act sooner, or come after you directly. Watch your back, Detective. And bring it home safe."

Leilani smiled, slow and mean. "Count on it."

She hung up, put the phone down, and watched the glow of Akira's laptop. Tomorrow, they'd go to war.

The day before the gala, the old farmhouse command post changed from silent to seismic in five minutes flat.

Naalei swept through the door, hair wild, sweatpants tucked into muddy garden boots, a canvas bag bulging with books on one arm, and Kai trailing after, lugging a portfolio that was nearly as big as he was. The house felt different with them inside. The panic dropped a notch, and the rooms warmed up the way they used to when the whole family packed into a single Ohana kitchen after a funeral.

Naalei didn't pause. She walked straight to the war table, dumped her haul, and started opening folios with the authority of a librarian on the last day of the world. "Move your laptop, Isaac. We need more space."

Isaac, startled, nearly spilled his energy drink but obeyed without comment.

Kai, eyes wild with sleep deprivation and pride, started yanking out sheets of printer paper covered in graphite and colored pencil. "I did the cross-section like you said, Nana!" he crowed, spreading out a hand-drawn, three-level schematic of Iolani Palace. "The tunnels are real. You've gotta know where to look."

Leilani grinned, letting the pulse of exhaustion fade. She pulled Kai in, kissed his temple, and ruffled his hair. "Show me."

He beamed, then started laying out the sheets like cards. "There's a servant's stair here, by the main kitchen, but if you follow this closet through the wall, there's a ladder to the basement. It's not on the plans, but it's on the old maps in the library books Nana got."

Naalei thumbed through a battered book and stabbed a finger at a yellowed diagram. "During the overthrow, the kings had to hide their people, sometimes themselves. The servants built escape routes. The city sealed most of them up after, but not all. This one runs under the palace yard, comes up in the old jailhouse across the street." She smiled at Kai. "My grandson remembers everything."

Kai bounced on his heels. "There's more. The boards in the king's office are hollow, but you gotta step on the right part to open it. I found it in the oral histories. Nana knows the stories."

Isaac, now fully awake, looked at Leilani. "You think Mastermind could know about these?"

Leilani shrugged. "Possibly. But he's not from here. He's not family. My bet is he's working off the posted blueprints and whatever he bribed out of the archives. This is next level."

Flores and Matsumoto, who'd been quietly sipping coffee and prepping gear, now leaned in, hungry for every word. "That's our edge, then," Flores said. "We know the inside. He doesn't."

Iosefa took a marker and started blocking out points of interest on the sketch. "We'll use the servants' stairs as a fallback. Team Two can post in the basement. If the time comes, we move through the closet into the main gallery." He glanced at Kai. "You did good, Detective."

Kai glowed, and even Naalei looked like she might cry.

Akira scrolled through the palace feeds, but even she studied Kai's drawings. "You ever want a job in network security, you let me know," she said, all respect.

Kai grinned, turned to Isaac, who crouched beside him, close and direct, their eyes level. "Have you ever open a secret door before?" asked Isaac.

Kai's face was serious. "Once. At the Bishop Museum. The janitor showed me where the door is, but you can't tell anyone or they'll close it up forever."

"Your secrets are safe with me," Isaac said, pinky-swearing with him.

The war room buzzed as everyone snapped into action. Naalei walked around the table, narrating the stories behind each map and blueprint, the language of kings and servants and hidden lives. She marked the crawlspace entry under the grand staircase with a sticky note, circling the pantry in the east wing. "This is where they hid the feathered gods. My tutu's tutu helped carry them," she said, pride burning in her voice.

Leilani watched her son with an ache that was equal parts terror and awe. She'd spent so much of her life trying to shield him from the violence and the grind, and now he was here, front and center, making the difference nobody else could. She squeezed his shoulder and kissed the top of his head again. "Best partner I ever had," she whispered, and he blushed, pretending not to hear.

As the afternoon sun filtered in, a tactical haze settled over the house. Kaipo, Flores, Matsumoto and Iosefa suited up in their disguises, three as caterers, one as a janitor, each rehearsing their cover stories with the grim humor of men going to a wedding where everyone was packing. Akira set up a portable server in the hall, her laptop and four monitors running hot, stealing bandwidth from a neighbor's router and bouncing signals off five different countries.

Leilani met with the team, mapped every angle, drilled contingencies until nobody could think straight. But the whole time, her eyes kept drifting to Kai and Naalei, deep in their own huddle at the kitchen counter, mapping history and futures at the same time.

When the sky finally slipped toward dusk, the tempo shifted. They ate a hasty dinner, the best the freezer could offer. Leilani tried to memorize the taste of her mother's pickled mango and the sight of Kai's hands flying over his diagrams.

Later, when the house had gone quiet save for the sound of wind through the louvered windows, Leilani found Isaac standing by the back porch, staring out at the lights that stitched Honolulu together like a net of diamonds.

She stepped beside him. For a while, neither spoke.

"Did I ever tell you about the first time I saw you?" he asked, voice softer than usual.

She smiled, leaning on the rail. "In the parking lot at Kapalama. I was undercover, buying fake IDs. You almost blew my op."

Isaac grinned. "You had this look. Like you knew the plan before anyone else even showed up."

She shrugged, trying not to let him see the nerves. "That was before I started falling behind."

"You're not behind now, Lei. Not this time."

She smiled at him, his face in the half-dark. "Do you ever tire of being the only honest guy?"

"I get tired of losing."

She reached over and took his hand, squeezing hard enough that he winced, just a little.

"Tomorrow," he said. "We finish it."

"Tomorrow," she agreed.

They stood together, with the wind in their hair, looking out at the city where everything mattered and nothing was ever truly safe. And inside, Kai slept next

to his blueprints, Naalei brewed coffee for the dawn,
and the world turned one last time before the endgame.

# Chapter Seventeen

## Gala Undercover

No one ever accused the Iolani Palace of subtlety. The entire grounds glowed under spotlights set up to bathe the three-story façade in impossible gold, every arch, and ionic column shivering against the dark like a hallucination of royalty. The air smelled of fresh cut ginger and perfume, the city's usual funk rinsed clean by a power-washed night and the storm that, until noon, had threatened to drown the party in mud. It hadn't. These people did not cancel. There were rumors that the original King Kalakaua would paddle through a hurricane for a party, and the modern descendants of the court lived that myth at full throttle.

Leilani arrived in a black town car, rented for the evening from an anonymous agency and driven by a cousin she saw at funerals or urgent care. Her gown, a champagne sheath that glittered like rainfall when she moved, fit so tight it threatened to snap a rib, The slit in the side running almost to her hip. She looked stunning, but the real trick was the hair. It was black, intricate, curled up in a style so elaborate it could have hidden a Swiss Army knife, three hairpins, and, in this case, a bone-white communication bud that snaked just behind her ear and vanished under a constellation of bobby pins.

The doormen nodded her in, no check of the clutch, no body scan, just a flat, "Welcome, Ms. Kealoha," and the perfunctory smile reserved for beautiful women with clearances. No one saw the badge, but everyone knew it was there. In this room, the difference between cop and thief was the quality of your shoes.

The inside was madness. Every foot of the main ballroom was polished to a molecular shine, the ancient koa wood floors buffed until the parquet became a dance of reflections. The ceiling, twenty feet up, disappeared in a riot of fresh orchid arrangements, spider-webbed spotlights, and twin crystal chandeliers larger than her first apartment. The noise, voices, laughter and the clash of forks on bone china slammed into her all at once. The palace band played a waltz, the genuine kind, three-quarter time, conducted by a man with a PhD in ethnomusicology and a visible distrust of the upper class.

She walked in like she was born to this, heels clicking, gown rustling, every motion choreographed to look accidental. The crowd parted a little, not out of respect, but in the way a sea anemone recoils from an electric current.

She scanned fast, bankers, politicians, TV anchors and a man who owned half the Big Island and dressed like he'd gotten lost on his way to a Jimmy Buffett audition. There were judges, their faces powdered so thick she could have dusted them for prints, and old school uncles in secret Aloha shirts under rented tuxedos. The elite. The target audience. Everyone here was on someone's payroll or planning to start one by morning.

She drifted toward the drinks table, not because she needed one, but because the first rule of surveillance was to always look a little distracted. The line was four deep, and the woman ahead of her spent the wait time livestreaming to her 90,000 followers. The camera aimed off Leilani's shoulder, accidentally immortalizing the crime scene before it even happened.

A voice in her ear, so low it could have been a thought. "You're ten seconds early, Detective."

She resisted the urge to smile, keeping her face neutral. "You don't sound happy to see me, Isaac."

The response was a hiss of breath. "You're overdressed. It's distracting."

"Didn't want to stand out."

A brief laugh. "Too late. With your picture plastered all over the internet, lots of folks are checking you out."

"Thanks for reminding me. I hadn't thought about that for at least five minutes."

She knew he was watching. Somewhere, Isaac was close enough to see her through the windows. She perused the wall mirrors, the big baroque ones hung at every interval, and caught the quick flash of a security uniform. Isaac, or a clone, making his rounds. He'd buzzed his hair tight for this, skin almost gleaming under the LED, and the lines of the uniform hugged his body in a way that screamed not-a-rental.

She let her gaze flick past him, all cool indifference. The crowd hid its criminals well, but to her eye, the difference between predator and prey was obvious. She spotted the first one on the dance floor, late thirties, Japanese American, in a tux that fit too perfectly and with a face so generic it could have been auto generated. The second was harder, shorter, ex-military by the posture, with a nervous tic in his left hand where he ran his thumb over his palm, as if counting down something only he could see.

A third and fourth moving together. Both white with the pale, slightly off color of longtime ex-pats, the kind who never quite assimilated but still knew how to score free drinks at every Honolulu bar. The woman, tall and severe, wore her hair in a braid so tight her eyebrows arched upward, and the man never stopped looking at his watch, even when he smiled at the governor's joke.

That was four, and she bet there were at least two more.

The line advanced, and she accepted a flute of something sparkly, then melted sideways into the flow of the room. The governor's staff was on patrol, herding guests, making sure the real VIPs weren't cornered by lobbyists or worse, the press.

She slipped between a pair of uncles arguing about land rights and approached the gallery, where the glass doors opened onto the lanai. She took a second to breathe, scanning the outer perimeter. Every ten feet, a uniform, state police or HPD, it was hard to tell at this distance, but their stances were textbook. All at parade rest, all with comms in their left ears.

A soft buzz at her wrist. She glanced down. A coded text, three letters, from Akira. The tech was watching the feeds from the server van across the street, patching in through three layers of firewalls and one unlucky cable box in the state archives. The message was a single pulse. BVI.

Blue Vest Inbound.

Leilani stepped back inside, holding her flute in her left hand, her right resting at her side, fingers curled. The signal was micro, but she saw Isaac pick it up from across the room. He angled his path to intercept, cutting a wedge through the crowd like a shark in open water.

"Two on you," he whispered over the comm. "Tagging third, east side."

She murmured, "I see them."

The blue vest, a junior staffer, twenty-five, nervous and sweating under the palace lights, cut through the dance floor with a tray of canapés, but his eyes tracked straight to the artifacts display in the adjoining gallery. He moved too slowly for a real runner, but too fast for a kid on the clock.

She followed, letting three feet of space breathe between them. The blue vest stopped at the base of the grand staircase, adjusted his earpiece, and waited. He scanned the crowd, met eyes with the Japanese man from earlier, and gave a nod so small that it would take a trained eye would spot it.

At that moment, the room changed. The governor, resplendent in his $3,000 suit and with a smile so wide it threatened to split his face, mounted the steps and tapped the mic. Instantly, the band cut. The crowd rotated as one, and every phone in the place came up with a wave of rectangles to record the speech.

She ducked to the left, feigning an interest in the

paintings on the wall, but really locking on the blue vest, who was now joined by the nervous ex-military guy and the tall woman with the severe braid. The three of them formed a loose triangle at the base of the steps, close enough to move as a unit but loose enough to vanish if someone called for a photo.

The governor started his talk, a riff on Hawaiian heritage, the future, the obligations of the past, and the critical need for unity. It was well-written and meaningless, and even the true believers in the crowd spent more time watching their reflections in the chandeliers than the actual speech.

Leilani swept the room, saw Isaac posted at the far wall, arms crossed, his weight shifted so he could pounce if needed. He was watching the triangle, too.

All at once, the hand signal, a touch to the temple and a drop of the hand to the waist, palm facing out. It happened in sequence, blue vest first, nervous next, then the tall woman. All three moved together, splitting off toward the service entrance in the northeast corner.

She whispered, "They're moving. Northeast service corridor. Another two heading for the gallery."

Isaac's voice: "I'm on it. You take the gallery, I'll tail the vests."

"Copy."

The governor wrapped up his speech, and the applause rose like a cyclone, covering her exit as she cut through the crowd, tossing her flute on the first half empty tray she passed. She ditched her heels in a coat closet. She never planned to keep them anyway, and moved fast across the marble, each step measured for noise, stride, and cover. The world narrowed to a point, and she relished the moment.

There would be no do-overs tonight.

She heard Isaac's footsteps over the comm, the soft hiss of movement, and the low grunt as he shouldered through the swing door to the service corridor. The earpiece transmitted every detail, and she allowed the sound to settle her.

She reached the artifact gallery as the two other suspects, both male, one wearing a caterer's jacket and the other in a tailored suit that hung too stiff to be real, ducked through the cordon and into the velvet roped zone where the king's sword and the feathered cape were displayed.

She pressed up against the old koa wood panel, feeling its chill through the silk. Her hands never shook, not even now. The game was on and she wasn't a pawn.

The velvet rope was less of an obstacle and more of a suggestion. Leilani hopped it without slowing, the hem of her gown catching for half a heartbeat before she kicked it free, splitting the seam a good four inches up her right thigh. The pain would come later. Right now, she needed speed.

The two men ahead barely registered her until the taller one glanced back, did a double-take, and whispered something to his partner. They peeled left, ducking behind a Polynesian mural and into the hallway that led to the executive washrooms. A dead end, unless they were counting on some hidden exit she didn't know about.

She gave chase, left hand up to steady the little clutch that held her badge, her phone and a SIG tucked in a holster that would have passed muster at any Las Vegas showgirl audition. The corridors of Iolani were all the same in the dark. Endless wood and glass, echoes bouncing off tile, the air going cold and then hot in patches as the AC tried and failed to keep up with the bodies inside.

On the first turn, the men had a ten yard lead. She caught a whiff of something chemical, faint but familiar, burned plastic, solder. She filed it for later.

She took the turn, gun now in hand but pressed flat to her thigh, and almost collided with a catering cart left abandoned in the side hallway. She used it as cover, crouched low, and saw them, hands pressed flat to a decorative panel set in the wall. The shorter man jabbed at something, a catch, or a lever, and the panel popped open with a low, satisfying click. A hidden door.

She waited for them to step in, then sprinted, bare feet slapping the old, worn hardwood. The edge of the panel bit her palm as she shoved in after them. The seam shut behind her, and the world changed. This wasn't a corridor. It was a time capsule.

There were no lights except the weak glow from an emergency strip taped to the floor. No sound but her own breath, louder now in the dead silence. The walls were raw stone, wet in patches, and overhead, latticework of copper pipes and exposed conduit. She followed, moving slowly now, letting her eyes adjust.

A voice in her ear, garbled by the stone: "West corridor. They just split. I'm with security, but they're amateurs. You got eyes?"

She whispered back, "In the old tunnels. Two suspects ahead."

"Backup in two. Don't get dead."

She smirked. Isaac and his timing.

There were footprints in the dust, impatient, not careful. She moved faster, careful not to sound out her own pursuit. The tunnel twisted, then dropped, a sudden slope ending at a wrought-iron gate left half ajar. The men had tried to lock it, but the bolt was rusted out. She eased it open and walked through, listening for any clue of their location.

Voices, echoing. "Down there. Fast. They'll be on us in a minute."

She followed the sound, every step slower, deliberate. The tunnel kinked left again, then opened to a landing that overlooked a boiler room, the kind no one ever talks about unless a pipe bursts or a rat chews through a line.

Below, one man hunched over a black Pelican case, hands working a bundle of wires and a device the size of a toaster. The other paced, gun drawn, scanning the upper reaches with a jittery energy that reeked of amateur hour. She stayed low, used the shadows to move around to the steel ladder bolted to the wall. One step at a time, letting the vibration of their voices mask the metallic click of her descent.

Isaac's voice came through again, clearer this time.

"I'm in the corridor, but I lost visual. You got anything?"

"Boiler room," she hissed. "One with a device, one with a gun. I can take them."

A two-beat pause. "Don't risk it. I'll be there."

She smiled, predatory. "Copy."

She dropped the last two rungs and crouched behind a barrel, SIG at the ready. The device the men were prepping looked like a jammer. At least, that's what the warning stickers on the casing suggested. The logo on the side was military surplus, the kind you see in procurement nightmares and police corruption scandals. They were prepping it for a short, fast kill, take out palace comms, crash the feeds, and let someone else move while everything was dark.

She waited until the man with the gun turned away. She stepped out, smooth and silent, and said, "HPD. Hands where I can see them."

The gunman spun, raising his weapon, but his finger never made the trigger. She put two rounds through his chest, neat and low, dropping him like a sack of sand. The second man tried to close the case, but she leveled the SIG at his chest.

"Move and you're done," she said. "On the ground. Now."

He raised his hands, palms open, eyes wet and wide. The air was still, the only noise the gurgle of the old water heater and the gunman's gasping. Isaac's footsteps echoed from the tunnel above, fast and growing louder. She glanced up, saw his shoe, then the man himself, sliding down the ladder two rungs at a time.

She kicked the gun out of the first man's hand. Leilani zip-tied both suspects with the flex cuffs from her clutch. She never diverted her gaze from the device, still humming and alive.

Isaac joined her, breathless but steady. "You good?"

She nodded. "Device is active. Looks like a comms kill switch. We need Akira to walk us through disabling."

"Copy," said Isaac, already pulling out his phone. He patched Akira in, and the hacker's voice came through, dry and clinical.

"Open the case. Don't touch the blue wires. Cut the red one at the base, then hold the ground plate for ten seconds until the light dies."

Leilani kneeled, and Isaac handed her a small knife he kept in his pocket. She flipped her gown to the side, exposing more of her amazing legs than she would have liked to, so she could move, opened the pelican case, and did exactly as told. The device whined, then faded to black. The threat was over.

The gunman, bleeding but not in shock, stared at her with a look that said more than words ever could. His breathing was labored, and blood dripped from his mouth. She crouched next to him, eyes flat.

"Who sent you?" she asked.

He looked away, then spat blood onto the floor. "You already know." He coughed up blood, his eyes closed and his breathing stopped.

She did.

She hauled him to his feet, ignoring his whimpers. "Let's go," she said to Isaac. "Someone else is in the system. This was a distraction."

He nodded, and together they moved the remaining suspect through the tunnel, leaving the dead device and the dead suspect behind. She noticed the palace shifting above them, the balance, the attention, the game.

It wasn't over. Not even close.

She climbed into the light, and she was ready for anything.

The man in black ran with a speed that was both practiced and desperate, zigzagging through the underbelly of the palace as if the blueprint were burned behind his eyelids. Leilani ditched the cuffed gunman and gave chase, vaulting through the side door and back into the maze of old service tunnels. Every sense screamed at her to slow down, to wait for backup, but the high in her blood said otherwise.

She matched him turn for turn. The space got tighter, wetter, a rush of cold air blowing through cracks she knew were there but had not seen. The corridor ducked left, turned right, and ended at a caged stairwell that led up into blackness. Her quarry didn't hesitate. He scaled it with animal fluidity, hands, and feet working in unison, a shadow with a grudge.

She followed, every rung ringing in her bones. At the top, a sliver of yellow light cut through the gloom.

He was there at the threshold, one gloved hand on the latch of a maintenance room door, the other clutching a matte black tablet against his chest.

She drew the SIG. "Stop. Turn around, hands up."

He did neither. Instead, he yanked the latch and dove through, slamming the door behind him. She heard the metal bar drop into place, then the sharp crunch of something heavy being dragged across the floor as a barricade.

She exhaled through clenched teeth, holstered the gun, and pressed her shoulder to the door. It didn't budge. The cold on her bare feet was now a bite, and her adrenaline was burning off. She paced the hall, looking for a weak spot, then noticed a crawlspace vent above the door, old mesh half-rotted, wires loose.

"South end, level three. He's barricaded. I'm trying to flank him."

"On my way. Two minutes," said Kaipo.

She reached up, fingers scrabbling at the mesh, then tore it free with a rush of decayed dust and the tang of old mice. She hoisted herself up, arms shaking with the effort, and squeezed through, feeling the vent scrape between silk and skin in equal measure. The shaft was two feet across, but she used her elbows and knees to inch forward, following the muffled shouts from below.

Through the grill, she saw him. The man in black was now unmasked, pale skin beaded with sweat. He'd propped a mop and two buckets under the door, forming a barricade, and was hunched over a gray control box, working a bundle of cables into the palace's hard wired network. Every movement was frantic but sure, like he'd done this a thousand times in his head.

She waited until he plugged the last cable in, then slid down the vent with a thud, landing catlike behind a stack of cleaning supplies.

He heard her but was too late; she crossed the space in three strides, gun up.

"Freeze. Now."

He didn't freeze. He spun, swinging the tablet at her head. It glanced off her shoulder, hard enough to sting, and he lunged for the vent she'd exited. She fired, missed by a hair, and dove after him, grabbing his ankle as he tried to snake through the opening.

He kicked back hard. Her vision popped with white heat, but she held on, yanking with all the adrenaline left in her arm. He tumbled backward into her, and they crashed together into the mops and buckets, a slow motion landslide of chemical and plastic and pain.

She pinned him, pressing her knee to his chest, one hand grabbing his wrist, the other aiming the SIG between his eyes. He didn't struggle. Instead, he lay still, lips curled in a half-smile.

"You're not the only one who can fake it, Leilani," he said, the voice distorted but unmistakable.

Her whole body stiffened. She ripped off his mask and stared down at the face. It was Tommy Nakamura. Her old partner. The one they'd buried two years ago. The one who'd sworn to her a hundred times that he'd never sell out. The shock punched the air out of her. She let go of his wrist and almost dropped the gun.

"Tommy…what?"

He smirked, face mottled from the chokehold, and the emotion she saw flicker there, brief and gone.

"I was hoping it wouldn't be you," he said.

She felt her hand tremble on the grip. "You're supposed to be dead. I saw the damn photos."

He rolled his head back, looking at the ceiling. "Sometimes that's the best cover of all."

The silence was total, other than the far-off hum of the palace and the drip of some forgotten leak. She wanted to say a thousand things, none of them fit for company. Instead, she reset her finger on the trigger, hard enough that the plastic creaked.

He smiled, and there was the old Tommy, with the smirk, the stubborn glint, the edge that could have cut steel.

"It's not about the money," he whispered. "It's about the story."

She felt the world tilt sideways. "You're working for them."

"I'm working for myself." His smile was so sad it almost broke her. "You can shoot me if you want, Lei. Or you can figure out who's playing both sides."

She stared at him, at the man she thought she'd known, the brother-in-arms she'd grieved, the ghost in all her best and worst dreams. She remembered the old days. She cuffed him double tight, and hauled him to his feet.

"Move," she said, barely trusting her own voice. "We're going to have a long talk."

He became silent, with a limp now in his gait that hadn't been there before. Behind her, she heard Kaipo's footsteps echo up the stairs. She turned, SIG steady in one hand, Tommy Nakamura's fate in the other. And she wondered if she really knew the difference between hero and villain. Everything was spinning, and she was dead center in the spiral.

# Chapter Eighteen

## Mastermind Unmasked

When the sun breached the clouds over downtown, the palace grounds looked like the aftermath of a failed revolution and an open bar brawl, which in Honolulu was usually the same thing. Isaac ran the show, herding HPD and FBI agents like they were kindergartners at a field trip check-in. Every museum-grade artifact was logged, tagged, double-gloved, and zipped into foam-padded evidence bags by two sets of hands and a third set of lawyers hovering behind the barricade. In the courtyard, a line of suited conspirators, most of them looking like they'd lost a high stakes poker game to God himself, sat cross-legged in the grass while SWAT stood over them with coffee and glazed malasadas.

Leilani leaned against the trunk of her battered Explorer, a shivering Tommy Nakamura handcuffed in the back seat. Her hair was a Medusa's nest, and the split seam on her dress was up past mid-thigh, but she smiled. It could have been the cold morning air. Perhaps it was the shock of catching a ghost. Or it was the sound of Isaac's voice on the radio, low and warm, as he called out assignments like a short-order cook. "Forensics to Gallery C. Evidence bag to loading dock. Get a statement from that wailing PR hack and, for God's sake, tell her the press is not allowed inside until the coroner leaves."

The window was rolled down, and Tommy leaned his head out, grinning that old, incorrigible smile.

"You ever think we'd end up like this?" he said. "You on the hero's side, me with the cuffs?"

She sipped cold black coffee, arms crossed over her ruined bodice. "You always were a drama queen, Nakamura."

Tommy had been a good cop before the shooting that she thought had left him for dead outside the bank. He was cocky and arrogant and had the looks to go with the charm. He flirted with every woman he met, but he was never a leader. She knew he wasn't the guy in charge, not the Host or Mastermind, but she figured he was close to them.

He laughed, rolling his wrist to show off the zip tie. "You could've asked me to surrender, you know. We could have had a pleasant chat, reminisced about old times. It wouldn't have wrecked your pretty dress. David is a lucky guy."

Her brain blanked out. "I asked," she said. "You don't remember the part where you tried to bash my head in with a mop handle?"

Tommy winked. "Instincts. Hard to retrain."

She finished the coffee, watching Isaac pace out the last perimeter check. He caught her glance, gave a half-nod, and pointed at the back seat.

"Ready?" she asked.

He grinned. "But I get to pick the music."

She let him stew on that, then slid into the driver's seat, the leather cold and stiff against her bare thighs. Tommy shuffled in the back, still cuffed, making a show of stretching his arms and craning his neck. "You remember the time at Kapalama, the dry cleaner heist?" he said, like they were old high school buddies instead of cop and traitor.

She started the engine, letting the idle tick while she waited for the media van to clear the driveway. "I remember you got the informant's name wrong, and we had to spend three hours chasing a guy with one shoe through four lanes of rush hour traffic."

Tommy snorted. "I meant the part where we both realized the suspect was a confidential informant for Vice, and we laughed about it over beers at Rainbow's. Good times."

Leilani drove in silence for a block, eyes on the road, the wet glimmer of the asphalt bright enough to make her squint. Tommy kept talking, voice getting softer as the city bled past the windows. "You ever wonder if it all could've been different? If we'd walked away that day, started our own P.I. gig, lived the dream?"

She didn't answer. She didn't trust herself.

He leaned forward. "You're angry. I get it. But you should know I didn't have a choice."

She braked hard at the light, then looked at him in the mirror. "Everyone has a choice, Tommy. That's the one lesson that matters."

He held her gaze, and she noted the tired in his eyes. The old Tommy had never looked tired, not even when they'd pulled three straight doubles and then got called to a homicide before the end of the shift. Now, there was an edge of something new. Guilt. Or the certainty of being on the wrong side of the badge.

When they pulled into the underground lot at HQ, the world felt colder, emptier, as if even the city's junk DNA knew it was the endgame. She parked in her old spot, half-blocked by a stack of broken barricades and a security guard sleeping in a golf cart.

She yanked open the back door. "Out."

Tommy stood, stretching again. She led him up the ramp and through the security checkpoint, smiling at everyone, as if he were on a guest list. Two officers at the desk looked at them, one with a look of recognition, the other with confusion.

"It's Nakamura," the first one whispered. "Didn't he?"

"Yeah," said the other. "But he looks good for a corpse."

She hustled him down the corridor, past the elevator, past the bullpen, to Interview 4, a windowless, coffin-shaped room with two chairs, a battered Formica table, and a camera mounted in the corner that had never once worked properly. She shoved him in, made sure he sat facing the mirror.

"Can I get a coffee?" he asked, as if they were still equals.

"You can get a lawyer," she said. "But I doubt they'll show up before lunch."

He smiled, then watched as she cuffed him to the bolt. He looked at his hands, turned them over, flexed them, then smoothed the fabric of his sleeve like a man preparing for church.

She sat and folded her hands. She pushed the record button on the tape deck and read him his rights. He chose at this point not to ask for a lawyer. She felt like he was playing a game, but she played along.

"Why'd you run?" she asked, keeping her voice flat.

He shrugged. "Didn't think you'd let me walk out. You never did like to lose."

"You didn't have to go full heist movie, Tommy. You could've turned yourself in, made a deal. We'd have figured it out."

He nodded, lips thinning to a line. "There was never a deal for people like me. The Host made that clear."

She let the word hang, testing his reaction. He flinched. "The Host," she repeated. "That's your buyer? Or your boss?"

He smiled, eyes drifting up to the camera in the corner. "Could be both. Or neither. You think this is about the money? We weren't planning the heist last night for money. You'd best get your mind right Kealoha, or you're never gonna figure this out."

She kept her hands still. "You were always about the game. The chase. That hasn't changed."

He looked away, staring at the wall. "The Mastermind was smarter than all of us. You included."

"Not that smart," she said. "I've got your tech girl in holding and your muscle in the morgue."

He grinned again. "I said smarter, not luckier."

They were silent. The AC kicked on, and the room dropped five degrees in a minute. Tommy's voice was softer now, an echo off the cinderblock. "You don't get it, Leilani. I already told you. This was never about art, or the feather cloak, or whatever bullshit the news wants to sell. This is about power. It's about whose story gets told, and who's left on the cutting room floor."

She drummed her fingers. "You were in the room with the former chief. Did you know about the inside leak?"

He nodded. "We all knew. It was the worst-kept secret in the HPD. You didn't think the spiral started with Makani'olu, did you? You were never part of the inner circle. Bet you didn't even know there was an inner circle. I bet David never told you."

"David wasn't part of some police cabal," she said with anger in her voice. "He was a good cop."

Tommy laughed. "David is smarter than everybody. You never saw it."

She felt the anger spike up, then clamp down. "The Chief ran you. Who was running her?"

He smiled, tired and thin. "That's the wrong question. The right one is, why?"

She leaned forward. "Why?"

He waited a beat, like an actor letting the line breathe. "Because it's the way you get out. You and I both know that, no matter how good you are, the system is a meat grinder. It chews you up and shits you out as fertilizer for the next crop of idiots. So, when someone comes along and offers you a chance to write your own ending."

He shrugged. "You say yes."

She stared, feeling the sting of that truth in her own bones.

He caught the look. "It's not personal, Lei. It's never been personal."

She waited.

"You're not even close to the real endgame. You think Mastermind is some old school kingpin? He's a ghost. Doesn't even exist. The person you're chasing is someone you already know," he said.

The words hit her hard.

He smiled, watching her face. "You want to hear something crazy?"

She nodded.

He leaned in, his voice almost too soft to hear. "You remember your husband, right?"

The world tilted. She tried to hide the reaction, but he saw it.

Tommy shrugged. "He's dead. Yeah. But you never saw the body. It was a closed casket and a lot of talk about how you ID'd the body from his tats. Tats are easy to fake."

She tried to kill the hope before it sprouted, but Tommy kept going. "What if the Mastermind was someone who knew every case file, every evidence locker, every safe house? What if he was trained to vanish, and knew exactly how to play you and the system?"

She fought to keep calm. "You're saying it's him? You're saying he faked his own death? Why? He was a good cop at the top of his game, and he had a beautiful son. Nobody gives that up. He's dead, Tommy. He was what was left after the sharks got to him. I identified the tattoos. I saw the DNA test."

He shrugged and smiled that cocky smile that always won him favor with the ladies. "But you never saw the body. I'm saying that sometimes the best cover is a headstone. And sometimes the only way to beat the spiral is to get out of it. It worked for me until this morning."

"Why fake your own death?" she asked.

"Had to. It's the way to get into the ghost squad."

He leaned back, letting the chair rock on two legs. "You want names? I'll give you names. But you'll be shocked."

She glared at him, feeling the room shrink, the air curdled. "Do it."

He smiled, eyes closing. "Come back tomorrow," he said. "After you've thought about it. After you've figured out who you're really chasing. Promise me I can be there when you figure it out. I want to see the look on your and everyone else's faces. Should be good for a laugh."

She pushed out of her chair; the legs screeching on the tile. "You're not in charge here, Tommy."

He opened his eyes, half-lidded, like a cat sunning itself. "I never was. Never would have been, but I can still win if I make you see what you don't want to see."

She unlocked his cuffs, then nodded to the two uniforms waiting outside. "Put him in holding. No visitors. No calls."

As they led him away, he called out over his shoulder, "It's always the last person you want it to be. Think about it, Detective!"

She walked out, shutting the door behind her, the cold of the hallway eating the heat from her face. She had a case to finish. But there was a new knot in her gut, and it was growing tighter with every step.

She stepped into the restroom and looked at herself in the mirror. Her gown was ruined, and she looked like she'd gone twelve rounds with a middleweight champion. She was sore as hell and royally pissed. She washed her face and then leaned closer. "There's no way David would have faked his own death. He wouldn't have left me and Kai for anything in the world. We were happy."

She dried her face and pulled open the door. Suddenly, the world around her wasn't as clear as it had been a little while ago.

The road home was a long, straight slash through darkness, cutting between ghost cane fields and low drainage ditches, the air thick with night-blooming jasmine. Leilani set the cruise at seventy and had all the windows rolled down. She drove one-handed, the other arm thrown across her lap, knuckles grazing the bandage where Tommy's mop handle had torn her muscle raw. She counted the telephone poles as they blurred past, one, two, five, infinity. On the fourth pole after the state park turnoff, the phone lit up with HPD's main number.

She answered with a grunt, expecting Isaac or Kaipo or someone else to ask if she was bringing back malasadas for the morning.

Instead, a voice she didn't know: "Is this Detective Kealoha?"

"Yeah," she said. "Who's calling?"

The voice was flat, feminine, mainland accent with a hint of nervousness. "I'm with Honolulu PD, custody desk. We, uh, need you to come down to the station. It's about your prisoner."

What she heard was the road hum, the whisper of wind in the mirrors. "Tommy Nakamura?" she said. "Did he try to roll someone in holding, or flirt with a matron and get his ass kicked?"

The pause was pure bad news.

"He's dead, Detective. He hanged himself an hour ago."

The car drifted over the line, tires rumbling on the shoulder strip. She corrected by instinct, but her brain was gone somewhere else, racing through the list of things she hadn't said, things she'd never get to say. All she saw was the way he glared at her in the interview room, that cocky smile and the glint of old brotherhood, and then how the last words out of his mouth had been a dare to see the truth.

"Thank you," she said, voice iron-flat. "I'm on my way."

She ended the call, then stomped on the brakes,

fishtailing gravel in a hailstorm behind her. The SUV rocked as she whipped it onto the dirt road, gunning for the farmhouse. She slid it to a stop by the porch, half the headlights aimed at the mango tree where Kai once built his spy fort, the other half flooding the front steps where Naalei sat in a plastic chair, reading by the porch light.

Naalei looked up, took in her daughter's face, and set the phone down without a word. "I'll make coffee," she said. She didn't ask what had happened. She stepped inside, the screen door banging once.

Leilani marched up the porch, her ruined gown catching on a nail and tearing another two inches of hem away. She kicked off her heels, almost threw them into the bushes, and stormed inside.

The house was a mess of food containers and evidence folders, the kitchen table buried under a drift of photographs, blueprints and maps. The board was still up on the wall, with a dozen strings radiating from the center. Now, in the off-kilter light, the whole thing looked less like a case and more like a curse.

She tore the dress off, leaving it in a puddle by the fridge, and grabbed the first jeans and T-shirt she found on the laundry pile. Her utility vest was in the hallway; the same one she'd patched up from the last raid. She cinched it on, not caring if the Velcro gave her new scars. She grabbed a backup SIG from the drawer, checked the mag, and slammed it home. She was already gone, out the door, before the coffee had finished brewing.

She took the old road to the city, burning the

speedometer needle. The world was two colors: the black of the hills and the radioactive gold of streetlamps. As she hit the city limits, the sky was already hinting at dawn.

At the precinct, the parking area was half full, most of the cars marked but one or two unmarked, easy to spot by the way they pretended to be nothing at all. She stomped up the steps, past the rookies working the desk, and into the holding corridor.

The station was quiet, voices muted behind closed doors. Standing in the lobby was Acting Chief Mori, in a black suit that looked like it cost less than the shoes but fit her perfectly. Mori had a clipboard in one hand, a folder in the other, and a tired, careful smile.

"Detective," she said. "I heard about the palace. You did good work tonight."

Leilani didn't slow down. "Where is he?"

Mori followed her, matching stride. "The ME is with him now, but they haven't moved the body. We're running the tapes and getting statements from the lockup crew."

She turned and walked past the battered vending machine and the old beat-up lockers, into the cellblock.

The cells here were modern, all glass, and steel, but the old holding tank was where they put the problem inmates, the ones too smart or too crazy to sit with the drunk and disorderlies. Tommy was in there, lying on the cot, eyes closed, arms folded over his chest.

He looked peaceful. Like someone who'd finished a long swim and was catching his breath.

The ME, a round woman with a graying braid, nodded at Leilani. "We haven't bagged him yet. You want a minute?"

She nodded, and the woman stepped back. Mori hovered by the door, arms folded.

Leilani stepped into the cell and stood over the body. The ligature mark was clear, high on the neck, deep enough to bruise but not to break anything. The sheet he'd used was still looped around the bars, a careful, professional knot.

But it wasn't the neck that caught her.

It was the right hand, palm up, the fingers still curled. On the skin, written in ballpoint, was a spiral, blood beading around the edges. It wasn't drawn; it was pressed in, as if he'd scored the flesh with a pen, then traced it until the lines bled.

She looked at his hand. Tommy was right-handed. She'd seen him write reports, sign warrants, even throw darts with the right hand. But the spiral was on his right, and the line was smooth and precise. If he had used his left hand to make it, it would have been shaky.

She studied his face, at the line of the jaw, the set of the mouth. There was a hint of a smile. Or she imagined it.

Mori cleared her throat. "Do you want to see the log? The footage?"

She didn't move, but kept looking at the hand.

He'd said, "Sometimes the best cover is a headstone." He'd said, "Come back tomorrow, after you've thought about it." He'd wanted her to see this.

She turned to Mori. "He didn't commit suicide. He didn't have the balls. But he was also right-handed. He couldn't have drawn a perfect spiral with his left hand. He was murdered. Lock down this wing of the building. Nobody in or out until we sweep every inch."

Mori nodded, her voice crisp. "Already done, Detective. The problem is, he was found right after shift change. I've got patrol units picking up everyone who had already left the building before we found him. You think Mastermind ordered this?"

"Yes, ma'am," she said. "Looks like we still have some housecleaning to do."

The acting chief stepped out of the way so the morgue attendants could roll out the gurney.

Leilani walked out of the cell, her stomach churning, and found herself back in the main hallway, staring at the board through the glass of the evidence room. The spiral was everywhere, on the wall, on the case files, in the palm of a dead man who was still running the game from six feet under, but this time she knew he was dead.

She pressed her hand to the glass, feeling the cold. She shut her eyes, and wondered if she was ever going to get free. What she thought if Tommy was right. What if the spiral never ended? For people like her, it was the single thing that mattered.

# Chapter Nineteen

## Justice and Reconciliation

The conference room at HPD headquarters hadn't been this full since the rail line murders, or the mayor's DUI. Every TV station from the Big Island to the mainland had sent someone, and the microphones on the podium looked like a bouquet for a deranged wedding. The crowd buzzed with a flavor of hunger that was part anticipation, part old vendetta; you didn't get a crowd like this unless someone important had gone down.

In front of the microphones, were the evidence binders. Blueprints, financial ledgers, two printouts of banking routes with colored arrows like a child's puzzle, and, in the center, a photo array of every key suspect, their faces lined up like a firing squad for the cameras. In the front row, reporters clutched notepads or squinted at phones. In the back, a half-dozen HPD officers leaned against the wall, their uniforms too new or too tight, the room's heat baking out the nervous sweat.

Leilani was center stage, flanked by Isaac on her right and acting Chief Mori to her left. She wore a suit jacket that covered her pistol, and her hair, usually ocean-wild, was tamed in a knot at the nape. If you looked closely, you'd see the fatigue in her eyes. One intern from the paper did, and scribbled something about battle weary, but her posture never gave an inch.

Mori opened with the statement, "Thank you all for

coming. This morning, after a joint investigation with the FBI, we have made multiple arrests in connection with the recent criminal conspiracy targeting both the city and this department." Her voice was low and strong, the tone of someone used to giving bad news in good sentences.

Leilani stepped up next, feeling the pressure of a dozen lenses. She started slowly, voice steady as she pointed at the evidence behind her. "Over the last two months, individuals operating within city government, private security and our own department coordinated a series of financial crimes and attempted thefts targeting state infrastructure and the Iolani Palace."

The room stilled. A hush you'd get at an accident or a funeral.

"We recovered more than a million dollars in fraudulent wire transfers," she continued. "We have audio logs and emails connecting the leadership of Makani'olu Development and multiple shell companies to the events at the sugar mill and the attempted heist at the palace."

A reporter from Channel 4 barked, "Does this implicate the previous Chief of Police?"

Leilani let the question hang, then answered. "Yes. The evidence directly implicates former Chief Higa in a pattern of obstruction and conspiracy. She was taken into federal custody as of this morning in Los Angeles, and we are working on extradition."

A flash of cameras hit her face, a synchronized burst of attention.

Another reporter from KHON asked, "And the connection to the mayor's office?"

Isaac picked this one up, cool and federal. "At this time, the U.S. Attorney is reviewing evidence involving several city officials, including at least one member of the city council. We'll have more once the grand jury returns indictments."

He kept his eyes on the crowd, but Leilani caught the way his hands flexed at his side, the only sign he wasn't made of concrete.

The Channel 8 woman pressed, "There are rumors this involved a national syndicate. Can you confirm?"

Leilani glanced at Mori, who gave the barest nod. "Yes," Leilani said, voice firmer now. "There is evidence the conspiracy reached beyond Hawaii. We are working with our federal partners to track the financial flow and pursue other targets as they are identified."

That got the crowd going, a wave of questions crashing onto the table. But the main show was over. The rest would be clean-up, spin, and whatever the internet remembered by evening.

Leilani stepped back from the microphones. She watched as the news cycle vultures circled the evidence display, snapping pictures of faces and figures. An old guard detective caught her eye, a guy who'd never liked her, but he stared at the evidence array and then at her and gave a silent nod. Another young officer looked as if she wanted to sink through the tile.

Acting Chief Mori took over, reading a prepared statement about departmental reform and zero tolerance. "This department has suffered a wound, but it is not fatal. We have learned from our mistakes. Effective today, all sworn officers and civilian staff will undergo new ethics and compliance training, and a third-party commission will review all active cases from the last year."

Reporters wrote this down, but the story was in the room's corners, the suspicious glances, the whispered rumors. Two officers traded looks over the heads of the media, one clearly thinking, I always knew. The other, sweating and pale, looked like he was counting the days until the next shoe dropped.

When the presser ended, Isaac leaned in, keeping his voice low. "You handled that better than most feds I know."

Leilani kept her eyes on the crowd. "Comes with the territory. The trick is to never let them see you sweat."

He grinned for a heartbeat. "We should celebrate," he said. "Or at least not drink coffee out of a paper cup for one night."

She nodded, the dull ache behind her eyes. "We can do that," she said. "But first, I need to check on something in holding."

He knew better than to ask. Instead, he laid a hand on her shoulder, quick and careful, then left her alone at the podium as the last few reporters lingered, hoping for an off-record slip.

Leilani watched the room clear out, the press

trickling toward their vehicles, the officers disappearing into side doors and elevators. She stood alone, looking at the photo grid, at the way every crime and every suspect seemed to lead to the same spiral, no matter how many times she tried to flatten it.

She took a breath, and when she looked up, Isaac was waiting for her by the door, holding two coffee cups. They locked eyes, and she saw the same thing she always saw, the sense that the story never ended, that it was always one case away from the next. But the world was quiet. And for Leilani, that was enough.

The hall outside the jail wing stank of burned coffee and microwaved popcorn, a permanent condition of the ventilation system. Leilani balanced on the windowsill, cell pressed to her ear, one eye on the bullpen where the morning's news still reverberated like aftershocks from a quake. The ME's voice was a low drone, calm and unhurried, relaying facts as if reading from a recipe card.

"Results are conclusive, Detective. Rohypnol in his blood, enough to knock out a linebacker. No bruising on the larynx, so it's consistent with asphyxia while unconscious. Either Nakamura did a number on himself after dosing, or someone helped him along."

Leilani traced the spiral of a fingerprint smudge on the glass. "He had visitors?"

The ME coughed, a tired sound. "Two guards on shift, one civilian overnight, and an attorney visit that morning. All by the book, far as the log says. But he was out for at least two hours before he stopped breathing. Your toxicology request will be in your inbox by lunch.”

“Thanks,” Leilani said, and meant it.

She ended the call, then hit Mori’s number. The acting chief answered in half a ring. “You got the autopsy, Kealoha?”

“Yeah. Suicide’s not adding up.”

“It never does. Listen, we’re already on it. Two hours before shift change, a rookie guard called in sick. His replacement, with no background in detention, spent a year on Makani’olu’s security detail before flunking out.” A paper shuffling sound and the faint whir of a scanner. “He and one other are at large, along with an inmate released early this morning on a clerical error. I’ve got people I trust tracking them down as we speak. I’ll let you know when we have something.”

Leilani could taste the frustration in Mori’s voice. “You want me to run the interview with Kamaka, anyway?”

“Yeah. See if the city councilman knows anything useful, or wants to feel sorry for himself.”

Mori hung up without saying goodbye, as was her style.

Leilani rolled her neck, heard the bones crack, and walked the length of the corridor to the interview suite. The old rooms were unchanged since her rookie days. Beige walls with an institutional texture that defied scrubbing, two chairs on either side of a table scored with knife marks, and overhead, the bulb that could turn anyone’s skin the color of a cold roast pork.

Kamaka waited, hands folded. He wore the

standard-issue jumpsuit, but even in bright orange, he radiated something regal, a carriage that didn't break. His lawyer, a woman with salt and pepper hair and a stare that could freeze an ocean, sat next to him but left the talking to Leilani.

She placed a thin file in front of her. "Results are in. You want the short version, or the dramatic one?"

Kamaka smirked. "Just the facts, Detective."

She liked him better that way. "Higa is gone, and she's sitting in federal custody. Your guy at Makani'olu is on a plane to a federal lockup. The other dominoes are falling faster than we can count. You can help, or you can fade into the same spiral as the rest."

He studied her for a long time. "You know what I always admired about your father?" he said. "He never let the badge own him. Even when the world turned against him, he stayed true."

Leilani held his gaze. "That's not how I remember it."

"Of course not," Kamaka said, leaning forward. "You're better than he was. You chose a side."

She opened the folder. "You were a kingmaker, Councilman. When did you lose the script?"

His fingers trembled once before he laced them tight. "One favor leads to another. A phone call here, a handshake there. And before you know it, you're so deep you forget what the air smelled like before you drowned." He looked down at his hands, then at her. "I wanted to fix things. But the machine doesn't let you repair it. It keeps chewing."

"Was it worth it?" Leilani asked, voice a shade too soft.

He shrugged, like a man admitting to a parking ticket. "In the end, the thing that matters is whether you can look your family in the eye." He turned to the lawyer. "Isn't that right?"

She didn't answer.

Leilani closed the folder. "You still won't name the Host. Or the Mastermind."

"There's nothing I could say that would protect you, Detective. Or me." He leaned back, face crumpling, the mask breaking. "You should leave it alone."

"That's what Tommy Nakamura thought," she said. "Oh, and by the way Tommy didn't kill himself. He was murdered. Something to think about if you'd like to change your mind."

He looked up, sudden and sharp, but said nothing.

She stood. "Thanks for your time."

Outside, the hall was even colder than before. She walked slowly, the thud of her shoes on the linoleum echoing louder than the voices that trailed behind. She rode the elevator down to the lobby and stepped into the open air, the sky already gone to morning, the sun glaring off the windshields of a hundred parked cars.

She put on her sunglasses and drifted toward the curb, the day so bright she felt her own shadow shrink. The sidewalk was a blur of tourists, flowered shirts, sand-blasted shorts, the smell of coconut oil and fried malasadas. She kept her eyes on the glass of the precinct entrance, using the reflection to check the street behind her.

At the crosswalk, she stopped, sensing it before she saw it, a pulse in the crowd, a vibration near the limits of vision. She turned slowly, and there, half a block down, between the shaved ice stand and the ABC store, a man stood, hands at his sides, staring directly at her.

He was ordinary. Tourist ordinary. Khaki shorts, a red tee, sunglasses, and a ball cap pulled low. But when he saw her looking, he removed his sunglasses and tapped two fingers to his forehead, a lazy salute.

She felt her stomach drop through the sidewalk. The face was a shade older, tanner, but the line of the jaw, the half-smile, the eyes. She'd know it anywhere.

It was David.

She blinked, and the crowd swept between them, but the man was still there, watching. She ran across the grass, feeling her pulse rise, and the world narrowed to him. She moved faster, the distance between them closing with every step. He didn't move, simply waited, hands loose, eyes locked on hers.

Thirty feet away, a family with a stroller cut her off. When she stepped past, the spot was empty.

She stopped, breath ragged, the noise of the street roaring in her ears. She spun, looking for him, looking for anything, but he was gone. There was only the drift of strangers, the heat of the day, and the whisper in her head that she hadn't seen a ghost. She stood there for a long time, unmoving, until the sun finally burned the image out of her eyes.

The rain started after six and hadn't let up by the

time Leilani turned into her mother's street. The pavement glimmered in the yellow run-off from the porch lights, the air thick with plumeria and the scent of charcoal from someone's barbecue three blocks away. Leilani cut the engine, letting the sound of the rain erase the city's noise from her bones.

Kai ran up to the door ahead of her, hood bouncing against his backpack. She followed, each step feeling heavier than the last, and entered without knocking. Inside, the house was a slow riot of comfort. Warm lamplight, bowls and plates stacked on the kitchen table, and the smell of fresh-baked manju leaking through the cracks of the old oven.

Naalei was there, moving from stove to counter, her movements a kind of low music. She looked up and saw them, face open in a way that didn't need words. "E komo mai," she said, shooing them toward the table. "You're right on time."

The house had been repaired since the last time she was there, the night her mother had been kidnapped. Uncle Edward had sent over some cousins, and they cleaned out the trash and the broken furniture, picked up some usable furniture at the thrift store, and bought her a new television. Not the little thirty-six in model she'd had for fifteen years, but a brand new sixty-five inch one with surround sound. Kai was in heaven.

Kai dropped his bag and circled the table, peering into each bowl like a museum curator. "We're having poke?" he said, eyes bright.

"Three kinds," Naalei said. "And steamed uala, and the poi is fresh. Not that bagged nonsense."

Leilani fell into a chair, her body slumping of its own accord. She watched as her mother worked, hands steady, voice low as she explained each dish to Kai, even though he'd eaten them a hundred times before. Every gesture, every garnish, was a history lesson you could eat.

The kitchen walls were a gallery of memory, sepia photographs of generations past, wedding leis braided and hung on hooks, a painting of the old valley before the condos and the bulldozers. Leilani let her eyes wander, and she could sense the echo of laughter from years before, when the house would be packed with cousins and the biggest argument was who got the last piece of haupia.

Naalei lit two candles, then turned off the overhead so the kitchen glowed in soft gold. The rain tapped the windows, a steady percussion.

"Did you talk to the councilman?" Naalei asked, folding herself into the seat beside Kai.

Leilani nodded, picking at the rim of her bowl. "He didn't give us much. It was the usual regrets."

"He was always a sad man," Naalei said. "Never looked anyone in the eye, not even his own kids."

They ate in silence, broken by Kai's quiet commentary on the food. The poi was tangy and cool; the poke, deep red, spiked with chili and green onion. Leilani ate slowly, letting each mouthful distract her from the spiral in her head.

When the meal was half finished, Naalei poured tea and handed the cup to her daughter. "You look tired," she said, voice gentle. "Not the regular tired, either."

Leilani observed her mother, the lines around her eyes carved deeper than she remembered. She thought of the man on the street, the face that looked like David, and she let the feeling come up instead of shoving it down.

"I saw someone today," she said, voice brittle. "Someone I thought I'd never see again."

Naalei didn't flinch. She had heard the story of Tommy Nakamura coming back from the dead and sensed what was coming. She reached across the table and placed her hand over Leilani's. Her palm was warm, skin soft as taro leaves. "Sometimes the past isn't done with us," she said. "Sometimes, we're not done with it."

"It wasn't a ghost," Leilani said. "He looked the same. H looked older. Like he'd been living a whole other life, right here, out of sight."

Naalei squeezed her hand. "There's an old story," she said. "About how the sea never gives back what it takes, but sometimes, if you listen, you can still hear the lost ones in the surf. It's possible he's trying to tell you something."

Leilani blinked hard, and Kai, who'd gone silent, reached over and hugged her arm. "You're not sad, right?" he asked, voice high and small.

She hugged him back, pulling him onto her lap. "Not sad…confused."

"Confused is okay," said Naalei. "Confused means you care."

The candles flickered, throwing shadows over the photos on the wall. Leilani watched them dance, memory and present merging into the glow.

After dinner, Kai dozed on the couch with a blanket, a video game controller resting on his chest. Leilani helped her mother clear the table, the quiet between them a comfort rather than a wound.

"Do you think he's alive?" Leilani asked, her voice almost lost in the sound of the rain.

Naalei considered the question, hands deep in soapy water. "I think sometimes the world needs us to believe in things we can't prove. It's what keeps us moving forward. But I also think you'll know the truth when you see it, even if it takes a while."

Leilani dried a bowl, traced the edge with her finger. "It's hard. Understanding one's emotions."

"You don't have to decide tonight," said Naalei. "Ohana is about holding space for each other. Even when we bend, we don't break."

Leilani smiled and set the bowl aside. She hugged her mother, burying her face in the scent of salt and starch and safety.

"Mahalo, Mama," she whispered.

"Anytime, baby," Naalei answered, her voice full and fierce.

Outside, the rain softened to a mist. The city still waited, still needed saving, but inside this little kitchen, the spiral loosened its grip enough to let the world back in.

Waikiki at sunset was the world's best con job. Even with the city bleeding behind it, the ocean was always blue, the air always honeyed with fried shrimp and suntan lotion. You could forget the politics and the blood and your own life for the stretch of an evening when the sun painted everything gold.

Isaac waited beyond the lifeguard stand, toes digging in the sand, a folder tucked under his arm like a security blanket. He looked less like a fed and more like a local boy off the leash, in board shorts and an untucked Aloha shirt. But the pacing gave him away. He kept glancing out at the water, then back at the crowd, never standing still for more than two beats.

Leilani crossed the lawn barefoot, the grass wet under her feet, the last rays of light slicing through the palms. She wore a loose tee and gym shorts, her hair wild from the drive, and every muscle in her body wanting to turn and run. She made herself keep walking.

Isaac spotted her and stopped, his face easing into a smile that lasted until she got close. He studied her, searching for damage. "You look better," he said, "but not good."

She let out a noise that might have been a laugh. "That's my brand."

They walked down to the water, picking a path between sunburned tourists and local teens showing off. The tide was out, leaving tidepools that reflected the sky. Leilani let the cool water numb her feet and kept her eyes on the horizon.

Isaac waited until they were clear of the crowd.

"You want to talk about it?" he asked.

She hesitated. "I saw David."

Isaac didn't react but kept walking. He was good that way.

"He was alive," Leilani said. "Or someone who looked like him. On the street. I ran, but he was gone before I got there." She dug her toes into the sand, the memory raw. "You ever see something you knew wasn't possible, but it felt true anyway?"

"All the time," said Isaac. "Usually right before things go to hell."

She turned to face him. "Do you think I'm losing it?"

He didn't smile. "No. But I think you've got unfinished business." He paused and held up the folder. "So do I."

He handed it to her. She took it, heart pounding.

"It's a promotion offer," he said.

She opened it, saw the letterhead, the federal seal, the words "Senior Special Agent, Washington Field Office." She read the fine print, skimmed the rest, and closed the folder. "D.C.?" she asked, voice sharp.

He nodded. "Big promotion. A desk and a window. Staff. The whole thing."

Silence filled the space between them. "Congratulations," she said, the word tasting like soap.

"But?" he said, reading her as if she were a case file.

"But you're not sure you want it," she said.

He shrugged, then looked out at the surfers lining up for the last sets of the day. "I'm not sure I want to leave this." He gestured at the sand, the skyline, and at her. "I've always been the guy who gets bored and moves on. But I don't want to run from this."

She waited, unsure what to say.

Isaac glanced at her, something wounded in his expression. "I meant what I said before," he said. "You're better at this than anyone I've ever met. You care. It scares me sometimes."

She almost smiled. "You should be scared."

They stood in silence, letting the waves eat their words.

Isaac said, "I won't take it. Not until we finish what we started. You, me, and this." He pointed at the city, at the lingering smoke in the air, the mess that never stopped. "We're not done."

Leilani let the words settle somewhere deep, not as a burden but as a possibility. "I'm not sure it'll ever be done."

"That's why we're the ones who have to do it," he said, and for once there was no joke in it.

They walked until the sun was gone and the sand grew cold. They sat down where the tide had drawn a perfect line between day and night. Leilani leaned into him, and he let her, saying nothing. The darkness was slow and absolute, but they didn't move.

Somewhere, the spiral would start up again. There would be another job, another wound, another impossible truth to swallow. The Mastermind was still out there, lurking in the shadows. Manipulating people to do his bidding. But for tonight, the horizon was blank; the world was quiet, and Leilani believed, that this time they could win.

# Chapter Twenty

## Honolulu Healing

Leilani reached the road and let the last of the city's tension lose its grip. She parked on the verge, under a breadfruit tree that had split the county curb with its roots. All around her were blue shadows and gold light; the sun was slipping fast toward the waterline. The only sounds were the chatter of birds and the far-off slap of surf.

She sat for a minute, hands resting on the steering wheel, staring at the basket in the passenger seat. It was woven from lauhala, thick with the scent of rain, and crammed with every token her mother had suggested. Orchids, palm ferns, a small gourd bottle of pa'akai, and a fresh bundle of ti leaves still glossy from the market. At the last moment, she'd thrown her badge in, tucking it under the fold of her windbreaker, a private dare she hadn't quite worked out in her own mind.

A breath. In, out. She grabbed the basket, locked the car, and followed the sand-cut path through a stand of hau trees toward the ocean.

The beach here was a secret, not in the official sense, but in the way the oldest uncles and aunties remembered, a pocket of sand bracketed by lava outcrops and scoured of tourists by bad signage and the total absence of anything to buy or rent. The tide was low, and the surf rolled in lazily, the horizon so clear she could count the clouds between here and Moloka'i.

Kai was the first to spot her. He'd been digging

trenches along the shoreline, a pale blue bucket at his feet and the entire front of his shirt streaked with wet sand. He called out, "Mom! Watch this!" He hurled a chunk of coral into the receding foam. It splashed, and he watched the ripple fade as if he had started a tidal wave.

"Don't go out too far!" Leilani called, but she knew he wouldn't. Not here, not with Nana in sight.

Naalei was a hundred yards down the beach, hunched over a patch of driftwood and stone that she'd cleared for the night's work. She wore a pareu over black shorts, hair up in a braid that had started tight and now bristled with wild gray. She didn't wave, but pointed to the spot next to her, a commander's summons, if not an invitation.

Leilani crossed the beach, the sand sucking at her shoes. For once in months, nobody followed her, no TV trucks, no neighbors craning to get a look at the hero cop. She hadn't let herself feel it until now, the burden of being everybody's public property, and the bruises it left behind.

She dropped the basket near the driftwood circle and crouched next to her mother. "Anything I can do?" she said.

Naalei grunted, jabbing a thumb at the lauhala mat she'd laid out. "You can help by sitting. Rest your bones, girl."

Leilani obeyed, setting herself on the mat and running her fingers over the weave. Naalei worked with the sure, slow rhythm of someone who'd made a hundred of these circles, tucking ti leaves in a spiral, layering flowers and salt. Each movement was a kind of music, a small choreography. She sprinkled the last of the pa'akai in the center, then nodded.

"It's good you came," Naalei said, voice low.

Leilani shrugged. "You made it clear I didn't have a choice."

"That's what moms are for."

They watched the waves for a while; the silence broken by the caw of a distant mynah bird and the thump of Kai's bucket as he upended a day's worth of shells onto the sand.

"Bring your treasures here," Naalei called out, and Kai, delighted, sprinted to obey. His knees were caked with wet sand, and he smelled of the ocean and faintly of peanut butter.

He dumped his haul by his grandmother. Coral branches, two conchs, a feather and a golf ball-sized hunk of beach glass. "I found a secret cave," he announced, as if he had discovered a continent.

Naalei examined each item, giving them their due. She held the feather up to the light. "Pueo," she said. "Good luck. You could give that to your mom."

Kai did solemnly, as if knighted into the service. Leilani tucked the feather behind her ear and ruffled his hair.

A shuffling of feet behind them made her look up. Isaac stood in front of the mats, hands jammed in the pockets of khaki shorts, a gray polo stretching across his chest. For a guy who could slip into any crowd, he stood out here, his posture too upright, shoes too clean, like a Labrador in a field of feral pigs.

He held up a small paper bag. "I brought mango and lychee. Also, sorry I'm late. The northbound lane was shut down by a water main break."

Naalei snorted, but it was a forgiving sound. "You think you are the first haole who ever showed up late to a ceremony?"

Leilani smiled, the warmth catching her off guard. "Glad you made it," she said, and meant it.

He stepped onto the mat, hesitating a second before dropping to sit cross-legged. His knees cracked, and he shot her a look. "You really want to do this?" he said, sotto voce.

Leilani nodded. "I need this," she admitted.

He smiled, handing her the bag of fruit. "Let's do it right."

The sun was lower now; the sky going orange at the edges, pink above the water. The breeze had picked up, and it swirled around the four of them, carrying the brine of the ocean and the perfume of the flowers that Naalei had laid out.

Kai settled on his mother's lap, arms wrapped around her knee. Naalei arranged the mat so all four faced the water, then set the circle with the basket of offerings at its heart. She began the chant, an oli about healing and renewal, her voice starting in her chest and rising like smoke. It didn't matter that Leilani caught half the words; the music of it was enough. Her eyes closed, letting the sound sink into her bones.

Isaac's hand grazed hers, the touch light but steady.

She looked over, saw his eyes closed, lips moving as if memorizing the language. When she looked past him, she saw her mother watching, not the way moms usually watched, but with a kind of pride that didn't need any words. This was the smallest family she'd ever had, and she believed it could be enough.

The sun touched the water, and the sky turned the color of Kai's wildest drawings. The ceremony wasn't official yet, not until the fire was lit and the food was shared. But in that moment, Leilani noticed the last months loosen their grip, the old fear losing its teeth. She squeezed her son, reached for her mother's hand, and let the world shrink to this, the four of them, a circle on the sand, as the day drifted into night.

The first time Leilani had ever been to a hoʻoponopono ceremony, she'd been five years old and angry at the world. She'd watched her mother and grandmother build a circle out of old poi bowls and cracked ʻopihi shells, forcing the whole extended family to sit for hours until every quarrel was confessed, every apology dragged out like a tooth. She remembered the air getting tight, then light. That first taste of magic, the way it made her believe you could mend anything if you tried hard enough.

She was thinking about that as her mother started the work of the ritual, voice lifting into the cadence of the oli. It was ancient, but each verse had a shape, a meaning, a reason for being here and not repeating old wounds in the same tired spiral.

When the chant ended, Naalei clapped her hands once. "Okay, now listen. All of you. This is not for show, yeah? We do this for real." Her eyes flicked to

Isaac, a dare and a lesson in one. "We bring what we need to let go. We share it. Next, we offer it to the sea or flames. It's the way."

Isaac nodded, caught the gravity of it. He watched Leilani for cues, and she sensed his eyes like a weight, steady and never judging.

Naalei motioned for them to take the circle. "Sit close," she said. "No spaces between." She scooted in until her knees brushed Leilani's. Kai, delighted, wriggled into the gap, curling his arms around his ankles.

"This part is for talking," Naalei said. "No secrets here."

She started the round herself, picking up the feather Kai had brought and turning it slow in her hands. "I offer this for protection," she said. Holding it up to the sky, let the dusk wind take it, and set it in the ring of flowers.

Next, she picked up a smooth, black lava pebble with a spiral scored into one face. "This is for my father. For the things he never got to say." Her fingers trembled for half a second. She set the stone on the sand and looked at Leilani. "Your turn."

The badge was cold in her palm. She set it on the mat, right next to a wedge of lychee and a folded orchid. "This is for all the times I was supposed to be brave and wasn't," she said. "For every kid who still has to live in the shadow of what we can't fix."

She knew Kai's gaze was on her, big and round. He'd never seen her cry before, not like this, not in public. She drew a breath and steadied herself.

Isaac spoke next. He hesitated and took his credentials from his pocket. His badge was clipped to a battered plastic card. He set it next to Leilani's. "This is for the people I left behind. For every case that didn't have a happy ending." His hand hovered, but he closed it, quick. "Some burdens are better carried together," he said, looking straight at her.

She smiled, raw but real. "Guess we're in it now."

Kai, when his turn came, didn't pause. He picked the biggest shell from his pile, a broken but still beautiful cowrie, and set it down. "For Daddy," he said, simply and certain. "And for everyone who is scared to talk."

Naalei nodded approval. "Good boy," she said, and he straightened with pride.

When the circle was complete, the center a mess of color and hope and failed prayers, Naalei reached for the bundle of ti leaves she'd set aside. She tore one in half and handed the strips around.

"Now, everyone write his or her fear," she said. "On the leaf. If you cannot write it, say it. The fire will take the rest."

Kai looked at his leaf, brow creased. "I don't have a pen," he said.

Naalei smiled. "Bite it," she said. "The teeth know."

He did, leaving a neat row of dents along the midrib. "This is for monsters under the house," he said.

Leilani took a Sharpie from her windbreaker and

wrote in block letters, FAILURE. She handed it to Isaac, who wrote after a long pause, ALONE.

Naalei, for her part, didn't write. She tore her leaf clean, then whispered something into it, too soft for any of them to hear.

With the leaves ready, she reached into her pack and produced a coconut shell, already loaded with dry grass and a scrap of charcoal. She struck a match and touched it to the edge. The shell took the flame slowly, licking at the air, a soft crackle lost in the sound of the surf.

"One by one," Naalei said.

Leilani fed her leaf to the flame, watching the word curl and blacken before it burned. Kai did the same. He clapped his hands as if he'd performed a magic trick. Isaac followed, quiet, eyes steady. When the last leaf ignited, Naalei tossed the shell into the ring of stones, where it glowed, a tiny sun on the beach.

For a long time, nobody spoke. They sat, letting the fire eat their troubles, the ocean beyond swallowing all sound. The sky was indigo, and the moon had started its climb, silvering the wet sand where the tide reached highest.

Kai was the first to break the silence. "Do we do this every time we're sad?" he asked.

Naalei barked a laugh. "If we did, the world would be a better place."

Leilani reached for Isaac's hand, felt it close around hers. "It's easier with help," she said, and he squeezed back, the lines at the corners of his eyes deepening.

She gazed at her mother, at Kai, at the last curl of smoke from the coconut shell. The badge still lay on the mat, but it felt lighter now, not the anchor it had been for so long.

In the glow of the dying fire, Leilani imagined what came next. A case that didn't end in blood, a night that didn't bring new names to mourn, a world where the past could be honored and released all at once. The wind shifted, blowing the last of the embers toward the sea. She let them go. They all did.

It was nearly dark when Naalei finished weaving the cord, hands moving with the stubborn confidence of someone who had done this for every major event in the family, birth to burial and all the storms in between. She looped the ends together, twisting the ti leaves into a thick braid and tying it off with a perfect square knot.

"Come," she called, and the circle closed in. Leilani took one end, then Kai, then Isaac, then back to Naalei. No one said a thing. The ocean worked its slow magic, rolling up the sand, then pulling back, every wave erasing the last as if the world was determined to keep starting over.

"This is to show we're still here," Naalei said, holding the knot tight. "Still Ohana. No matter what comes."

Kai grinned, cheeks smudged with charcoal. "Even if I forget to take out the trash?"

"Yes," Naalei said, ruffling his hair.

Leilani felt the knot dig into her palm, grounding

her. It had been a long time since she could remember a physical sensation that wasn't pain or fatigue. She leaned into it, eyes closed, listening. Her son's laughter, her mother's low hum, the soft, conspiratorial way Isaac's breathing shifted when he wanted to say something but didn't want to interrupt.

As the shadows grew long, Leilani stood and dusted off her hands. She caught Isaac's eye, and together they wandered down the beach, away from the dying fire, shoes forgotten behind them. The sand was cool, the wind rising, and the world felt open for the first time in a very long while.

They stopped at the tide line, where the water shivered with moonlight and small crabs hunted for lost scraps. Isaac stared, her face as unreadable as ever.

He didn't start with words. He put an arm around her shoulder and let her lean into it, matching her slow exhale with one of his own.

"I heard you," he said finally. "Back at the circle. About the badge."

She kicked a shell and watched it tumble into the froth. "Yeah. Guess it was overdue."

He waited. "I turned down the transfer."

She froze, not quite believing. "D.C.? You said it was your shot."

"It was," he said. "But there's more important work here." He shrugged, as if it were another piece of the puzzle. "And I'm not done chasing ghosts yet."

She turned to face him. "Are you sure?"

He nodded. "Absolutely."

She studied his face, all angles and shadows, the old wound near his hairline catching the light. "You know this place breaks people, right?"

He grinned. "I'm counting on it."

She laugh; the sound rolling out over the water. "You're a strange man, Torres."

"Takes one to know one."

They gazed at the waves for a while, the city behind them reduced to a glow, the beach empty but for their own prints and the promise of more to come.

"So," she said at last. "What now?"

His gaze fell upon her, softer than before. "Now? We get ready. Because the spiral always comes back, and the island never stays quiet for long." He squeezed her shoulder almost like a promise. "But this time, we don't let it eat us."

They walked towards the circle, where Kai was trying to teach Naalei how to throw a spiral with a lump of driftwood. He waved when he saw them, eyes bright. "Mom! Nana says I have good instincts. I'm gonna be a detective like you!"

Leilani smiled at her son, at Isaac, at her mother, and something inside her realigned. She reached out and grabbed the ti leaf cord, pulling everyone in for one last knot.

The sky was black now, but the horizon still glowed faint, a line of fire waiting for tomorrow. They stood together on the sand, a family of four, the cord linking them hand to hand. For the first time, the circle felt unbreakable, not by blood or by law, but by the simple act of choosing each other.

Leilani shut her eyes, holding the knot, and let the new world take root. The spiral would keep turning, and she would keep chasing it, but tonight, the one thing that mattered was this circle and the promise that they'd face the dark as one.

When the wind came in off the water, the cord snapped taut between them, and Leilani laughed, loud, wild, free. And when her family laughed with her, she knew it would always be enough.

# Chapter Twenty-One

## Aloha and Aloha

Sunrise, and the city, were still wringing out the dregs of darkness when Leilani parked the ancient Explorer on the side of the road. The beach was a crook of sand between a tangle of kiawe and a seawall pocked with generations of initials, but it was theirs. The air shimmered cold for the tropics, seventy, seventy-two, and for once the clouds hadn't caught the sun yet. Kai unbuckled before the car had stopped, vibrating in the back seat like a tuning fork. "Let's go, let's go, let's go!" he sang, already wrestling his towel around his waist to prepare for the board shorts quick-change.

Isaac grinned, pulling the foam-topped surfboard from the roof rack and handing it off to Leilani. She balanced it on her hip like a third child and said, "Easy, Tiger. If you break a fin before you hit water, Nana's going to disown us."

"I thought you said 'ohana never broke for anything," Isaac replied, hauling his own beat-up longboard out with a practiced roll of the shoulder.

Kai made a face, exaggerated for effect. "Rules are different if you're late for school or if you damage property," he said. "Or if you forget to feed Nana's cat. Or if you."

"Forget to brush your teeth," Leilani finished, cutting a glance at him with a smirk.

The sand was chilly underfoot and perfect for running. Kai tore down the slope, board leash bouncing at his ankle, and Isaac loped after, leaving Leilani to bring up the rear with her own slender, battered board. The lineup was empty except for two ancient uncles trading turns on the outer reef. Closer to shore, the sets rolled lazy, glassy, and now and then a faint pulse would send a thigh-high wedge straight to the sandbar. Perfect for a ten-year-old learning to read the ocean.

Kai threw his towel on the sand, then, realizing the day's first wet was on offer, sprinted straight into the shore break and flopped with a theatrical shriek. "First blood!" he howled, paddling in the half-foot of foam like he'd conquered the North Shore. He stood, shaking droplets out of his hair, grinning madly. "C'mon, Mom, bet you can't beat me to the blue buoy."

Isaac, meanwhile, set his board on the sand, crouched, and popped up in a wobbly facsimile of a surf stance. He glanced at Leilani, who leaned her board against a driftwood log and folded her arms, watching. "Like this, right?" Isaac called, pitching his hands for balance.

She squinted, lips twitching. "If you want to face-plant on the drop, sure. Try not to use your hands like a T. rex."

Kai snickered, rolled his eyes, ran over, and plopped down beside the board. "Show him, Mom."

"Gladly." Leilani's demo was no nonsense. She kneeled, hands flat, then rose in one smooth movement, shoulders over knees, back foot angled.

Years of practice, thousands of pop-ups. She stayed there, poised, then exaggerated a hip twist to ride an imaginary wave down the line. She held the stance, eyes on Kai, who watched with a look that was pure hero worship.

Isaac tried again, this time with more discipline, and promptly toppled sideways into the sand. Kai howled, rolling over in hysterics. "You look like a drunk flamingo!" he managed through giggles.

Isaac, face coated in sand, glanced over at Leilani. "It looked easier on the YouTube videos," he laughed. "See? I'm building his confidence. That's good coaching."

Leilani extended a hand and hauled him up. "Stick to investigating financial fraud," she said, patting him on the back. "You'll save your knees."

They worked in concert, like a little pit crew, rigging up the leashes, double-checking the wax job, and running fingers along the rails for any dings or splinters. Kai narrated every step, the way ten-year-olds can. "If you don't check the leash, you'll lose your board, and if you lose your board, you'll have to swim all the way to China, and if you swim to China, you'll never get back in time for pancakes", until Leilani shushed him by mussing his hair.

"Let's stretch," she said, and they stood in a loose triangle, toes pointed at the sea, arms overhead, the morning sun clearing the top of the condos down the coast. There was a smell, somewhere between coconut sunscreen, board wax and the sweet rot of washed-up driftwood, that could have been bottled as a cure for stress.

Kai bounced on his feet eagerly. "Go?"

Leilani nodded, and he sprinted to the waterline, the board tucked awkwardly under his arm, every step flinging sand backwards in rooster tails. Isaac jogged after, more measured, while Leilani took a moment to breathe, eyes on the horizon. There was a time, not so long ago, when she would have read every shadow on the water as a threat, every unaccounted for shape as a potential danger. Today, the danger was the chance of sunburn or a bruised ego.

She followed, board underarm, and the world shrank to the hiss and hush of shore break, the slap of bare feet on cold sand, and the sound of her son's laugh as he tumbled through the first foamy wave.

In the lineup, it was a different country. The city faded away. There were the three of them and the two uncles out on the reef, trading turns, and whistling whenever one of the kids botched a takeoff. Kai paddled hard, jaw clenched, determined to keep up with his heroes. When Leilani or Isaac caught a wave, he whooped and tried to follow, wiping out in spectacular fashion, re-emerging, spluttering, more energized than before.

Isaac surprised everyone by catching the second set of the day. His pop-up was textbook, and he managed a wobbly ride straight to the sand, beaming with triumph as he looked back for witnesses. Leilani and Kai both clapped.

Back on the sand, Leilani showed Kai how to dig the tail of the board to keep it upright, how to check for hairline cracks, how to stand with feet perfectly spaced on the waxed deck. It was the slow unfolding of a ritual she'd learned from her father, one she'd rarely had time to share until now.

Isaac hovered nearby, towel slung over his shoulders, pretending not to watch but not missing a moment.

"You think he'll be as good as you?" Isaac asked, pitching his voice loud enough for Kai to hear.

Leilani glanced at her son, who was busy drawing spirals in the sand with the tip of his board. "He's already better," she said. "I never had the guts to charge the big sets when I was his age."

Kai looked up, grinning. "You didn't want to get sand in your mouth," he said, parroting something she must have said years before.

They kept at it, set after set, until arms and legs trembled and bellies rumbled with the promise of breakfast. The sun was well up, burning the tips of the whitewater, and the beach had populated with other families, all claiming their little squares of paradise.

Leilani sat on the sand, towel around her shoulders, letting Kai climb into her lap though he was way past the age where he pretended to need it. He was shivering, skin bright with salt and sun, but she wrapped her arms around him and held tight. Isaac sat to her left, picking sand from his hair, the two of them sharing a silence that was more comfortable than any conversation they'd ever had in a squad car or at the scene of a crime.

Leilani forgot the spiral of old grudges, the city politics, the endless grind of crime and consequence. For a minute, it was this: family, sun, salt, and the next perfect wave.

Kai drifted off, head on her shoulder, still damp from the water.

Isaac nudged her, his voice barely above a whisper. "You're a good mom," he said.

Leilani shrugged, but her eyes were wet, and the thing she noticed was the endless blue horizon waiting for them all.

In the lineup, time dilated, the minutes stretching and slowing until the rest of the world blurred away. The three of them paddled out, Leilani and Kai in the lead, Isaac close behind, his arms churning a practiced rhythm that still couldn't match either of theirs. The water was glassy, the early wind having died down, leaving a mirror-sheen on the shoulder of each swell.

Leilani kept Kai to her left, between herself and the shore. She watched every dip of his arms, every squint of determination as he eyed the little sets rolling in from the outside. "Not too far," she called, but it was mostly out of habit. He'd learned from her before he'd learned from school. The ocean could love you or kill you, but it never did anything on purpose.

A long lull, then a bump in the blue. Kai pointed, excitement sparking through his whole body. "There! That's the one!" His voice was loud enough to carry, over the slosh and hiss.

"Easy, wait for it," Leilani said, the words like a

benediction. "Pick your line. Time the peak."

He nodded, arms tensed, head low, watching the wave lift under them. He started too early, missed the drop and slid sideways off the foam. The second time, he almost caught it, lost his balance and tumbled, the board spinning in a lazy arc.

The third time was perfection. The wave, a waist high right, soft as a sigh, reared up, and Kai dug in, hands gripping the rails. He sprang to his feet, clumsy but upright, and for a glorious three seconds, he rode the wall, arms outstretched, chin up, the future shining in his eyes.

Leilani whooped so loud it startled a frigate bird overhead. "Go, Kai!" she yelled, pumping her own fists above the deck. Isaac, straddling his board in the channel, let out a cheer, caught up in the moment.

Kai carved a wobbly path down the line, made it all the way to the sand, and crashed with a belly flop into the shore break. He popped up, both fists raised in victory. "Did you see? Did you see me?" His grin threatened to split his face.

"Like a champ!" Leilani called back, paddling in after him. She basked in the pride, sharp and sweet and almost too much for one heart. Isaac slid off his board and waded through the foam, standing calf deep as Kai splashed back toward them.

"You see how he stuck the landing?" Isaac said, gesturing with exaggerated approval. "Could've taught those Olympic kids a thing or two."

Kai grinned, hugging the board to his chest. "Mom

taught me how to read the shoulder," he said. "And you taught me how to get up if I wipe out." He smiled at Isaac, who blinked, surprised and a little touched. "Team effort," Kai finished.

Leilani ruffled her son's hair, then looked out at the horizon. The sun was well up now, painting the line of water gold and silver. She squinted, scanning for rips or cross currents, the old vigilance kicking in. But the sea was kind this morning, and she let her guard drop half a notch.

They paddled back out, taking turns catching the little peelers. Each time Kai caught a wave, Leilani tracked every move, ready to react if he got into trouble. She kept her voice steady, coaching and coaxing, but mostly watching, memorizing every second.

Between sets, they bobbed together, feet dangling in the cool water, the salt air thick on their tongues. Isaac floated close, one hand steadying Kai's board, the other tracing idle circles in the water.

"Better than the FBI gym," Isaac said, kicking gently to keep upright.

Leilani smiled, chin resting on her arms as she straddled the board. "Less paperwork, too."

Kai said, "I wish we could do this every day." He meant it.

"Me too," Leilani said, and for once she believed it. "If the world spun off its axis tomorrow, there would always be this morning, this salt, this family."

They stayed out until their arms ached, after which

they turned back, catching the next wave in together. The ride was short, but they landed in a pile, all tangled up in foam and laughter and the wild relief of a world that, for the moment, was exactly as it should be.

The sand was already hot as they staggered back up the slope, each of them trailing saltwater and success. The three surfboards made a bright row, planted upright in the sand like sentries. Kai collapsed on his towel, barely wringing out his shirt before launching into a high-velocity replay of every ride.

"Did you see that second wave?" he asked, body vibrating as he mimed the exact drop and pivot with both arms. "I almost wiped out but then bam! I totally saved it! I was like, whoosh!" He shot a glance at Leilani, hungry for validation.

She leaned over and shook the excess water from her own hair, then reached for Kai's with the towel, scrubbing hard enough to make him squeal. "I saw it, Kaimana. That was a pro-level recovery. Style points for the arms," she added, wagging her eyebrows.

Kai grinned, flushed with pride. "You think Nana will let me surf the outside next time?"

"If you eat three servings of poi at dinner and promise to do your homework every night for a week," she said, kissing his damp forehead.

Isaac sprawled beside them, propped on one elbow, with a look of lazy satisfaction on his face. He'd pulled off his rash guard and was now taking full advantage of the sun, letting it erase the pale lines that never quite faded from mainland winters. "Next time, we're bringing a video camera. The world deserves to see your technique," he said to Kai.

Kai groaned, burying his head in the towel. "Promise not to post it on the internet."

Leilani handed Isaac a bottle of cold water from their cooler. Their fingers brushed in an accidental touch, and for a second she felt the echo of something she hadn't known how to want until lately. They shared a glance, comfortable, teasing, like they'd been doing this for decades.

The morning's ocean had left salt on their skin, and the breeze stuck the dampness to every crease and hair. Leilani stretched, back arched, feeling the pleasant fatigue settle into her muscles. She looked out at the water, where the two uncles from earlier had been joined by three more, all of them passing waves and good natured insults in equal measure. The world felt safe.

They spread out the picnic, last night's musubi, some still-cool papaya, and a handful of clementines. Kai inhaled the musubi, barely pausing to breathe between bites. Isaac peeled an orange, flicking each segment into his mouth with the precision of a marksman.

Leilani was about to join them when her phone buzzed from the zippered pocket in her backpack. She hesitated, reluctant to break the spell, but checked anyway. The number was unlisted; the message brief.

*THE WEB IS BIGGER THAN YOU THINK. SOME SPIDERS ARE STILL SPINNING THEIR WEBS. WATCH YOUR BACK.*

No sender, no emoji. Only words, like a fishhook catching her mind.

She felt her body tense, a tightening between her shoulders, an old cop's habit she'd never outgrow. She checked the sender details and the call log, all in one smooth motion. When she looked up, Isaac's eyes were on her. He'd seen the change, when no one else had.

He didn't say anything, but offered her half his orange, the gesture easy but loaded. She took it, smiled, and tried to shake off the chill that the message had left behind.

Kai, oblivious, was stacking clementine peels into a wobbly tower. "Did you know the tallest building in the world is in Dubai?" he asked out of nowhere. "It's like a thousand feet high."

Isaac ruffled his hair. "If you keep eating like this, you might catch up."

Leilani squeezed Kai's hand, looked back out to sea, scanning the horizon. She wasn't expecting trouble, not really. But the old instincts never left. She drifted, wondering who the message was from, and whether the ghosts of old cases ever really stayed buried. She'd won this round, but the game continued.

She laughed at one of Isaac's dumb jokes, watched Kai finish the clementines, and decided, for now, the best thing to do was keep building towers in the sand.

The lunch was mostly gone, and Kai had abandoned his fruit tower in favor of building a fortified sand castle, complete with a moat and improvised driftwood drawbridge. Leilani watched him for a while, admiring the way he was already marshaling resources, negotiating with the tide, testing the walls for weaknesses.

She glanced at Isaac, who was busy pulling shards of shell out of the towel and feigning indifference, but she could tell by the set of his shoulders that he was thinking about the message, too. She waited until Kai was deep into an engineering crisis, a rogue crab invading the north wall, before rising with a stretch.

"Need help with the cooler," she said, jerking her chin toward the car. Isaac caught the hint, dusted off, and followed.

They walked side by side, silent for a bit. The sand was warm and uneven underfoot, the sun a little too bright now that the clouds had burned off. When they reached the shade of the kiawe at the edge of the lot, she pulled out her phone, held it so he could see.

His eyes flicked over the message, then up to her. "Heard from the peanut gallery, huh?"

She nodded. "Same number as before?"

"Nope. New one." She scrolled, showing him the blank contact history. "Nothing else. Whoever it is, they're good at hiding."

Isaac took the phone, thumbed through menus with the easy suspicion of a man who used to read other people's mail for a living. "Could be a bluff," he said, but he didn't sound convinced.

Leilani took a breath, tasting brine and uncertainty. "I know it's not over. There's always a bigger web." She trailed off and admired the horizon. The blue seemed endless, but she knew enough to read the signs. Storms never stayed gone for long.

Isaac handed back the phone, then leaned against the hood of the car, arms crossed. He wasn't much for speeches, but when he spoke, it was quiet and solid. "We're not going back, Lei. We don't have to play defense forever."

She measured the truth in his words. He didn't flinch, didn't smile. He waited for her to decide what she needed him to be, backup, partner, whatever.

She stepped closer, the space between them small and intentional. "If something comes, I'll need your help," she said.

He shrugged. "Always," he said. "Even if you break my case clearance stats."

She allowed herself a laugh, low and private. They stood like that, side by side, not quite touching, their eyes trained on the distant shimmer of the surf. A flock of plovers cartwheeled along the tide line, then scattered, shrill as a siren. The sound snapped her to the present.

Isaac broke the moment. "We should get back to Kai before he conscripts another tourist."

Leilani nodded, pocketed the phone, and together they walked down to the sand, letting the waves lick their feet as they walked. She thought of the message, of the invisible lines that tied the past to the present. She thought of how much she wanted this peace, and how hard she'd fight to keep it.

When they reached Kai, he looked up, face radiant,

and shouted, "Mom! Come check out the castle!"

She kneeled beside him, hands on his shoulders, and Isaac hovered behind, close enough to cast a single shadow.

"We've got your back, Kaimana," she said.

And she meant it.

The day bled into evening in increments. First the light shifted, going soft and syrupy, the gold you got on the right side of the island. The crowds thinned, the volume of the world dialed down to a couple of beach walkers, a stray paddleboarder, and the three of them. Kai dug into the last phase of castle construction, hands caked with damp sand, brow furrowed in intense calculation.

Leilani sat on the towel, picking at the corner of a musubi, watching her son's singular focus. Isaac stretched out beside her, ankles crossed, sunglasses perched on his forehead. The noise was the gentle slap of the tide and the distant cackle of a mynah bird scavenging near the trash bin.

Kai stepped back from the moat, brushing his hands on his shorts. "Do you think detectives ever have to investigate sand castles?" he asked, earnest as ever.

Isaac considered. "I once heard about a case in Santa Monica. Someone stole all the flags from the championship castle. Devastating."

Kai giggled, pivoting to Leilani. "You'd catch the bad guy, right, Mom?"

She smiled, a real one, letting her shoulders drop. "I'd try my best, but if you ask me, the best detective is the one who doesn't leave fingerprints on the evidence."

Kai's face grew serious. "Could I be a detective? Like you?"

She reached out and pinched his chin as if weighing it in her hand. "You already are," she said. "You always ask the best questions." She meant it, and the look in his eyes said he knew.

He returned to his castle, this time recruiting Isaac to find the right shells for battlements. Together, they searched the tide line for the perfect pieces. Kai issued instructions in a voice that echoed every police chief and teacher she'd ever admired. Leilani listened, half amused, half in awe of how much had changed, and how quickly.

The sun slipped lower, painting the sky in bruised orange and pink. Shadows stretched across the beach, making every footstep an event, every word echo a little longer.

When the castle was finished, Kai pronounced it the Fortress of Investigation, complete with a drawbridge and a lookout for spies. He and Isaac planted the driftwood flag, and Leilani took a photo, wanting to capture the way the moment felt, fragile, beautiful, unrepeatable.

The wind picked up, cooler now. The tide crept higher, licking at the bottom tier of the fortress. Leilani watched the water eat away at the outer wall, a slow and inevitable siege.

Isaac sat beside her again, arms looped around his

knees. "You think it'll last until morning?" he asked.

She smiled. "Nothing does. But that's okay."

He nodded, reached for her hand. For a while, they sat, shoulder to shoulder, watching the waves.

Kai lay sprawled on his back, staring up at the first stars. "Can we come back next weekend?" he asked, voice thick with fatigue.

"Count on it," Leilani said.

As darkness gathered, she stood and walked to the water, letting the chill bite at her ankles. The castle was already slumping, battlements softened, the tide erasing every trace of construction. She stood alone, silhouetted against the last scraps of daylight, and closed her eyes.

The old fear was still there. She'd never lose it. But it didn't own her anymore. Not while Isaac was behind her, not while Kai was laughing, not while the ocean kept its own secrets and promised to wash the rest away.

She whispered, "Aloha," to the sea, letting it carry both her gratitude and her challenge. Goodbye and hello, in the same breath.

She turned back to her family, and together, they walked up the beach toward the night, leaving behind footprints and the memory of a perfect day.

A chill ran up Leilani's back, and she looked around, wondering if she was being watched. She never saw the guy down the beach watching them. He put the opera glasses in his backpack and followed them to the parking lot, watching as they drove away, laughing.

# Acknowledgments

A special thank you to my daughter Christina J. Morgan, my unofficial collaborator.

Any mistakes the reader may find are solely the responsibility of the author.

Special thanks to my daughter Stephanie Morgan, my beta reader. Stephanie has read every novel in its rough stages and rarely gets to see the completed product. Her insight and critique have been critical in making sure the stories make sense.

Also, I would like to thank my family for their encouragement. I have been telling them stories since they were little, and I always told them that someone should be writing this stuff down. I decided to write it down myself.

I want to thank my closest friend, Trish Moakler-Herud. She has been encouraging me for years to write my stories down. I hope this will make her proud.

Special thanks to my late wife, Jane. She pushed me for years to become a writer, and my biggest regret is that she didn't live long enough to see it happen. I love her with all my heart and miss her every day. I think she would be pleased.

Finally, thanks to the readers. Without you, none of this would be important.

# About the Author

**2019 Pacific Book Awards Best Mystery Finalist . . .** *Crime Delayed*

**2020 Pacific Book Awards Best Mystery Winner . . .** *Crime Denied*

**2020 Chanticleer International Book Awards: 1st Place Blue Ribbon, CLUE Book Awards for Suspense, Thriller Fiction . . .** *Crime Denied*

**2021 Chanticleer International Book Awards Finalist, CLUE Book Awards for Suspense, Thriller Fiction . . .** *Crime Conspiracy*

**2021 Chanticleer International Book Awards Finalist, Book Series, CLUE Book Awards for Suspense, Thriller Fiction . . . Crime Series, The Buck Taylor Novels**

**2022 Chanticleer International Book Awards Finalist, CLUE Book Awards for Suspense, Thriller Fiction . . .** *Crime Exploded*

**2022 Chanticleer International Book Awards Finalist, CLUE Book Awards for Suspense, Thriller Fiction . . .** *Crime Spree*

**2023 Chanticleer International Book Awards Finalist, CLUE Book Awards for Suspense, Thriller Fiction . . .** *Crime Scene*

**2023 Chanticleer International Book Awards Series Finalist, Mystery & Mayhem Book Awards**
*. . . Crime Series.*

Chuck Morgan attended Seton Hall University and Regis College and spent thirty-five years as a construction project manager. He is an avid outdoorsman, an Eagle Scout and a licensed private pilot. He enjoys camping, hiking, mountain biking and fly-fishing.

He is the author of the Crime series, featuring Colorado Bureau of Investigation Agent Buck Taylor. The series includes *Crime Interrupted, Crime Delayed, Crime Unsolved, Crime Exposed, Crime Denied, Crime Conspiracy, Crime Unknown, Crime Exploded, Crime Spree, Crime Family, Crime Scene, and Crime Victims.*

He is also the author of *Her Name Was Jane*, a memoir about his late wife's nine-year battle with breast cancer. He has three children and four grandchildren. He resides in Lone Tree, Colorado.

# Other Books by the Author

Dear Reader, thank you for reading this novel. Please enjoy the other books in this series and follow Colorado Bureau of Investigation Agent Buck Taylor and his team as they investigate new and sometimes unusual crimes in the Colorado mountains. Each novel is a separate story, and they can be read in any order, but you might find it more enjoyable to read them in order.

Happy Reading,

*Chuck Morgan*

**"Crime Interrupted: A Buck Taylor Novel by Chuck Morgan is a gripping, edge-of-the-seat novel.** *Right from page one, the action kicks off and never stops, gaining pace as each chapter passes." Reviewed by Anne-Marie Reynolds for Readers' Favorite.*

**Finalist . . . 2019 Pacific Book Awards Best Mystery**

*"This crime novel reads like a great thriller. The writing is atmospheric, laced with vivid descriptions that capture the setting in great detail while allowing readers to follow the intensity of the action and the emotional and psychological depth of the story." Reviewed by Divine Zape for Readers' Favorite.*

*"Professionally written in the style of a best-selling crime novelist, such as Tom Clancy, Crime Unsolved: A Buck Taylor Novel by Chuck Morgan is a spellbinding suspense novel with an environmental flair. Intriguing subplots of fraud, survivalist paranoia, and murder weave their way through the fabric of the plot, creating a dynamic story. This is an action-filled, stimulating tale which contains fascinating details that are relevant in our present climate." Reviewed by Susan Sewell for Readers' Favorite.*

*"Chuck Morgan has a unique gift for plot, one that makes Crime Exposed: A Buck Taylor Novel a hard-to-put-down book. From the start, readers know what happens to Barb, but they become curious as they follow the investigation, wondering if the characters will find out what happened to her. The descriptions are filled with clarity, and they offer readers great images. The prose is elegant, and it captures both the emotional and psychological elements of the novel clearly while offering vivid descriptions of scenes and characters. This is a fast-paced thriller with memorable characters and a criminal investigation that is so real readers will believe it could happen." Reviewed by Romuald Dzemo for Readers' Favorite.*

**Winner . . . 2020 Pacific Book Awards Best Mystery**

**2020 Chanticleer International Book Awards: 1st Place Blue Ribbon, CLUE Book Awards for Suspense, Thriller Fiction**

*"It's really progressive to see a female serial killer portrayed with such intelligent writing and depth of character*, and the cat and mouse chase dynamic is thrown off nicely by the switching of genders. What results is a really enjoyable thriller and crime mystery novel, and overall Crime Denied is certain to please fans of both hard-boiled detective tales and action/adventure crime novels." Reviewed by K.C. Finn for Readers' Favorite.

**2021 Chanticleer International Book Awards Finalist, CLUE Book Awards for Suspense, Thriller Fiction . . . *Crime Conspiracy***

*"This makes for a truly dynamic story where anything is possible, and a hero you can root for even when it looks like all is lost."* Reviewed by K.C. Finn for Readers' Favorite.

*"This is a book you can't put down, which will entertain you on many levels, and at times make your skin crawl; the kind of book that remains in your thoughts long after you*

**2022 Chanticleer International Book Awards Finalist, CLUE Book Awards for Suspense, Thriller Fiction . . . *Crime Exploded***

*"**Action-packed and fast-paced, I was sucked into the story the moment I opened the novel.** The author built the story to perfection. Chuck Morgan gave just the right amount of suspense, mystery and action to keep readers' attention on Buck and his team. There was never a dull moment in the story. The narrative ran smoothly until the end; it followed the development of the story and the pace set by the characters. I enjoyed the twists and turns. What I loved more than anything else in the plot was how calculating Buck was. He was smart; he didn't let the FBI discourage him and kept his head in the game. The action gave me an adrenaline rush. Absolutely brilliant!" Reviewed by Rabia Tanveer for Readers' Favorite.*

## 2022 Chanticleer International Book Awards Finalist, CLUE Book Awards for Suspense, Thriller Fiction . . . *Crime Spree*

*"It is one of the best crime novels I have read in a long while, with real characters developed in a way to let you get to know them intimately, understand them, and appreciate their strengths and weaknesses.* The plot is tight, exciting, and tense, with plenty of action, and it will grip you from the start. The bizarre storyline is enthralling, written in descriptive prose that lands you right in the middle of the action. Forget sleep; once you pick this book up, you won't want to put it down until it's finished. Fantastic story, and highly recommended for fans of high-octane crime thrillers." *Reviewed by Anne-Marie Reynolds for Readers' Favorite.*

**"Crime Family is the tenth book in the Buck Taylor series. Chuck Morgan had me hooked from the first page until the end.** *There was never a dull moment with all the action; one chapter flowed into the next. The story was fast-paced and kept me on the edge of my seat. I kept turning the pages to find out what would happen next. I was intrigued, and with all the twists and turns, I could not predict what was looming. The characters were well-developed. Each had a background description, and it was fun getting to know some of them. The story was excellently written with a fitting ending." Reviewed by Alma Boucher for Readers' Favorite.*

**"Crime Scene is a must-read for lovers of mystery sleuth and**

murder tales with a touch of conspiracy." *Reader's Favorite review.*

**"Crime Scene has a carefully designed intrigue that deepens with every unforeseeable turn of events, and a dynamic narrative."** *Reader's Favorite review.*

**"This is a great book. Holds your attention and you don't want to put it down. I would recommend this book to anyone who loves a good crime novel."** *Amazon review.*

**"Spellbinding, gripping, powerful, and relevant are just a few words that come to mind after turning the last page of Crime Scene: A Buck Taylor Novel, book 11, by Chuck Morgan."** *Amazon Review.*

**"A riveting plot and good pacing keep the reader in suspense as Buck Taylor and his team establish evidence beyond a reasonable doubt.** *The author sustains interest by skillfully showing the art and intuition involved in crime investigation and the science behind it, as well as the elements that can delay or confound it. There are a lot of quirky characters in the novel and the author gives them mannerisms, voices and descriptions that make them distinctive and realistic. The details and descriptions of the work and everyday life of the players are both pleasantly appealing and revolting, depending on the scenario. What's most captivating and intriguing about the character development is the backstory of the unhinged*

*characters and how the author uses them as part of the perplexing trail of a horrendous crime. Themes of sadism, cruelty, grief, forensics, police procedures, and even a little bit of romance can be found in this installment of the Buck Taylor series. Highly recommended for crime story fans who especially enjoy the information as well as the twists, turns, and the untangling of intricate and cold case crime sprees." Reviewed by Carmen Tenorio for Readers' Favorite.*